Also by K.L. Slater

Safe with Me
Blink
Liar

FINDING GRACE
K.L. SLATER

GRAND CENTRAL
PUBLISHING

NEW YORK   BOSTON

Grand Central Publishing
Hachette Book Group
1290 Avenue of the Americas, New York, NY 10104
grandcentralpublishing.com
twitter.com/grandcentralpub

First published in 2019 by Bookouture, an imprint of StoryFire Ltd.

First Grand Central Publishing edition: May 2020

Grand Central Publishing is a division of Hachette Book Group, Inc. The Grand Central Publishing name and logo is a trademark of Hachette Book Group, Inc.

The publisher is not responsible for websites (or their content) that are not owned by the publisher.

The Hachette Speakers Bureau provides a wide range of authors for speaking events. To find out more, go to www.hachettespeakersbureau.com or call (866) 376-6591.

ISBN: 978-1-5387-1826-1 (mass market)

Printed in the United States of America

OPM

10 9 8 7 6 5 4 3 2 1

CHAPTER 1

Lucie

Sunday afternoon

I stir from my nap, feeling something soft on my cheek. When I open my eyes, my husband, Blake, is crouching down at my side, his fingertip gently tracing down my face.

"I made you some tea," he says. "You seemed restless, were you dreaming?"

I shake my head. Try to push away the memories that managed to steal up on me while I slept, but then panic seizes me.

"What time is it? Grace..." Still feeling a bit groggy from sleep, I struggle to sit up.

Our daughter has been on a trip to Alton Towers with her best friend, Olivia, and her parents, Bev and Mike, as a birthday treat for her turning nine years old yesterday.

"Relax! Oscar's at your dad's, but Mike just called and that's why I've woken you. They're back now from Alton Towers and he says Grace will be setting off to walk home in two or three minutes, so I'm just going outside to watch for her."

We live on the same street as Bev and Mike, but it's a long

road and our houses are separated by a steep bend. Grace's constant mithering finally paid off at her birthday party, when I caved in and agreed she could walk home unaccompanied. Unbeknown to her, Mike and Blake will be watching her every move.

"How long have I been asleep?" I bend my arm up in front of me and squint at my watch. "Two hours!"

I definitely feel a bit off through sleeping so deeply and for too long. I shuffle around until I'm comfy and pick up the hot drink.

"You must've needed it. Mike said they left the park early in the end as it was dropping cold." Blake stands up and heads for the hallway. "Right. I'm going out to hide behind the hedge to monitor her. God help us if she sees me watching. She's 'nine years old now,' you know."

I grin at his impression. It's been Grace's favourite phrase since her birthday; she's making full use of her new status while several of her friends at school are still eight. I take a sip of my tea. It's hot and sweet and I feel instantly better.

It's been a difficult week for one reason or another and I'm ready to put it behind me.

I set my favourite Ed Sheeran playlist going on Spotify, put my cup down, and relax back into the cushions.

It's the last few quiet minutes before Grace will rush in like a tornado. I'll hear everything about the day in that wonderfully vivid way she recounts things she's loved doing, so I'll feel almost like I've been there with her.

I've been unsettled since the upset this morning in our local café with Mrs. Charterhouse. It feels like anxiety is always just a heartbeat away from pouncing, and once it gets a hold, it's hard to shake off.

But what Barbara Charterhouse said and did can only keep its power if I continue to analyse her words and constantly turn them over in my mind. She was completely out of order, there's no doubt about that.

But she obviously just saw red and is probably already ruing her spiteful words and actions.

I can't wait to cuddle Grace and feel everything in my world is right again.

I decide to quickly pop to the bathroom, so I can give my daughter my full attention when she bounces through the door telling me all about her day out.

I turn up the music a little so I can still hear it and haul myself up from the couch, singing along to one of my favourite tracks. I jog upstairs for the extra exercise, thinking how much better I feel now, after my sleep.

I'm so lucky to be back here in my lovely home after this morning's upset. And when Blake picks baby Oscar up from Dad's, I'll be ready to spend an evening with the people I love the most in the world. I feel resolved not to let that bitter Charterhouse woman spoil it.

I wash my hands, apply a little Molton Brown hand cream, and take a moment to enjoy its luxurious creamy feel on my skin. I splashed out on it on a recent shopping trip, reasoning that it's the little things that give the most joy. That's what I told Blake, anyway, and he doesn't have to know how much it cost.

I inspect my skin in the small mirror over the sink, twisting my mouth to one side and then the other. I can't spot any new spots or wrinkles.

I know I'm lucky. Blake never forgets to tell me he loves me before leaving for work each day, and I always feel so grateful for that. My only problem continues to be truly accepting that someone could genuinely care for me, but I'm working on it.

It's been a long road, but I do believe I'll get there.

Blake has been outside for a little while now, so I'm expecting to hear Grace thundering in any moment, bursting with excitement and stories of terrifying rides.

I hear the song begin to fade out, but just as I'm about to leave the bathroom, I spot an errant eyebrow hair sticking out at the wrong angle. In the short pause before the next track starts, I open the cupboard and reach for my tweezers.

And that's when I hear it.

"Lucie!" Blake sounds startled, his tone containing rising panic. "Lucie, come quick!"

I drop the tweezers in the sink and dash to the bathroom door, dread nipping at my throat.

I think I hear him shout again.

"Coming!" I bound downstairs and rush to the front door.

My husband is standing at the open gate, one hand supporting him on the post. He looks odd, like he's winded.

"What's wrong?" I rush up the damp, mossy path in my bare feet, and then I realise. "Where's Grace? I thought Mike said she was on her way?" My words sound hoarse, like there's a lump of gristle suddenly wedged in my throat.

Blake half turns, limping badly on one leg.

"He did say that, but she hasn't appeared from around the bend yet. My phone distracted me, and I slipped on the moss...twisted my ankle. I've been shouting you for what seems like ages, but—"

"Oh God!" I rush back into the porch and jam my feet into my mucky old trainers, then run out again, flying past Blake through the gate.

"Call Mike, make sure she's left."

"I already did," he shouts after me. "He watched her leave the house five minutes ago."

His final words fade to nothing as I sprint down Violet Road towards the bend in the middle that signifies the halfway mark. From there I'll have a clear view of the rest of the road.

My shoulders are hunched up under my ears, every muscle in my body feels taut enough to snap.

I must've walked this route a thousand times with Grace, and at our nice easy pace, it's never taken more than five or six minutes to get from Mike and Bev's house to our own front door. Grace should have certainly at least reached the bend.

I get there, panting. I can visualise her surprised face as I bump into her...She'll chastise me for checking up on her. *I'm not a baby, Mum. I'm NINE now!* Her new favourite phrase echoes in my head.

My eyes are clouded with fear as I round the bend, but I force myself to focus. To breathe.

There's a woman walking a dog, a young mum with a toddler in a pushchair, and a couple of teenage lads who've just hopped over the fence from the small park.

But I can see immediately that there is no sign of Grace.

CHAPTER 2

I run. I run faster than I've ever done in my life, down to Mike and Bev's house.

Mike rushes out before I even reach their front door.

"Is she back?" His face is etched with concern, and for a moment I feel light-headed, like I'm watching the two of us from a distance.

Bev dashes out of the house behind him, and I spot Grace's best friend, Olivia, standing in the hallway, hugging her arms around herself, big brown eyes wide in a pale face.

"Have you got Grace?" Bev shrieks.

My legs begin to shake and I stumble, skittering forward until I grab at the hedge.

"No, she's not back yet...Oh my God, Grace...Which way did she—"

Wordlessly, Mike rushes past me, his face a mask of determination. He begins jogging up the road, looking into every garden he passes.

"Lucie, come inside." Bev takes my arm gently.

"No! I can't. I have to look for her." I turn around full

circle, scanning the road, the houses, the gardens. "Which way did she go?"

Bev stands at my side, an arm around my shoulders as we look up the road. "Mike brought her outside, then watched her go up the street towards the bend. He came in smiling, said she looked like a little soldier marching up there."

I stare up ahead. A car crawls past, its occupants taking in our alarmed expressions with interest. A dog barks in a garden somewhere close by. My feet feel fused to the asphalt.

Mike is almost at the bend himself now.

Bev says something in a soothing tone, but all the sounds around me are starting to fade out, as if I'm drifting away.

"I have to go. Have to look for her," I mumble. Breaking away from Bev's touch, I begin to stride away.

"I'll get someone to watch Livvy," Bev calls out urgently. I can hear the strain in her voice. "I'll be with you very soon."

I try to focus on my breathing.

I put one foot in front of the other.

This can't be happening. It just *can't*.

I move up the road, looking, searching every possible place.

Grace loves animals. She might've stopped off to stroke a cat or a dog, or a lonely old lady might have asked her in for a chat. She's such a gregarious, caring girl, is my Grace. She loves people, too...She'd always find the time to help someone in need.

My vision grows blurry with tears. I pull a tissue from my sleeve and look to my right, where Abbey Road branches off from Violet Road. I stumble on a few more yards and look through the gap in the houses towards Florence Road and Priory Road.

All these side roads, houses...All the hidden places Grace might be.

I stumble and grasp on to someone's gatepost. I feel sick, dizzy...I can't bear the terrible feelings that are rising up inside me.

What if...what if someone has taken her, is hurting her just yards from where I'm standing now? I press the heels of my hands into my temples. I can't bear it. I can't stand the thoughts.

"Come on, Luce, it's OK, we'll find her." Mike appears in front of me, helps me stand upright. "Take a minute and just breathe. That's it. Grace is a sensible girl, she'll have seen someone she knows, or—"

"She knew she had to come straight home, Mike." My voice is rising. "She knew we'd be worrying. She...Oh no, oh my God...her medication, her insulin!"

"She had it in her pocket, Lucie," Mike confirms. "I handed it to her myself before she set off."

That's something. It's something at least.

Bev reaches us, breathless from running.

"Sue from next door is watching Livvy for an hour or two," she tells Mike. Then, "Where's Blake?"

"He's twisted his ankle really badly," Mike says grimly. "It's swelled up to twice its normal size. I've told him to just stay put, but he's insisting on limping down here now."

"He was on his fucking phone *again*." I squeeze my fists tight and grit my teeth. "He should've been watching out for Grace."

I see Mike and Bev glance at each other, but I don't care. Blake is virtually surgically attached to the damn thing.

"Your front path is really slippery with moss," Mike offers limply.

"We have to ring the police," Bev says.

"Blake agrees we should check the whole street first, knock on a few doors," Mike says. "It won't take us long."

"But what if she's already in a car?" I cry out, stepping away from them. "We have to ring the police *now*, so they can put a roadblock up or—"

"I'll do it now." Bev pulls her phone out of her jeans, jabs at the screen and holds it to her ear.

Blake appears at the bend, his face twisted with pain. He leans on the park fence to get his breath.

Mike goes to him, and I stand there, staring at the street that now seems a hundred miles long with a million places Grace might be. What were we thinking of, letting her walk up alone?

Mike scales the small park fence and disappears. Blake looks at me and says something, holds out his arms, but my feet are rooted to the floor.

Bev is speaking rapidly on the phone. Giving facts, times, places, although I can't seem to process any of it. My head is full of static, my body uselessly shaking and cold. I feel so cold.

"Grace! Grace!"

A terrified voice screams in my ears, seeming to flood through my entire body. I see Bev's concerned expression and I look around frantically.

But there is no one else to see because the person who is screaming is me.

CHAPTER 3

People emerge from their front doors. Cautiously at first, peering out enquiringly before walking slowly, arms folded, to their gates.

They discreetly murmur the dreadful news between them, like a Chinese whisper.

But as we pass by, I hear the disjointed phrases, see the incredulous expressions and their disbelief that something like this could actually happen here, in our middle-class leafy bubble.

On our very own street.

A little girl is missing.

Walking home alone.

Everyone must search their gardens.

People spill out onto the street, spread out over the other side of the road.

All eyes seem to be on me as I move frantically with Bev, knocking on doors, searching. Looking. Trying to find Grace.

Blake and Mike are over the other side of the road. Blake

isn't much use, but Mike scoots ahead, dashing up and down paths.

"Where are the police?" I whisper to Bev.

"They're on their way. Keep focusing, Lucie; we'll find her, we will. You're doing brilliantly."

But I know she's just saying it, because with every "no" we get, from resident after resident, I watch my friend's face grow a little more pale. With each shake of the head when we ask if they've seen a nine-year-old girl dressed in jeans and a pink coat with a red bobble hat and yellow gloves, I feel her conviction that Grace is nearby wane just a touch.

I beat back the bile rising in my throat.

We get to the park and I think about my dad and Oscar, both oblivious to what has happened to Grace.

A group of residents behind us fan out and walk in a line across the park, calling out, kicking areas of undergrowth, wet leaves. I don't want to think about why they're doing that.

I stand at the fence, my wild eyes scanning the sparse trees that edge the grassed area for a pink coat, a red hat.

We came here last August, in the final few days of the school summer break, when I was about six months pregnant: me and Grace, Bev and Livvy. We packed up a simple picnic, which made us all laugh as we were still effectively on our own road.

We spread out a tartan blanket, and we had the best after-noon sitting in the sun putting the world to rights: debating whether Mike would get his long-awaited promotion to national sales manager of the high-end kitchen manufacturer he works for; whether the community would get behind new councillor Blake; and most importantly, what sex the new baby might be.

The girls played happily around us, weaving in and out of the trees and hiding from both us and each other.

That was barely six months ago, and I hadn't a care in the world.

All I had to fret about was a dinner Blake wanted to host at home for the people who had helped run his campaign. And I can remember worrying whether, having left a shopping trip a bit late, I was going to get Grace her new school uniform in time.

I'm aware of the noise level increasing behind me, a flurry of movement responding to authoritative voices. But I can't break the spell.

I stand and stare at the spot where we picnicked, and something writhes up from the bottom of my stomach. I retch and vomit at the side of the fence.

"Sorry," I mutter, mortified with myself. "Sorry, I..."

"Lucie?" Bev touches my arm. "The police are here."

I turn to see two police cars behind us. Mike is helping a limping Blake across the road and back over towards us. Bev steps forward and identifies herself as the person who called in "the incident," as the policeman refers to it.

She moves next to Mike, but I watch as she reaches out to Blake, grasping his hand. They don't say anything, just look at each other, and I can almost see the pain radiating between them.

A police van pulls up and a platoon of uniformed officers emerges, their faces grim and focused. Their uniforms are dark; most of their faces are white. They all look the same, like a small army drafted in to help.

I feel frozen, as if I'm standing on a flimsy platform of ice that could give way at any moment. I just can't move.

I watch, my throat burning with stomach acid, as Mike and Blake join Bev in talking to the officers. They all turn and glance at me, then look back at each other and nod.

I bring the cuff of my sweatshirt up to my mouth and blot my vomit-spotted mouth.

Blake limps over, envelops me. His arms feel cold,

unyielding. I want him to stop holding me, but I can't find the strength to push him away.

He looks at me, his eyes pleading, his face impossibly pale and drawn.

"They want us to get into the police car, Luce. They're going to take us home."

"No," I say with steely determination. "I'm not going home without Grace."

"We have fifteen officers out here looking for her and carrying out door-to-door inquiries, Mrs. Sullivan." The uniformed officer looks young, as if he's just finished university. "And most of the local community are out too, by the looks of it. If Grace is here, we will find her."

If. He said *if* Grace is here.

Blake reaches for my hand, grips it so I can't easily slip away. He starts to lead me to the police car, but I stand firm.

"And if she's not here, what does that mean? Someone has taken her into a house, or driven her away in a car?" I can't dampen down the panic that's filling my chest. "She could be on the motorway by now. She could be anywhere!"

Suddenly I'm wailing. Pushing concerned hands away. My face is wet with tears and I'm coughing so hard it feels like I'll rupture my windpipe.

I can't do it. I can't leave this place until I find Grace.

People surround me, in a supportive but firm manner. We're all moving together. Hands on my back, my shoulders. Words of reassurance murmured in my ears.

I feel weak with desperation, with rage. Sound and movement flicker in and out of my circle of attention like an ebbing tide. None of this feels real. None of this can be happening . . . *It just can't.*

I'm sitting down in a soft seat. I'm in the police car, and

Blake slides in next to me. Doors are slammed, concerned faces line up outside the window.

An engine starts, purrs as the car starts to move.

We're going home. Just Blake and me, without our little girl.

Without our precious Grace.

CHAPTER 4

Before: Saturday afternoon

I stood by the riding school practice field, watching as my daughter's party guests paraded past us parents.

I could hardly believe Grace had turned nine today. The years had passed in a blur, like a long car journey where people and buildings seemed to merge together and lose their sharp detail as you watched them from the window.

My Grace was bright, clever, and kind. Our world turned on her smile, and seeing her happy was as vital to me as the air I breathed.

I took a step back from the fence and inhaled a deep breath of fresh air mixed with damp earth and the unmistakable aroma of horse manure and hay. Grace had left ball ponds and bouncy castle parties behind a while ago; yet another sign she was growing up fast.

I smiled and waved as she trotted past on her sleek black horse, side by side with her best friend, Olivia. Both girls were perched perfectly on their placid mares. Grace's eight other young invited guests followed in procession, supervised by the two riding school staff.

My dad had offered to look after Grace's baby brother, Oscar. Dad suffered from emphysema, the legacy of working in a chemical factory for nearly forty years. He put in the requisite claim after being hounded by legal companies hungry for a cut, and after nigh on two years of wrangling, he did receive a modest payout. But nothing to compensate for the restricted quality of life he now endured.

Of all the variables that could affect his health, cold weather was the worst. He could barely walk a few steps these days before he was gasping for air. So when Grace begged for a riding party, I knew Dad would struggle to attend.

Little Oscar was just getting over a bad cold himself, and when Dad suggested, quite rightly, that he was better off staying wrapped up warm at home while we celebrated at Grace's party, Blake and I both readily agreed.

Life had been busy for us, especially since Oscar came along unexpectedly, and to be honest, we'd both thought it would be nice for us to focus on Grace for a few hours on her special day.

It sounded trite, but I did feel blessed. Two gorgeous kids and a husband who cared deeply about us all; it was honestly far more than I ever expected for myself. The empty black space inside myself felt soothed, even if it could never be fully healed.

The horses circled again, and this time as Grace passed us, she turned slightly, her face animated with joy. The energy and passion for her beloved riding buzzed around her like an aura as she paraded in front of us, her friends and family.

A delicious sweet scent distracted me, and when I turned around, I saw that Blake was standing there holding up two steaming mugs of hot chocolate like trophies.

"There we go. And before you ask"—he extended one

towards me, his soft brown eyes twinkling with mischief—
"I didn't put any marshmallows in yours, so there are hardly
any calories in it."

I grinned and accepted the mug gratefully. I didn't mention that I'd seen the owner of the stables making the hot
chocolate with full-cream Jersey milk before we went outside. I was probably about to consume an entire day's points
in the next few minutes, but after the first tiny sip, I knew it
was going to be worth it.

I'd joined an online slimming club a couple of months
ago. Apart from the odd blip, I'd managed to stick to my
diet, and to date, I'd lost nearly a stone. Blake had been
really supportive, as he knew how steadily piling on weight
over the last few years had badly affected my already flaky
self-confidence.

Over the past months, I'd watched as Blake became more
and more absorbed in his work. When we were invited to a
black-tie ball at the Council House after Christmas, I felt a
bit nervous, as I didn't know anyone there. If I'm honest, I
thought about making an excuse.

"It doesn't matter that you won't know anyone." Blake
had swiftly dismissed my fears. "I'll introduce you to everyone, and besides, I want them all to meet my amazing wife.
You have to come. No excuses."

I'd expected low-key, but when we got there, I'd been surprised how much effort the other female guests had put into
their dresses, makeup, and hair.

I'd been forced to buy a new dress because I simply
couldn't comfortably fit into the two or three cocktail dresses
I'd bought a few years ago, when I had evening corporate
events of my own to go to at The Carlton. They were still
hanging in the depths of the wardrobe, because I insisted on
kidding myself that one day I'd get back into them.

We'd just about scraped by for money the last few months. There was hardly anything going spare while Blake was investing in his political career, as he put it. Certainly no money allocated for a spending spree on a fancy new dress I'd probably wear only once or twice.

I ended up ordering one in a bigger size than I'd have preferred, from an online clothing catalogue. More than I wanted to pay, but still. I opened an account to spread the cost over a few months.

It didn't make any difference; I still felt utterly crap at the ball. When the dress arrived a day before the event, I could just about do the zip up, but it was very much on the snug side. I felt shocked. Since Oscar's birth, my at-home uniform had consisted mainly of stretchy leggings and tunic tops, which I jazzed up a bit with costume jewellery and high heels on the rare occasion we went out socially.

Somehow, an additional few extra pounds had crept on over Christmas without me even noticing.

I'd done my hair and makeup myself for the ball to save cash, although it was painfully obvious that most of the other women had pulled out all the stops to look fabulous. Worst of all, they gravitated to Blake like bees to a honey pot.

He kept pulling me into his conversations—"Meet my lovely wife, Lucie"—and they'd smile and say hello, but I couldn't miss the disapproving sweep of their sooty false lashes, taking in my unvarnished toenails, my mismatched handbag, and the way the front of my new dress pulled unflatteringly around my tummy.

How come a man like Blake Sullivan has such a dreary wife? How has such a frump bagged a catch like him?

I swear I could hear their judgemental thoughts as if they'd actually said them out loud.

To be fair, I never saw Blake eyeing anyone up or flirting.

Not once. He behaved impeccably, never left me on my own at all, but I still felt all chewed up inside.

I didn't say anything when we got home that night, but I sort of made a pact with myself to get back on track with a healthier lifestyle. Blake was working hard for all of us, and he was only human. If I didn't make myself a better prospect, how long might it be before his head was turned?

I returned my attention to family and friends who were clustered around the riding practice field, chatting amongst themselves and waving to the girls as they trotted past.

As I surveyed all the bright, happy faces, a solitary figure standing near the riding school office caught my eye.

I nudged Blake discreetly. "Isn't that Jeff over there, from next door?"

"Looks like him, yeah," Blake agreed quickly before looking away. "Fancy a bit of lunch tomorrow when Grace is out?"

I narrowed my eyes, instantly suspicious at his manner.

"Don't tell me you invited him here today?"

"No!" Blake frowned. "Well, not exactly..."

He was a terrible liar. "Oh, Blake!"

"I didn't invite him to the party, OK? I happened to mention we were coming here, and he said he used to love horse riding when he was younger and he'd often wondered what it was like here..."

"Save it, Blake. You basically invited him."

He hung his head bashfully. "I didn't see any harm in it, Luce. Sorry. I told him to come and have a piece of birthday cake with us, that's all."

My husband was a sucker for an underdog. According to his mother, Nadine, he'd always been the same. Good-looking, tall, and sporty at his all-boys grammar school, he liked to take the new starters who were finding life difficult under his wing. Nadine once proudly told me, not long after we met, how Blake would occasionally wade into disputes at school in order to protect the more vulnerable boys.

"He could've made their lives a misery and joined in with the bullying, but that's just not Blake's way. He's the last of a dying breed: a true gentleman," Nadine boasted, stroking his hair in a proprietorial way.

He was still the same now; got a real pleasure out of putting right injustices and helping people who found it difficult to stand up for themselves. Councillor Blake Sullivan.

It was an admirable quality most of the time, but at other times it could grate. We, his family, needed him too, and I'd have liked him to focus a bit more on us. On me.

Jeffery Bonser was our middle-aged neighbour. When we moved into our semi-detached house on Violet Road three years ago, he'd just lost his mum.

He became really awkward about the shared driveway at first, insisting on putting out the bins at the end when we were out at work, so we couldn't get our car back on without having to move them. And he'd play what he told Blake was his mum's favourite Frank Sinatra album on full blast upstairs, often until midnight, in the room right next to Grace's bedroom.

"He's just hurting from his mum dying," Blake had insisted, making me feel like a witch when I suggested contacting the antisocial-behaviour department at the local council. "Cut him a bit of slack, can't you? I think his heart's in the right place, under the prickly exterior."

More like *weird* exterior, I thought at the time.

But Blake had other ideas about how to get Jeffery onside.

"He reminds me of some of the boys at school," he told me. "They'd purposely get into trouble over the silliest things. It's a cry for attention really. He's lonely, Luce. That's all it is."

Over time, he casually befriended the man, spending a few minutes chatting at the fence when he got home from work and Jeffery just happened to be out in the front yet again.

I heard him asking Jeffery's advice on what to do with the overgrown garden, even though we'd discussed plans to pave over the patchy square of grass and straggly borders, favouring the easy option to keep it neat.

Then one day, it occurred to me that the bins were no longer blocking the driveway and the Sinatra had stopped.

Now, our neighbour seemed to see my husband as a true friend and often popped around for a chat with him... often at the most inconvenient times.

As if he could feel our eyes on him, Jeffery looked over now from where he stood by the riding school office and raised his hand. We both waved back.

"Our girl is loving the attention." Blake nodded towards Grace, who had just embarked on her third loop around the practice field. The horses seem to have speeded up to a canter now. "I'm so glad everyone got here despite the bad weather."

There had been a light covering of snow over the last couple of days. We lived three miles from the city, and the weather never got too extreme here, but some of Grace's party guests had travelled down from north Nottinghamshire, where it could become pretty bleak at this time of year, and Blake's parents had come all the way up from London, where they claimed to have had a good covering of the white stuff overnight. Yesterday it was touch and go whether they'd get here.

"You'll just need to put your big coat on to survive up north, Mum," Blake had joked on the phone.

"I'm especially glad your parents managed to get here," I said archly and he shot me a stern look, tempered by a little amused twitch at the corner of his mouth.

"Luciee…" He elongated my name, admonishing me playfully. "Be nice!"

I widened my eyes and took another sip of hot chocolate. "I'll have you know, I'm on my best behaviour. Seriously, though, I *am* glad they could make it, for Grace's sake."

"Me too. I'm hoping it might encourage them to visit us a bit more."

"Steady on. You'll be asking your mother to approve of my parenting skills next," I sniped cheekily.

Right on cue, Blake's mother turned from her place at the splintering wooden fence and gingerly picked her way over to us, mindful of the mud spattering her glossy black court shoes.

"It's such a sweet little gathering, Lucie," Nadine said in the west London accent she'd adopted within weeks of leaving Nottingham six years ago when Colm, Blake's father, retired. "Did I tell you that Liberty rides, too? The stables near their home in Kensington are enormous, four times the size of this place. Prince Charles actually visited them a few years ago, you know."

"Yes, I think you might have mentioned it once or twice, Nadine," I said, feeling Blake's elbow nudge gently into my side. "Sadly, we don't have anything remotely as grand around here, but Grace loves to ride anyway."

Nadine nodded and glanced back towards the field, smiling affectionately at Grace. "Liberty has to have all the matching gear, you know. Pink this, sparkly that, whereas dear Grace, well, she seems happy to wear anything at all!"

Liberty was her other granddaughter: the daughter of Chester, Blake's brother, and his wife, Aisha. It was fairly obvious that Nadine saw a lot more of Chester's family than she saw of us.

Blake coughed. "The parents who come here make a point of recycling their kids' used riding gear amongst themselves, Mum. It's perfectly good quality, and kids grow so fast. All that fancy stuff is just a waste, in my opinion."

"Oh yes, *recycling*," Nadine murmured, as if the very concept of it baffled her.

Blake, as a local councillor for the Green Party, was passionate about walking the talk, and environmental living was very much part of our lives. I couldn't claim to be the world's biggest eco-warrior, but I had managed to absorb rather a lot of climate-change facts and figures from Blake over the years, and my opinion was that there was probably something in it. Climate change, I mean. Which always made my husband laugh.

"I should say there is." He rolled his eyes whenever I said it, and teased me. "In one short sentence you manage to be so effortlessly reductive of the world's finest scientific minds, my dear."

"Grace asked me something earlier." Blake interrupted my thoughts. He'd raised his voice a little, and I knew he was trying to distract his mother from saying something so offensive I wouldn't be able to hold my tongue. "As she says, she's *nine* now, and she wondered if—"

"Not the walking home alone thing again." I scowled. "Why can't she just let it go?"

Nadine had opened her mouth to speak when there was a scream from the field.

"Grace has fallen off her horse!" someone yelled.

I dropped my cup and rushed over to the fence. Blake was two steps in front of me, Nadine lagging behind us. When we got there, the riding instructor was bent over our daughter.

Blake scaled the fence easily and was the first to get to Grace.

"Is she OK?" I yelled breathlessly, clambering over after him. "Grace?"

"She's fine." Blake glanced up from where he was crouching next to our daughter.

I looked down and saw that her wet eyes were folded in on themselves. Her face was covered in a fine sheen of perspiration, and I spotted the telltale paleness of her skin right away.

"She's having a sugar low!" I plunged my hand into my anorak pocket and pulled out the small tube of glucose tablets I carried with me everywhere. I popped one into Grace's mouth and her eyes flickered open to look at me. "Chew it quickly, poppet."

The instructor looked at me, alarmed.

"She's a Type 1 diabetic," I explained. "Sorry, I should have mentioned it when we booked. She's had breakfast, but her blood sugar must've dropped with all the exercise and excitement."

The instructor lightly touched her own chest. "Phew, that was a bit of a scare. She just turned around to talk to the group behind and slipped."

I nodded. "Her concentration disappears when she has a low episode, but the glucose tablets bring her back to normal levels really quickly."

As if to prove a point, Grace propped herself up on her elbows and gave me a weak smile.

"Feeling better now, chick?"

She nodded, her face still pale. "Can I get back on my horse now?"

"I think this might be a good time to break for party food," the instructor remarked. "Thank goodness she's OK. Panic over."

I smiled my agreement and watched as Blake helped a slightly shaken Grace to her feet. The rest of the onlookers had gathered behind us. When I turned, everyone looked relieved, nodding and saying reassuringly that I shouldn't worry, Grace was fine, which was true.

Still, I felt really sick.

Ten minutes later, Grace was the one cradling a small cup of hot chocolate in her hands. It served as a pleasant way to further boost her blood sugar levels and was a real treat, as usually she had to stay away from sugary drinks and snacks.

They'd brought the registered first-aider in to check her over; she said Grace had bumped her head but she was satisfied there were no worrying signs of impact.

The girls all sat in the party lounge at a table festooned with colourful paper plates and tethered balloons bearing the number 9. Tinny-sounding party tunes played in the background. Blake and I stood next to Grace and her friend Olivia, with Olivia's parents Bev and Mike, who also happened to be our closest friends.

"Don't let it spoil your day, sweetie," I told Grace.

"I've not had a low for ages and then it happens on my birthday," Grace said crossly. "And now my head hurts and my horse will think I don't like her."

"I nearly fell off last week, Grace," Olivia said sweetly. "It's no big deal, and anyway, who cares, because we get to go to Alton Towers tomorrow!"

She managed to raise the first genuine smile from Grace.

"After a day at Alton Towers, I'm guessing me and Bev will be in bed before these two tomorrow night." Mike grimaced.

"Oh, you'll be done for, mate. No doubt about that." Blake grinned in agreement.

Grace and Olivia bent their heads together for a second or two before looking up at us.

"Muumm," Grace whined. "When we get back from Alton Towers, can I walk home from Livvy's house on my own?" Before I could begin my usual response, explaining all the reasons why that was still not a good idea, she continued with her bid for freedom. "I'm nine now, and Olivia's allowed to the shop on her own to buy sweets, aren't you, Livvy?"

Olivia nodded.

I knew the shop they meant. It was a small Nisa store about halfway between our two homes on Violet Road, managed by tubby Mr. Jaspreet and his lovely wife, Meena. Grace and I often had a wander down there if I'd run out of bread or milk, and somehow I always ended up buying her one of those ridiculously expensive comics with a free cute toy attached to it.

"Her dad watches her there and back, she just doesn't realise it," Bev told me from behind her hand. "We could do something similar...if you want to let her walk up."

"Pleease, Mum." Grace rubbed her sore head, sensing weakness now. "I'll be fine. I'm *nine* now!"

"What's all this about walking home?" Nadine fiddled with the gold buttons on the cuffs of her black wool coat as she gravitated towards us, her interest piqued.

"It's just from her friend's house, Mum. Grace maintains she's too old now for Lucie or me to walk back home with her." Blake looked at me beseechingly. "She reckons it's cramping her style."

I rolled my eyes. "I don't know, Blake. I think—"

"Nine is too young, in my opinion. Ten, perhaps," Nadine remarked sternly. "In fact, if I remember correctly, I think Liberty was at senior school before Aisha would consider it. She's such a competent mother, handles Liberty so well when she tries to push the boundaries."

I turned to my husband and saw that he'd noted the sparks flashing in my eyes.

"Do you know, Blake," I said pleasantly, "I think Grace *is* sensible enough to make a five-minute walk on her own now."

"Yesss!" Grace and Olivia high-fived together and it was smiles all round, my daughter's headache seemingly forgotten.

Apart from Nadine, that was. My mother-in-law looked like she was chewing on a wasp.

CHAPTER 5

You really couldn't blame anyone for taking her at face value. Standing there today at the party, watching her lovely daughter and playing the perfect mother and wife.

Clever enough to fool even those closest to her. She seems so plausible, so decent... and yet both she and I know that's not the case.

We're the only ones who know it, although she hasn't got a clue I'm aware of who she really is.

She's done well for herself, I'll give her that. Ambitious, good-looking husband, two cute kids, a boy and a girl— although the baby isn't here today, of course. She doesn't need to work, and lives in a nice area.

I know her routine inside out.

Oh yes, she's carved a reasonable life out of the unspeakable chaos she left behind her all those years ago.

I've known about her past for a long, long time. It's been hell to get so close and keep so quiet, but I knew I had to wait. I wasn't sure what for; I just knew there would come a time, an opportunity to set things straight, remind her of the awful truth she's tried so hard to bury.

She nearly succeeded, too, in erasing the evidence.

I suppose, if my own life had taken a different path, if I hadn't dug around a little, acted on my instincts, events would have blurred and eventually merged into a history that could be forgotten.

I've been close to confronting her so many times, but now I know there couldn't be a better time for me to act.

It would be easy to rush, but I've waited too long for that. I'm going to take my time, make sure everything runs like clockwork.

Then I'll sit back and watch her very carefully constructed life fall to pieces around her.

That moment can't come soon enough.

CHAPTER 6

Lucie

Before: Sunday morning

The morning after the party, I was thoroughly spoiled. Blake insisted I stay in bed another hour while he got up early to look after Oscar and get Grace ready for her outing.

I pulled my robe around me, turned off the lamps and popped across the landing into the bathroom. What a luxury, to actually take my time going to the loo without rushing to get back to Oscar, or being interrupted by Grace walking in.

I glanced in the mirror and wished I hadn't before padding back across the bedroom to open the curtains. It looked like another cold day out there, but with a blue sky, just like we were lucky enough to get at the party yesterday. I loved this sort of pre-spring weather.

Before Blake was elected as a councillor, we sometimes used to wrap up on mornings like this and walk by the river after taking Grace to school. There never seemed to be the time to do that now.

A movement below the window caused me to peer down. Jeffery from next door was in his front garden, waving up at me. I nodded and raised my hand, just so he couldn't tell

Blake I'd been rude—which he had been known to do on occasion, as if I was a kid—then turned away, shuddering as I stepped back from the glass.

Not even eight o'clock yet and he was already out there, pulling up invisible weeds. I swear he did it just to keep tabs on what people were up to on the street. He must have left the party early last night, as we made sure we said goodbye to everyone there but I don't remember seeing him hanging around outside, as he was earlier in the day.

I got back into bed and lay on my back listening to my husband and daughter banging around downstairs looking for everything she needed for her trip.

I smiled as I imagined them searching for Grace's other training shoe, or her gloves, which always seemed to separate the second she walked in the door. I waited for the eternal cry, which I was certain would come at any moment: "Muum…"

But to my astonishment, she didn't yell, and after about twenty minutes, they all trooped back upstairs.

I took baby Oscar from Blake's arms and propped him up next to me in bed with pillows. He gurgled, shaking his favourite yellow rattle.

Grace sat on the edge of the bed to eat her cereal.

"How's that bumped head feel now?" I asked, flicking the rattle to keep Oscar engaged.

"Fine. Olivia says that once you're twelve, you're allowed to get into Alton Towers on your own," Grace remarked as she loaded her spoon with Shreddies. "We'll just need a lift there and back then. No need for any adults to stay with us."

"That's three years away yet," I remarked drily. "Looks like you'll be stuck with us for a while longer, chick."

She suddenly seemed desperate to have complete autonomy. It was probably just her age; I remembered it as a difficult time, stuck between being a child and a pre-teen.

I glanced over to the doorway, where Blake stood tapping furiously on his phone, texting again. He literally never stopped. If he was awake, you could guarantee he'd be on that bloody phone.

He looked up and saw me watching. He slipped the phone into the back pocket of his jeans, winking at me when I frowned.

"You're walking home on your own later, Gracie-bob, what more do you want?" he said.

I sighed, still uncomfortable with our decision to allow her the increased freedom.

"She'll be fine, won't you, cherub?" Blake said reassuringly.

"Of course I will. It's no big deal, Mum," Grace added. "*Loads* of people in my class walk to school on their own now."

I shook my head firmly at Blake behind her back. There was no way I was going to be talked into letting her do *that*, with two busy roads to cross.

"Who were you texting this early in the day?" I said lightly.

"Oh, just replying to a couple of messages that I didn't get around to last night." Blake checked his watch. "Eat up then, Grace. They'll be here to pick you up in a few minutes."

"Yesss!" Grace scooped one more spoonful of cereal into her mouth and then dumped the half-eaten breakfast on my bedside table.

Blake helped her put on her outdoor clothing and soon she was a blaze of colour in a bright pink coat and red bobble hat, with her yellow knitted gloves sticking out of her pocket.

"Alton Towers will see you coming in that get-up," I joked.

Grace nodded happily. "See you, Mum."

"See you later, sweetie. Love you lots." I wrapped my arms around her as she leaned forward for a kiss. "Be careful walking home later."

"Yes, Mum," she groaned, heading for the door. "I'm nine years old now. Remember?"

"How could I forget? Oh, and Grace?"

She looked back at me.

"Got a kiss for your brother?"

She huffed and plodded back to the bed, clumsily landing a kiss on the top of the baby's head. Oscar responded with an ear-piercing squeal and a gummy grin as he shook the rattle harder than ever.

Blake smiled and followed her downstairs. A few minutes later, I heard the door open and close. In no time at all, he bounded back up to the bedroom.

"And relax...she's gone. Peace for the day!"

I nodded to our son. "Well...sort of."

"Fancy brunch at Copper at ten?"

"Lovely." I snuggled further down under the quilt, feeling deliciously indolent. Oscar squeaked and whacked me on the head with his rattle. "Oww!" I smiled lazily at Blake. "That's another two hours yet. You could set Oscar's new mobile going in his cot, so we can have a five-minute cuddle..."

He pressed his lips together. "There's nothing I'd love more, Luce, you know that. But I..."

My heart sank and I wished I hadn't hinted at making love. I knew I looked like shit. I'd felt too tired to remove my eye makeup last night and now resembled a panda. Plus, my hair was desperate for a wash and was sticking out at all angles.

I covered up my embarrassment by turning it back on him.

"Who have you agreed to run around for *now*?"

"Oh, just a favour for a colleague. I promised Steph Lawson yesterday that I'd check in on her mother first thing. She's had some kind of virus and is really weak at the moment, and poor Steph's at a conference all weekend."

The last time I saw *poor* Steph Lawson, she was done up like a dog's dinner and simpering over Blake at the Council House ball.

"Well, don't be long." I rolled my eyes. "You know, you're just a big softy, Councillor Sullivan. The one morning we don't have to get up and watch Disney videos, and you go and find yourself another blooming job to do."

"I know, I'm hopeless. Sorry."

He kissed me and I kissed him back, just to show there were no hard feelings, and he ruffled Oscar's fuzzy hair.

When he'd gone, I tried to savour the relative silence. Oscar was gurgling, but it still felt strange because there was no television blaring out from the lounge, or singing or stomping of Grace's feet.

I often craved a bit of time to sit quietly, like I used to do before having the kids. Yet only a few minutes after Grace and Blake had left, I started to miss the sounds that usually filled the house. Our daughter was such a bundle of energy, a joy, and I absolutely loved her to bits.

She'd been a good little helper since Oscar was born too, although I'd noticed lately that the initial novelty of having a brand-new baby brother seemed to be waning. At first she'd jump up to fetch and carry at the first sign I needed anything. Now, she sometimes had a little grumble to herself if I asked her to help.

It was possible she was feeling a bit left out, which was one of the reasons I'd agreed to my dad looking after Oscar yesterday.

Just recently, I'd been thinking about looking around locally for a little part-time job. Nothing too complicated, just a few hours when Grace was at school and hopefully Dad could have Oscar.

Lots of the mums at the weekly playgroup I took Oscar to

came dressed in their smart office clothes. After the session, they never hung around for a chat; just grabbed their babies and bolted out to drop them off with a relative or a childminder so they could go to work.

I wasn't judging them; needs must. We could really do with the extra money a part-time job would bring, but up to now, Blake and I both felt it was more important for me to be with the kids. Maybe I'd raise it with Blake, see what he thought.

I lay on my side, picked up Oscar's little tiger toy and waved it in front of his face. He always seemed particularly delighted with this game, his little body jerking with excitement each time he dropped the toy, in anticipation that it would magically reappear within seconds.

I felt guilty looking at his beautiful bright face as I thought back to how devastated I was when I found out I was pregnant last year. It was a total rookie mistake I'd made, too.

Blake and I had always planned to have two children, but after Grace was born, it never seemed to be the right time to try again, for one reason or another: lack of money, lack of space in our old house, my frequent attacks of anxiety ... We kept putting it off, and in what seemed like no time at all, Grace had turned five and started school.

Then Blake became engrossed in his plans to run for councillor at some future point, and with Grace at school, it seemed a big leap to go back to having a newborn around. I went back on the pill and we just settled gratefully for what we had, without really discussing it at length.

I still felt stupid now when I thought about how it happened. I'd had a hideous stomach upset one weekend after we'd been out with Mike and Bev to a new Thai restaurant in town, and spent what seemed like a whole day in the bathroom before sleeping it off. I didn't get out of bed until Tuesday.

When I was feeling better, I completely forgot to take my pill, and after another boozy night out a couple of weeks later, while my dad babysat Grace, the result was . . . Oscar.

It was a real shock to us both at first, but Blake readily adapted to the idea and I had to put a brave face on it, though in reality I had many sleepless nights and hours of worrying how life would be with a new baby again.

I came around to it in the end, and when we told Grace that she'd be getting a new brother or sister, she was apoplectic with joy.

"I want a sister . . . a girl, *pleeease*! I can do her hair and play her my favourite Little Mix songs!"

But she loved him anyway when he arrived.

I handed Oscar his rattle again and picked up my Kindle, opening the thriller I'd started reading last night. I'd managed about three pages before I fell asleep with the device on my chest. Oscar had been fractious and snuffly the last few days with his cold, but last night, when Blake brought him back home from Dad's, he'd rested really well so we were able to catch up on our own sleep a bit.

I idly picked at the hem of the quilt cover as I wondered what other plans Blake had for the day. He'd already mentioned he'd got to "pop out" later, which was shorthand for being gone a while; hours sometimes. It's not that I didn't trust my husband; I did. But just lately, his impromptu absences seemed to have increased substantially. I don't know . . . Blake often remarked that I had an over-active imagination. I supposed he might have a point.

Oscar let out an ear-curdling squeal, as if he felt frustrated, too.

"I can't just say no when people ask me for help, Luce,"

Blake said when I complained about the time council business took up at the weekends.

Anyhow, that was why I was so used to my husband being out of the house. He'd had to give up his job as a healthcare assistant at our local GP's surgery to focus on his work as a Rushcliffe borough councillor, but still, he never seemed to have enough hours in the day. It was in his nature to do over and above what was required and expected, which was what made him so good at whatever he turned his hand to, and so popular with people in the local area.

My head snapped up at the sound of an ear-splitting scream and a bump.

"Oh no!" I raced around the bed and scooped up my baby from the floor. He was already bright red in the face from screeching. "I'm sorry, I'm sorry, darling."

I sat down on the edge of the bed, stroking him and kissing his head, speaking soothingly to try and calm him. When he'd calmed a little, I propped him up on my knee so he was facing me. I looked him over.

An angry red welt throbbed on his left temple where he must have glanced his head on Blake's bedside table as he fell. Thank goodness it hadn't drawn blood, but I could tell just by looking that he'd have a mark there for a while and possibly some bruising.

I felt like the worst person in the world.

I spent the next ten minutes singing back-to-back nursery rhymes and tickling Oscar's stout little belly, never taking my eyes off him for a second. It didn't take long until he perked up. He was such a joy; he hardly ever cried unless he was hungry, ill, or needed changing. He just seemed to have a positive aura surrounding him that I felt certain he must have got from Blake.

Grace could be a little reserved at times; like me, I

suppose. For as far back as I could remember, I'd always had the feeling that the world was against me, that good things happened to other people, not to me. This ingrained belief meant I always tended to expect the worst, while Blake naturally gravitated towards more positive thoughts.

"Have you ever considered you might just get lucky one time?" he often needled me when I was fretting about how something or other would turn out. But he might not be as cynical if he knew why I felt that way . . .

CHAPTER 7

Sunday afternoon

I feel stifled inside the police car, as if there's not enough oxygen to breathe.

We must only be about 300 yards from our house but the police had insisted on accompanying us home. I'm desperate to be out there, on foot, looking for Grace but my protests fell on deaf ears.

During the short journey, I'm vaguely aware of Blake looking over at me and reaching across to touch my arm reassuringly several times.

I can't respond. I can't even press my lips together in a sign that I acknowledge him, never mind give a little smile. I can't look into his eyes and feel my own fear reflected right back at me.

I keep reliving the moment he went outside to meet Grace. The moment I decided to turn up the music, to visit the upstairs bathroom, rather than the downstairs loo. The self-indulgent moment I lingered to check for new wrinkles in the mirror.

And now, I can't stop thinking: *why?* What made me decide to do those things?

If I'd stayed downstairs and turned the music off, I'd have

heard Blake calling out the second he slipped. Crucial seconds would have been saved.

It tears me to pieces to think that so many wrong decisions had to be made in order to create the perfect scenario for Grace to be left completely alone on her walk back home.

Blake had to step on the patch of slippery moss at exactly the right angle to ensure an ankle sprain that he'd struggle to get up from. He had to check his phone at the precise moment he did, although that wasn't so unlikely, given that he is virtually surgically attached to the damn thing.

In those minutes before my husband went outside to meet our daughter, I'd been so smug in my life. Fondly making light of having to listen to Grace's incessant chatter when she returned home, looking forward to a fun evening ahead.

As the police car drives slowly up our own street, I look out hopelessly at the unusual profusion of local people milling around, talking with their hands in groups, discussing what might have happened to Grace.

I recognise some of the familiar faces staring at us sympathetically as we pass; we already have a new role as the poor parents of the missing girl. Bursts of radio static pepper the silence inside the car and I have to fight not to scream for them to open the door and let me out.

The houses, the gardens, the people; they all look exactly the same as they did yesterday and the day before that. How can that possibly be, when Grace has gone?

"We're here, Lucie." Blake squeezes my hand, studies my face. I know my expression is blank as I stare at the back of the driver's headrest as the car slows to a stop.

I turn and look vacantly at the house. At the path where Blake slipped. At the gate Grace should have run back through, full of stories of her day at the theme park.

The brickwork looks darker, the windows cold and angular.

It doesn't look like home any more.

There's a flurry of movement outside the car.

My door opens and a female officer helps me out. Our eyes meet and she gives me a sad little smile that says she knows how hard this is. She spoke to me earlier, told me her name before we got into the car, but I can't seem to remember anything she said.

I walk towards the house. There are police officers either side of Blake and me. I'm placing one foot in front of the other. One two, one two. The ground is solid and unforgiving beneath my feet but I feel as if I'm floating just above it. Untethered, somehow.

I hear the creak of the front gate, the shuffling of heavily booted feet on concrete. My eyes fix on the skein of moss that patches the path in front of me. The group pulls back for a moment as Blake stops walking and stares down at the cursed spot. I know he's thinking about the consequences of his accident.

There is a bottle of eco-friendly moss treatment fluid in the cupboard under the kitchen sink that he bought on special offer from B&Q last month. That he noticed the mossy path at all . . . was this a hint, a warning of the terrible event scheduled to happen? Or was it just another example of his good intentions being scuppered by his failure to follow through?

He has no such trouble at work, just in his domestic life. Rushing around ticking off his to-do list, trying to wear all the hats.

What does it all matter now? I return to my silent, exhausting quest of trying to make sense of what has happened. Yet in trying to search for a reason for Grace's disappearance, it feels like I'm about to topple over the edge of the normal life I took for granted only this morning, into a kind of relentless madness only I know is there.

The front door opens; a firm, reassuring hand on my shoulder guides me through into the hallway where every day Grace shrugs on her coat and puts on her shoes, then carelessly discards them again, sometimes several times throughout the day.

I stand next to the stairs, the end balustrade strong and unforgiving against my back.

The small space is full of people, yet it feels empty, lifeless, and the air is full of foreboding as feet shuffle and mouths cough. People try their best not to steal curious glances at me and fail.

They must be wondering why I let my nine-year-old daughter walk home alone. Why I chose to nap and listen to music instead of ensuring she was safe.

Thankfully, if they are, nobody is saying it out loud.

My heart yearns for Oscar. I need my baby in my arms, safe and warm. Perhaps I can ask them to call Dad and get them both back here.

"Get that door shut quick," an authoritative voice growls, and it swings closed, but not before I spot a photographer near the gate.

Then a woman in a red mac appears seemingly from nowhere and springs forward with a microphone, shouting something.

It seems the local press have already arrived.

CHAPTER 8

Olivia

Sue from next door had put the television on for her and made her a mug of hot chocolate, which Olivia hadn't touched yet.

She sat in this lounge every night with her mum and dad, but right now, with Sue here, it felt like she was in someone else's house.

Everything was upside down since Grace had gone missing on her way home. It was like someone had messed up a completed jigsaw puzzle and now the picture looked all wrong.

Sue was chattering on and on about her grandchildren, Elsa and Niall, who lived in Spain and visited her twice a year. Usually Olivia liked Sue's stories about the stuff Elsa and Niall got up to. And she'd usually laugh when Sue explained how she was trying her best to learn Spanish but kept pronouncing all the words wrong and getting them in the wrong order so her sentences made no sense.

But today, she wished Sue would just turn off the television and stop talking, because Olivia was trying very hard to think.

She stared out of the window, Sue's voice and the television both fading away into the background.

Their usually quiet street was buzzing with people, and lots of them were police officers. Men, women, and even children walked in groups, heads turning, necks craning this way and that, as if they expected to find Grace hiding under a hedge or even in one of the wheelie bins that people had put out for the council's scheduled rubbish collection tomorrow.

Her friend wasn't in any of those places; Olivia could have told them that. Grace wasn't stupid; in fact, she was one of the cleverest in Miss Barr's class, proven by a recent test they'd all had to sit.

There was no way Grace would hide somewhere or run away. If she was planning on doing either of those things, she would definitely have told Olivia. Olivia was Grace's best friend, after all, and they told each other *all* their secrets. Like at Christmas, when Olivia had taken half a cooked ham out of the fridge and the girls had smuggled it to the park. While their mums chatted, they'd dodged into the small copse and left the meat there, so the local stray cats could have a festive feed too.

Grace had never told on her, despite both their mums ganging up together and demanding the truth from them. That was what best friends did for each other, and if Grace had been planning anything daring or exciting, Olivia knew she'd have been the first person she'd have told.

Yet if Grace hadn't disappeared on purpose, then what could have happened?

Olivia swiftly pushed the shadowy thoughts away. She didn't want to think of what else might have happened to her friend. On Violet Road, people knew each other, spoke in the street and often got together, like they'd done for the royal wedding street party in May.

The girls often complained that nothing exciting ever happened to them like on the programmes they secretly watched on Netflix upstairs in their bedrooms. They both wished some sort of a crime would be committed so they could investigate it like in the Nancy Drew books that were in the school library.

But nothing ever did happen. Until today.

And now, it didn't feel exciting at all. It felt horrible to think Grace had somehow disappeared after leaving here, and it made Olivia's hands go all cold and clammy when she thought about her friend screaming on the rides earlier that day.

Sue was still droning on, something about what she planned on cooking when her grandchildren flew in from Spain next week. Olivia stared at her before turning her attention to the window again. Didn't she know this stuff wasn't important right now?

Grace was missing. It didn't matter that Sue was cooking all her family's favourite meals.

There were familiar faces in the crowd searching the street outside. Her mum and dad were there, and Olivia spotted that man Jeffery with them, who lived next door to Grace.

Sometimes, in the warmer months, they played out in the garden, and they'd spotted Jeffery watching from his upstairs window on more than one occasion. They'd stuck out their tongues and wiggled their ears at him and he'd soon disappeared. It had been so funny to see him scurry back from the glass.

But there were also lots of people out there that Olivia didn't recognise at all.

The adults had all banded together, trying to solve the mystery along with the police.

Nobody had asked for Olivia's help.

"Darling, did Grace say anything about not going straight

home when she left here?" Her mum bit her lip while her dad paced back and forth, to and from the window. "Did she mention she might call somewhere else first?"

Olivia had told them the truth: that Grace hadn't said a word about anything like that.

"Is there anything else you can tell us, Livvy?" her dad had asked. "Anything Grace has said or done that shows you she's been unhappy, or is worried about something that's happened at home, or at school?"

"No," Olivia had said.

She'd thought about telling her parents what Grace had whispered to her in the playground a couple of days earlier, but she didn't want to get her friend into trouble.

And once Grace was back from wherever it was she'd gone, Olivia was bound to wish she'd kept the secret to herself. If she told, even for the right reasons, Grace would more than likely get into one of her grumps, where she stopped talking to Olivia and was all sulky for a while.

Anyway, even though the thing that Grace told her had happened was horrible, it had nothing to do with her going missing this afternoon.

It couldn't have anything to do with it at all.

CHAPTER 9

Lucie

Sunday afternoon

I sit in an armchair in the lounge, alone for the first time in what seems like ages. It's a seat that Grace has christened "Dad's chair."

The people who ushered me in here don't know that. They don't know our ways, our routines, how we spend our time as a family.

I no longer feel like I know those things either. The room feels strange, unfamiliar. I'm uncomfortable here, like a reluctant visitor who doesn't know how to act or what to say.

What do you do, how do you react when your daughter is missing, when you feel utterly hollowed out inside?

The Jo Malone candle Blake's mother bought me last Christmas sits on the coffee table. I haven't lit it yet, still waiting for a good enough reason to enjoy its subtle fragrance. My eyes settle on the cluster of photographs on the fireplace...I dithered over those frames in Debenhams for ages. It actually felt like an important decision at the time.

I'm in a stranger's house because other people are now

in charge. My emotional connection to our home has been ripped away like a nail from a fingertip.

The door opens and uniformed officers stand aside as Blake comes into the room with two men, both wearing badly fitting suits. One is short and plump, the other tall and thin. They look like a comedy duo off the television. They don't look like the sort of people who might be capable of finding Grace.

The plump one steps forward and shakes my hand. His palm feels soft and warm against my own, but there is a steely strength in his fingers that underpins his seemingly benign grip.

"DI Gary Pearlman, and this is my colleague, DS Rob Paige." He perches on the edge of the couch opposite me, bows his head slightly. "Mr. and Mrs. Sullivan. I can only imagine what you're going through, but I want to reassure you that we'll do everything within our power to find Grace as quickly as possible."

It sounds so obviously straight out of the training manual, but the furrows on his brow show me he is genuinely concerned.

"Thank you," Blake says. "Please...call me Blake, and this is my wife, Lucie."

"Thank you. Blake, I know you're in a lot of pain with your ankle at the moment and you're going to need medical attention..."

"It's nothing, only Grace matters. Please, carry on."

The detective nods his approval.

"I can't emphasise how important these next few hours are in the investigation. It's crucial we make as much progress as possible..." His voice fades out as I recall the numerous times I've read in newspapers, watched on television, seen online the assertion that the first seventy-two hours are vital in finding any missing person alive, and terrifyingly, how that time frame plummets to just forty-eight hours when it's a child who is missing.

"...so I apologise in advance if my questions seem unnecessary, inappropriate, or invasive. Believe me, my only motivation is finding Grace. That's the aim of anything I ask, say, or do."

Blake nods and I stare at the detective wondering why the hell we're sitting here like this. We should all be out there, on the streets, searching for my daughter.

DS Paige takes out a small black notebook. He opens it at a blank page and his hand hovers above it with a pen.

"I know it can seem frustrating sitting here when you'd rather be out looking for Grace," he says, as if he's read my mind. "But your information is the most powerful factor we have in finding her. You are Grace's parents. You know her better than anyone."

"She's Type 1 diabetic," I say. "It's really important she takes her medication regularly."

"We do know she had her insulin on her," Blake adds. "She should be OK for a while; she knows how to measure her blood sugar levels and administer the insulin to herself."

"That's good," DS Paige murmurs, and it goes down in his notebook as though it's dealt with.

But it's not as simple as that. Grace could become very ill, very quickly, if for some reason she can't use the insulin.

The female officer who accompanied me into the house brings some tea through. She carries the cups and the sugar canister on a tray I'd forgotten I had, covered in an autumnal print of leaves and berries. I've had that tray for years and never thought to use it.

DS Paige asks us if we've searched the house and garden. "I don't mean just the obvious places," he adds. "Also cubbyholes and any garden sheds. Young children are able to squeeze into some seemingly inaccessible spaces."

Blake shakes his head. "We haven't had time to search the house, but like we told the other officers, Grace has been out all day. She was walking home from her friend's house when it happened."

"If it's OK with you, we'll get that done right away, then." He doesn't phrase it as a question.

"Of course," Blake agrees.

DI Pearlman looks towards the uniformed officers in the doorway and gives a sharp tip of his head. The officers immediately disappear in the direction of the stairs.

"It's a waste of time," I say faintly. "Grace isn't here."

"I understand that, Lucie, and I'm sure you're right. But certain boxes have to be ticked and I'm afraid there's no way around it. The quicker we get through this stuff, the closer we get to our objective."

Objective?

I open my mouth to tell him about Grace Susan Sullivan. My daughter.

I want to tell him how she has too much energy to sit still for any length of time, never mind stay silent and hidden in some tiny space in the house on her own.

How she's never hidden from us even once in her entire nine years on the planet.

"Let them do their job, Luce," Blake says, and I close my mouth again.

DI Pearlman clears his throat and begins to ask questions while his colleague dutifully scribbles down Blake's answers on his notepad.

How did Grace seem before she left home this morning? Had there been any arguments or disagreements? Is it possible she'd run away as a prank or because she felt unhappy or annoyed in some way? Could she have gone somewhere else on impulse: a favourite place or a friend's house, perhaps?

"This is all nonsense." I stand up, knocking over the untouched cup of tea at my feet. The female officer springs forward, her hands stretched out towards the spillage.

I feel dizzy and I can't stop shivering, like I'm freezing cold. Which I'm not.

"The tea is not what matters here," I screech, waving her faffing hands away. "Finding Grace is what's important."

"Lucie, please. Just stop!" I don't think it's possible for Blake's face to grow any paler than it already is, but it does. And two little spots of heat begin to glow, one on each cheek.

I'm embarrassing him, but that's just tough, because some things need saying.

DS Paige clears his throat. "Mrs. Sullivan, I understand how difficult this must be. I know—"

"But you don't know! You don't know anything and I'm just trying to save time here. *I* know Grace didn't hide or run off. *I* know she didn't go to a friend's house. Someone took her. Do you understand?"

"We do understand what you're saying, Lucie, yes." DI Pearlman's tone remains calm, steady.

It only serves to infuriates me more.

"You don't seem to have a bloody rush in you, sitting around scribbling in your notebooks. In the meantime, my daughter is—"

The detective speaks again, his voice level but firm.

"There are currently fifteen officers out making inquiries on this very street, Mrs. Sullivan. That number is due to be boosted to thirty within the hour as we take in the surrounding area. As we speak, the police helicopter is on standby for dispatch to begin a woodland search. The local community are gathering themselves for an organised search on foot."

A woodland search.

An image of a small, partly clothed body and staring eyes offers itself for consideration, but I won't let it in. I can't.

I sit down.

DI Pearlman looks over at Blake and then back at me. His tone softens a little.

"As Grace's parents, you two are doing the most valuable thing of all. You're providing us with crucial pieces of the jigsaw that nobody else can give us. The quicker you answer our questions, the clearer the picture becomes."

"Sorry," I whisper.

"There's no need to apologise, Lucie, no need at all." He looks at each of us in turn. "Now, if you could start at the beginning. This morning, after Grace left for the theme park..."

CHAPTER 10

Before: Sunday morning

I'd enjoyed my extra hours in bed, just me and little Oscar, but the time whizzed by and I realised that soon Blake would be back and it was time to get ready for our trip out.

I strapped Oscar into his little padded bouncy chair and placed it right next to the shower. I alternated five minutes of scrubbing with flicking water over at him and watching him chuckle.

Afterwards, I quickly dried my hair and dressed simply in leggings and a soft brushed-cotton tunic top. I smeared on a bit of tinted lip gloss and applied mascara.

I changed and fed Oscar, and when I heard Blake's car pull up outside, we were just about ready to go for brunch. I froze when I heard voices in the hallway.

As I carried Oscar downstairs, I saw that Nadine was there.

"Mum wanted to pop in and see Oscar on her way into town." Blake smiled.

"Thought I'd do a spot of shopping while I'm here," she said. "I still miss the small independent shops, living in London."

"Here he is." I handed Oscar over, but she looked startled, holding him at arm's length and away from her pristine coat.

"Goodness, who'd have thought a little chap could dribble so much?" She smiled tightly. "Do you have a tissue, Lucie? Their chins can get quite sore if you just leave them to drool, you know."

I bit down on my tongue and fished a tissue out of my pocket. I dabbed at Oscar's chin. "There. You should be acceptable for Grandma now."

Blake shot me a look.

"What's that?" Nadine tipped her head to study the mark on Oscar's temple.

"Oh, he took a little tumble off the bed," I said, trying to keep my voice light. "He's perfectly OK, but he caught his head on the bedside table, I think. I've smeared a bit of Savlon on it."

"How on earth did that happen? Weren't you watching him?" Nadine looked at Blake.

"Of course I was! I just dropped something on the floor, and when I went to pick it up, he chose that exact second to roll over." I didn't want to say I'd been lost in a daydream about Blake's recently increased absence.

"He was lucky, he could've really hurt himself." Blake frowned.

I knew what they were thinking, even though they hadn't said as much.

Grace had had one or two little accidents when she was a baby, silly things that should have been prevented. One time I forgot to close the stair gate behind me and she clambered up a few steps before tumbling down. Another time she pulled at the tablecloth and scalded her hand with hot coffee.

Fortunately, she wasn't badly hurt in either incident, but Blake and his mother had long memories, it seemed. I felt sure Aisha had never neglected Liberty for a second.

But I was going through a bad time back then; the trauma

of the past had a very tight hold on me. I was dealing with stuff Blake had had no idea about...stuff he *still* had no idea about.

I remember being constantly anxious and suffering panic attacks. I'd often wondered if I also had post-natal depression. Anyway, I wasn't the same person now, but try telling that to Nadine.

"How was Steph's mum?" I tried changing the subject.

"A bit subdued, bless her." Blake pulled a sympathetic face and tickled a now-jolly Oscar under the chin. "She's usually out and about litter-picking with the Rushcliffe ramblers on a weekend, but she's got to get her strength back up before venturing out in the cold."

"Well, I don't want to keep you." Nadine unceremoniously handed Oscar back to me.

"Why don't you come with us for a spot of brunch, Mum?" Blake suggested.

I held my breath.

"Thank you, but no, darling. I'm afraid huge breakfasts don't suit me." She patted her flat stomach with a gloved hand. "Us girls have to work at keeping slim."

I didn't meet her eyes, but I reckoned I could make a good guess at what she was thinking. Well, stuff the bloody diet. I was looking forward to a good nosh-up.

After air-kissing us all, Nadine finally left.

We wrapped up warm and tucked Oscar snugly into his pushchair, then made the ten-minute walk from our house to Copper Brasserie on Central Avenue. Blake unbuckled Oscar and took him inside the café while I grabbed his changing bag and followed them in, leaving the pushchair outside under the Perspex canopy of the external seating area.

While we were waiting for our food, predictably, Blake talked about his work.

"I'm really excited by the local support, Lucie. The chief executive of the council told me off the record that she honestly thinks I could run for MP once my term is up."

I nodded, sipping my latte and watching his amber-flecked hazel eyes light up as he spoke about the changes he'd already been able to instigate since being appointed councillor for the Trent Bridge ward a year ago.

He'd already told me last week about the chief exec's comment. He was so full of bounce and enthusiasm, he often forgot what he had and hadn't mentioned.

"See, the higher up the ladder I get, the better I can make people's lives." He took a gulp of his cappuccino, which left a line of froth on his top lip. "And the better *our* lives will be, Luce. With you, Grace, and Oscar at my side, I feel like nothing can stop me." He caught my expression and frowned. "What?"

I ran a finger across my own top lip, and he grinned and wiped his mouth with a napkin.

He started talking about local transport links to the city and beyond, and I'm ashamed to say I felt myself listening a little less closely. Oscar bashed his rattle on the high-chair tray as if he'd had enough too.

Zoning out was how I often dealt with Blake's unerring passion for his job. Of course I was interested in his work, but sometimes his relentless vigour exhausted me. He just never stopped *doing*. And when he wasn't actually doing, he was talking about it.

As his wife, I was often pulled into local initiatives like the Great Litter Pick, and I helped out at least half a dozen church and school fetes throughout the year.

I didn't mind, really. I was happy to play the good wife and I'd much rather remain in the background than the spotlight.

The waitress brought our food over. Eggs Benedict for

me and a full English for Blake. She rushed back to the kitchen and reappeared thirty seconds later with my fresh orange and Blake's tomato juice.

I'd brought half a jar of fruit puree for Oscar even though I'd fed him before we left, but he seemed more than happy bashing his tray and beaming at the other customers sitting around us.

As I began to tuck into my breakfast, Blake seamlessly recommenced his rant about rising train fares. I made sure I raised my eyebrows and nodded in all the right places.

Blake's ambition and drive fascinated me, always had. This was partly because I was so utterly the opposite. I tended to shy away from anything that took up too much of my time, family aside: events, meetings…particularly a career.

I hadn't always felt this way. There was a time when I was quite the academic, collecting consistently high grades in my GCSEs, then my A levels, enabling me to win a place at Newcastle University studying for a BA in accounting and finance.

My dad was so proud. He told everyone how he'd known I'd be bright right from when I was small, and that I had ambitions to open my own accountancy firm once I'd gained some experience in the field. He framed the local newspaper's photograph of my sixth-form college graduation, where I won the annual Student of the Year award, and hung it in the hallway at home.

I hated disappointing him.

I can still remember the small, plaintive cry of despair at the end of the phone when I told him I was pulling out of university.

"I can't handle it, even for another single day. I'm just not cut out for it, Dad."

It was like a grieving process for him. First came the

denial, then the anger, followed by a period where he seemed really depressed, and I felt so, so guilty.

Finally, he did accept it. He really had no choice when I moved lock, stock, and barrel back home. I knew it had finally sunk in when he took down my award photograph.

Dad, friends, neighbours...none of them could understand it. The local golden girl who'd showed so much promise; such a waste of talent to just throw it all away like that.

But of course that was because none of them knew the real reason why.

CHAPTER 11

"Earth to wife," Blake called, looking at me quizzically. "Your food is getting cold, Luce."

"Sorry!" I picked up my cutlery.

"You weren't half deep in thought there."

"I was just thinking about what you were saying." I cut another piece of toasted muffin and broke the yolk of the egg with it. "I don't know how you find the energy for it all; you're amazing."

Blake speared a bit of sausage with his fork.

"Couldn't do it without my family. You three are my world, you know that." He popped his loaded fork into his mouth, then leaned across the table to squeeze my hand. "Anyway, since we have a little time alone, I wanted to run something past you."

I nodded slowly, hoping the sinking sensation I felt inside didn't show. More often than not when Blake wanted to talk, it was to secure my consent to help out at some event, or to agree to him taking on yet another commitment in the local community.

"Do you fancy going on holiday, somewhere abroad, over Easter? Grace will be off school, and if I put it in my diary now, nobody can spring anything on me at the eleventh hour."

I put down my fork. "Really?"

We'd holidayed in the UK for the last five years. Blake had always wanted the least fuss possible. No airports or foreign currency. We'd toured Cornwall in all weathers, camped in Wales. I had to accept he just wasn't good at switching off and relaxing on a sunbed. So the thought of a holiday abroad sounded like heaven to me.

He grinned. "I take it you like the idea?"

"I *love* the idea." I grasped his hand. "But how will we afford it? I know money is—"

"Let me worry about that. I've had news of a bonus I didn't know was coming; councillors sometimes get them apparently."

A warmth spread into my chest as I realised there was a real possibility the fantasy of sunshine and sand and family time together could become a reality.

"Grace will be so excited. Do you think Oscar will be OK on the plane?"

"Course he will!" Blake tickled him under the chin. "You'll be absolutely fine, won't you, little man?"

Oscar gurgled in agreement, making us both laugh.

We should come out together for breakfast more often, I thought. I felt like I'd actually got my husband back for a short time.

"When we get back home, we can look online and decide where to go before we price some packages up. How's that sound?"

"Brilliant!" I couldn't keep the smile off my face. "Do you fancy Portugal? Apparently the west coast is—"

"I hope you're bloody well pleased with yourself!" A strident voice cut through my sentence, and I looked to my left, where a ruddy-cheeked middle-aged woman in a waxed jacket stood, glaring at Blake.

"Good morning, Mrs. Charterhouse," my husband said calmly, before nodding to the wiry man hovering uneasily some way behind her.

I'd seen this rather brusque woman a few times out and about. She'd always been quite pleasant and nodded over in acknowledgement of me, as if we were somehow acquaintances. But today, her belligerent focus was firmly pinned on Blake.

"Do you ever stop to think about the people behind your vicious little protests? Isn't it far more charitable to give folks a fighting chance?" She placed weather-worn hands on the edge of our table and looked at me, before turning back to Blake. "You've got yourself a nice comfortable life, I'm sure. Wife who doesn't need to work, two spoilt children enjoying all the privileges you so virulently disapprove of in others. Why interfere with *our* livelihoods?"

I tried to swallow down the lump that had appeared in my throat. She sounded as if she actually knew stuff about us. About our family.

Oscar squawked and shook his rattle as she turned to glower down at him.

Blake sat up a little straighter, his brow furrowing. "I don't appreciate your manner, Mrs. Charterhouse, but I'm happy to discuss the rejection of your plans if you'd like to make an appointment with—"

"I don't want a fucking appointment, thank you very much." She lifted a hand and slapped it back down on the table, and I jumped a little in my seat. Oscar's head jerked up, startled. "I want to hear what you've got to say about the campaign you started against us. Right now. In front of these good people."

The colour had heightened in her face as quickly as it drained from Blake's, but his voice was firm and calm.

"I'll thank you to watch your language in front of my son."

He glanced at me, gave me a tiny reassuring nod to signal he had everything under control. But I didn't feel convinced, and neither did the customers sitting at the tables around us, judging by the number of open mouths on display. I dug my nails into my palms in an effort to stop my hands shaking.

The woman's scowl deepened and she showed no sign of backing off.

Blake cleared his throat. "Mrs. Charterhouse. As you can see, I'm enjoying brunch with my wife and son and I'm not at liberty to discuss this issue with you right now. I can assure you that—"

"It was a vendetta, that's what it was." She turned to the other patrons of the café, seemingly in an attempt to get them onside. "Thirty-five years we've lived on Bridgford Road. *Thirty-five years!* A few purpose-built dog runs is all we wanted. To set up a little boarding kennel to supplement Harold's pension."

She jabbed a thumb at the mute man behind her, who looked as if he was willing the floor to swallow him up, then addressed the customers again.

"Is it too really too much to ask...to make a modest living from one's own land?"

A murmur rose from the other tables. I couldn't tell if it was in agreement or not. I now recalled Blake referring to the Charterhouses' planning application a few weeks ago. He'd spoken to a stream of concerned residents who'd approached him for help, unhappy at the couple's boarding kennel proposal for their back garden.

Blake sighed. "It was your own neighbours who objected to the planning permission, as you well know, Mrs. Charterhouse. I didn't—"

She raised her voice above his.

"It was *you* who whipped them up into a frenzy. Frightening them with tales of hounds barking through the night, and the non-existent wildlife being affected, all because of your ridiculous obsession with the environment. Anything that'll enhance your reputation you'll happily jump on board, no matter what the cost to others. That's about the size of it, isn't it?"

Oscar mewed, his eyes wide as he looked from his father to the angry woman. He was getting upset.

We were saved by a young waitress approaching, twisting a tea towel in her hands.

"Can you keep your voice down, please?" Her eyes darted around the room. "Sorry. People are trying to eat, and—"

"Don't worry, we're going." The woman pushed her face closer to Blake's. He didn't flinch, but I saw him clench his back teeth in an effort to keep his expression impassive. "You know, your life might not be quite as perfect as you think it is. Ever considered that?" She chuckled. "You act as if you're the golden boy around here, but there are plenty of us can see right through the facade. You're treading on a lot of people's toes on your way to Westminster, and making a lot of enemies."

She dropped her voice to a whisper and leaned closer still, so only we two could hear her words.

"Watch your back, Councillor Sullivan. That's my advice."

As she turned to leave, she swept her hand over towards me and knocked Blake's tomato juice into my lap. A collective gasp rose from the other customers as she strode out of the café, her husband scuttling after her.

I cried out and jumped up, my clothes wringing wet. Blake sprang into action, grabbing our napkins to dab at the spill.

"Are you OK, Lucie? What a cow. I can't believe she did that..."

Concerned people began milling round, offering more napkins. Unknown hands pressed towards me, touched my clothes. I could hear soft voices comforting my son. Oscar began to cry, and Blake plucked him out of the high chair.

I looked down at the small clumps of red, oozing flesh that clung to to my leggings as I tried to steady myself by gulping in air.

An avalanche of memories that I seemed to spend half my life trying not to recall filled my mind. Sixteen years instantly melted away and I was back there, just like it was yesterday.

My mouth filled with saliva and my heart seemed to be pounding at the base of my throat.

The other customers' concerned faces loomed in and out as I tried frantically to draw in more breath, but the smell of cooking and the lack of fresh air just made me feel worse. I felt a hand on my arm, and my husband launched forward as if in slow motion. It galvanised me into action.

I broke away and rushed towards the customer loo that I knew was located at the back of the café. But the contents of my stomach beat me to it, and I threw up there and then, all over the floor.

CHAPTER 12

Back home, Blake fussed around me.

I pushed him gently away and made to sit up. "Oscar? Is he..."

"Oscar's fine, I've strapped him in his chair for a few minutes." He placed his hand on my upper arm and I relaxed back again. "I'll make you some toast and strong coffee. You hardly ate a thing at the café and it'll help with the dizziness."

"No. Thanks, but I couldn't eat a thing. I'll just have some water."

He left the room swiftly, clearly glad to find something to do. It had been a long time since my spate of panic attacks, and I imagined he didn't want to go back there. Believe me, neither did I.

I could hear him murmuring reassuringly to Oscar in the kitchen. I was making such a mess of everything: worrying what Blake was up to when he was out of the house, neglecting to watch over my baby so he fell off the bed and hurt himself.

And now the incident at the café to add to the list.

I felt twisted up inside, making a spectacle of myself just because that mad old harridan tossed a glass of tomato juice in my lap. Lots of witnesses meant lots of local gossip. It wasn't the kind of attention Blake would want to foster, for sure. I was becoming a liability to have around.

"I'm sorry, Blake. I don't know what came over me," was the first thing I said when I stopped throwing up, every customer in the café gawping at me when I collapsed into a chair feeling dizzy and disorientated.

"Don't be silly, Lucie. Here, have a sip of water." He held a glass to my lips and I took a little.

"She's a bloody madwoman, that Barbara Charterhouse," someone called out, to a flurry of grunts of agreement.

"It's assault, that's what it is," someone else remarked. "You've plenty of witnesses here, if you want to report her."

"Don't let the nasty cow get away with it," another voice added. "She needs teaching a lesson."

"Thanks, everyone," Blake said grimly, jiggling Oscar in his arms. "I'm not worrying about all that right now. I just need to get my wife home."

There were several offers of lifts, and he gratefully accepted one. I'd never been so glad to walk through my own front door.

Now Blake came back through from the kitchen and handed me a small glass of water.

"This'll cheer you up. Look who's here, on the Smiler, of all things."

He held his phone in front of me, and Grace's face filled the screen, alive with terror and excitement on the infamous steel roller coaster. I smiled, despite a twinge of worry that she wouldn't be safe on the ride. I felt better already for seeing that she was obviously having a wonderful time.

"Mike's sent a text, too. The girls are both ecstatic because they're managing to scrape the minimum height restriction for the scariest rides. He says they're planning to leave about four."

I glanced at my watch. Still plenty of time until they'd be back. "I think I'd like a nap, if that's OK with you. I feel exhausted."

"Course it is." He reached for a folded blanket from the armchair. "Please don't feel bad about what happened today, Luce."

I shook my head. "I know. I just wish I didn't have such a dramatic reaction when something out of the ordinary happens. It wasn't that awful in the scheme of things."

My anxiety levels could soar from nought to one hundred miles an hour in the space of a few seconds. I seemed to have no control over it at all.

"You can't help the way you're made, and I for one wouldn't want to change a single thing about you."

I bit my lip.

"Those things Mrs. Charterhouse said...she knew I didn't work, and that comment she made about the children being spoilt. How does she presume to know anything about us?"

"Pure bluster, I should think," Blake said cheerfully, plumping a cushion and sliding it behind me. "She and the folk she chooses to hang around with are all big supporters of Len Broadman. She's just a bitter, nasty person and really not worth your attention, darling."

Len Broadman had been elected as councillor for the Trent Bridge ward three times in a row before Blake beat him hands down last year. He still had lots of support in the area and seemed to occupy himself by being the proverbial thorn in Blake's side whenever he had the chance.

Still, if Barbara Charterhouse's spiteful comments didn't bother my husband, then I reasoned I shouldn't let them bother me, either.

I lay down on the couch and Blake draped the fleece blanket over me.

"Try to get some rest. I've already called your dad, and he says he'll have Oscar for a few hours."

Dad loved having the kids, but now I felt like I was imposing on him, because he'd looked after Oscar all day yesterday as well.

"Can't you watch him while I nap?"

"I've got one or two things to do, but I'll be home long before Grace is, so don't fret." He kissed me lightly on the forehead. "An indoor picnic and a film later; I'm sure Grace will approve. I'll get some snacky bits while I'm out."

He brought Oscar over for a kiss, and then I heard the click of the latch as he pulled the front door closed behind him. The very faint hum of the Audi's environmentally friendly electric engine started up, and they were away. No doubt Blake was off to do more good in the community after calling at Dad's, despite the opinion of people like Mrs. Charterhouse.

Her words rattled around in my head.

There are plenty of us can see right through the facade.

What did she mean by that? My husband was one of the most caring people I knew, with the purest motivations for helping people.

How could someone like him breed the kind of resentment that puttered out of that woman like toxic fumes?

I pushed the unanswered questions away and concentrated on relaxing each part of me, starting with my fingers, palms, forearms, elbows...

Finally, I felt myself start to drift away.

CHAPTER 13

Sunday afternoon

For the next few minutes, Blake answers the detectives' questions and I nod my agreement.

I've been a bit distracted, thinking through the exact events of the day prior to Grace setting off from Olivia's house. I haven't shared all the minutiae with the detectives, of course. Blake has just outlined the main points.

I don't know how much longer I can stand this feeling. *Feelings.* Terror, grief, extreme frustration at the lack of control. Conflicting emotions all tangled up in my head like an unravelled ball of wool.

How can it have come to this? Only this morning, we had such an ordinary family life: thoughts of watching a movie later together, hearing all about Grace's day. Now that's been replaced by the prospect of a hellish existence without her. It feels like the devil flipped a coin on a whim and we just lost the toss.

Or perhaps this is my own personal penance to pay and not random at all.

I can hear the searching officers' feet stomping about

upstairs in Grace's room, interspersed with sliding, scraping, and thumping noises as they move furniture, peer into spaces, into shadowed, little-used corners.

There's a marked change in the location of their footfall before the furniture-moving noises begin again. I realise they've now started in Oscar's small bedroom, just above us.

And that's when it hits me.

They think we're lying. They think we've done something to Grace and hidden her body here, in her own home.

My body feels brittle, as if the slightest movement could break me into little pieces. I sit very still and hold my breath.

"Mrs. Sullivan?"

I pull in air. "Sorry. I ... I didn't hear ..."

"I wondered if you could take us through your movements after Grace left the house with her friend for the theme park. In your own words."

It seems so pointless when Blake has already covered this.

"I ... I just showered and then we went for brunch."

"And where exactly did you go?"

"Copper Brasserie, on Central Avenue."

DS Paige writes it down. I can imagine him walking into the café to ask for verification we were there this morning.

Suddenly Barbara Charterhouse's rant seems well timed. Everyone will remember seeing us there, no doubt about it.

But I don't want to go into that unpleasant incident right now. It really isn't relevant. Blake has said nothing about it, so I take it he doesn't think it's important either.

"And when you left the café?" DS Paige prompts me.

"Well, we came home and I was feeling tired and a bit out of sorts, so I had a nap."

"OK. What time was it when you took your nap, and how long did you sleep?"

"It was early afternoon and I slept for a good two hours. Too long, really."

I think about how upset I was at the time, and how inconsequential it all seems now.

"And while your wife slept, Blake, what did you do?"

"I went out to make a few calls, work-related. I have a lot of things to follow up in the local community. Issues from my monthly surgery, stuff like that."

DI Pearlman's phone rings and he takes it out of his pocket and glances at the screen.

Blake and I sit bolt upright. "Have they found Grace?"

"Sorry, I have to take this." It's only when he stands up that he seems to register the odd mixture of hope and fear that must be plastered on both our faces. "It's about another case, sorry."

"Another cup of tea?" the female officer asks tentatively, and I feel guilty for snapping at her earlier.

"Thanks. That would be lovely," I say. "Sorry I shouted, I…"

"No apology needed." She smiles and picks up the cup, still swimming in its saucer full of cold tea at my feet.

DS Paige turns to me.

"I was just thinking about something Blake said earlier. That today was the very first time Grace walked home alone from her friend's house."

DI Pearlman comes back into the room just as the female officer leaves to make our tea. He looks thoughtful, sits down again.

I catch a lightning look between the two detectives. So quick, I wonder if I might have imagined it. I'm seized by an unexpectedly hopeful feeling. It's now clear that these people are going to do their level best to help us find Grace. I can feel that they desperately want to help us. It's so important I start to really believe that, to try and break the cycle of mistrust I've had for most of my life.

"She...she's been asking us for a while now. Turning nine has seemed to be quite a milestone in her mind. We've noticed she's fighting for a bit more independence, to do stuff on her own."

DS Paige writes something in his notebook.

"So it's true to say her behaviour has changed recently?" DI Pearlman shifts in his seat a little. "She's been finding her feet, challenging your parental authority. Would you say that's a fair statement?"

A flame of annoyance sears my chest.

"Not in the way you're trying to imply." I control the urge to snap. He did say at the beginning that there would be uncomfortable questions he had to ask. "Please, just accept that there's no way Grace has run away from home. It's completely natural for her to try and push certain boundaries as she gets older."

"Of course," DS Paige says amiably. "My own daughter is ten, going on sixteen. Can't tell her anything she doesn't already know." I nod, offer him a weak smile. "Nobody's accusing you of anything, Lucie. We're just trying to ascertain Grace's state of mind in the hours before she went missing."

"I didn't want her to walk home alone." I bite my lip and glance at my husband. "Blake pushed as hard as Grace did for it to happen and I felt I couldn't just keep saying no."

It comes out wrong. Sounds accusing and I didn't mean it to.

"Lucie, that's not really fair. I—"

"I don't mean it's your fault, Blake. Just that...Well, you both convinced me really."

The detectives turn to look at him. Is it my imagination,

or have their expressions turned slightly wolfish, as if they've just realised they are on to something?

Blake looks at me pleadingly, his fingers twisting together. "Grace kept going on and on about walking home and we just thought it would be fine. We both did, right, Luce? We agreed that Mike would watch her leave his house and I would monitor her arrival home. I didn't pressure you to say yes, or go on about it, did I?"

"No. I...I didn't mean it like that." It must sound to the detectives as if I'm backtracking, trying to protect my husband, but it's true that I wasn't blaming Blake.

He did go on and on at me, though, in support of Grace's obsession with walking home alone. I told him I thought she was still too young, and he dismissed my concerns.

Mike effectively did his bit watching Grace leave, but Blake put checking his phone before his daughter's safety. Then he slipped on the path he'd failed to maintain because of his councillor duties and twisted his ankle so badly he couldn't get up for those fateful few minutes.

Unwelcome possibilities thunder through my mind.

So many times I've heard how the missing child's father is the first suspect in cases like this, and that's exactly what the detectives must be thinking now.

I stare at my husband, sitting there with his head in his hands. I'm certain he loves Grace every bit as much as I do. I just think he just worries less, believes she needs a little more leeway than I'm sometimes prepared to give her.

There are plenty of us can see right through the facade...

Damn Barbara Charterhouse and her vicious words that seem to have opened up a crevice of doubt in my mind.

My husband has no facade; what you see is what you get, and Blake would never do anything that might hurt our daughter. I believe that with every fibre of my being.

I open my mouth to tell the detectives that he didn't push for Grace to walk home alone, that he wasn't negligent in monitoring her progress back to the house.

"Blake, I wonder if it might be better if we continue our conversation down at the station," DI Pearlman suggests, breaking into my thoughts. He raises his hands to show he means no harm. "Nothing formal, nothing to worry about. Just that being away from the house might give you the space to—"

"You seriously think I've got something to do with my own daughter going missing?" Blake stands up, runs his fingers through his hair.

"Not at all, Blake. That's not—"

"The press are out there, and I'm the local councillor. What do you think people are going to say if you take me off in a marked police car?"

For a second, I detest him. That he could think about his image at a time like this is beyond belief...but then he redeems himself.

"I'm dying inside that Grace is missing. And who do you think I blame? *Me*. Of course I blame myself, for failing to watch her home safely." His eyes fill and tears career down his face. He doesn't look at me. "My wife has had the good grace not to blame me, but it must have occurred to her that I allowed this to happen."

"Blake..." I feel shamed by my secret thoughts about his phone obsession, the neglected path.

"It's only natural you would, Luce. I'm a fucking idiot. I should've realised, I should have..."

He squeezes his eyes shut and clenches his hands into fists as he tries to conquer his emotions. I've seen him do it before, when his grandfather died.

"Calm down, Blake. Sit down for a moment, please."

DS Paige's friendly tone has gained a bit of an edge. I can understand it: Blake is six foot two; the detectives won't want him losing it. "If you'd prefer not to go down to the station at this stage, that's fine. We can carry on with our interview here. But I will have to ask you some difficult questions. Try and think of it as part of the process of finding your daughter."

The more I think about this, the more obvious it is that they must suspect Blake had something to do with Grace going missing. It's ludicrous.

"I'd prefer to stay here." Blake blows air out of his mouth, seems to pull himself together and sits down again.

"Right then, sir, time to press on." It's *sir* now, not Blake. Is it my imagination, or has DI Pearlman assumed a slightly more formal manner? "Let's start with you telling us exactly where you went and who you saw during the two hours your wife took her nap earlier today."

There are three pairs of eyes on my husband's face as his cheeks fire up like someone lit a furnace beneath his skin. It's always been a physical reaction of his when he feels threatened or challenged in any way.

He meets my gaze and I wait for something—an unspoken message, a feeling—to relay between us, like sometimes happens when we're in tune.

But there is nothing, and his eyes look empty, cold even. It feels as though an invisible barrier has been erected between us.

Then, unexpectedly, he stands up, dusts down his already spotless jeans and gives one of his nervous sniffs. He keeps his eyes trained on DI Pearlman, who looks a little taken aback at his action.

"You know, I think it might be best if I come to the station after all," he says.

CHAPTER 14

I shuffle forward to get up out of my seat, but Blake puts a hand up.

"No need for you to come, Luce."

"But what about Oscar? I'll have to fetch him from Dad's and—"

"Stay here, Lucie," he says firmly. "Someone needs to be here for news about Grace. Just give your dad a call to explain what's happened. I can pick the baby up later."

The two detectives stand up.

"But . . . why are you going with them? Why are you . . . can't you just talk here?" My words have ragged, unfinished edges. This change in his attitude doesn't make any sense, and I don't know what it's about. "You said yourself the rumours will start flying if you leave in the police car."

"I've changed my mind, and what does any of it matter really? If it helps find Grace, then it's better this way. You're so stressed, and it might keep the newspaper hacks away from the house if nothing else."

I doubt that very much. The small gathering outside the

gate I can see from the window seems to swell every minute Grace remains missing. They're like jackals, waiting to sense an increased weakness in their prey.

"DS Fiona Bean is going to stay here with you, Lucie," DI Pearlman says hurriedly. He seems suddenly very keen to take Blake up on his offer. "Fiona is your designated family liaison officer; she's here to answer any questions you might have about the police process and to support you through it."

I've seen these officers on plenty of TV crime dramas. They're put in place to help with the parents' inevitable breakdown when the missing child is tragically found. They also watch and listen for any clues as to wrongdoing in the family.

My hand flies up to the hot wetness spilling on to my cheek. Blake rushes over.

"Come on, Luce. It'll be OK, I promise you. Grace will be back soon. There'll be some crazy explanation and—"

"You don't know that." I push him gently away. "Nobody knows where the hell she is."

He tries to pull me close, but my body is rigid with the tension that's also keeping me upright. If I relax my muscles, I fear I'll just collapse in on myself.

"Hopefully he won't be with us very long, Lucie," DS Paige says.

I don't say anything, but the word *hopefully* only serves to make me feel worse.

I stand by the window as they leave, watching the camera flashes as Blake reaches the gate. He stops to speak to the press as they drive forward en masse to swarm around him, greedily seeking the smallest nugget of information to base an article on.

DS Bean hovers around my elbow.

"Would you like a cup of—"

"No." I shake my head. "No more tea, thanks."

"Sorry." She rolls her eyes. "They teach us to constantly offer, you know. Tea often helps."

"I know. Usually I'd bite your hand off, but everything..."

"Yes. People have described it as an awful new reality, everything turned upside down, inside out."

"Yes," I say vaguely. "That's exactly how it feels."

"I've just had confirmation they've increased the number of officers on the street. They're carrying out comprehensive door-to-door inquiries and asking people's permission to search their back gardens. The local community are providing added manpower. You have some pretty supportive neighbours."

I nod. "People are generally good around here when help is needed. But what if..." I falter. Stop myself.

"You can ask me anything," Fiona says gently. "That's what I'm here for, Mrs. Sullivan."

"What if Grace isn't around here any more? What if she's miles away? Someone may have taken her away in a car and then everything that's being done out there is completely useless."

She presses her lips together. "Measures are in place for every eventuality."

I frown, wanting more.

"We've put out a national alert and we're in the process of informing ports and airports. You can rest assured, everything has been considered. But can I make a suggestion?"

I look at her. She's a no-nonsense woman, short brown hair, no makeup, tiny silver ear studs, and determined mid-brown eyes. She's probably a realist; deals with facts and nothing else.

I nod. "Please do."

"Don't let yourself dwell on that stuff. It will screw you up so fast, you won't even realise it's happening until you're on the floor. Take each step at a time. For now, we've no reason to believe Grace is anywhere but local. My advice is, don't let yourself slide into the abyss, love. Not yet."

A young, uniformed officer coughs in the doorway.

"Sorry to interrupt. We need to take Grace's hairbrush and toothbrush, is that OK?"

I nod. I don't need to ask what for. They'll need Grace's DNA on record for if they find a body and...

Fiona places her hand gently on my shoulder.

I suddenly feel a real need to escape other people's eyes; even her's.

"DS Bean, I think I might go for a lie-down upstairs, if you don't need me for half an hour or so."

"That's a good idea; you must be exhausted. And it's Fiona, by the way, Fi, if you'd prefer. I don't mind, to be honest. I'll answer to anything."

"And you can call me Lucie," I say as I go to the door. "Promise you'll disturb me, though, if anything at all..."

"Goes without saying. You'll be the first to know if I hear the slightest thing."

As I climb the stairs, I hear Fiona return to the kitchen and close the door behind her. She's obviously making a call, as after a moment or two, I hear her speak. She's probably reporting my mental state to her superior. I feel like her eyes are on me every second I'm in her sight: evaluating, trying to garner any clues I might have tried to hide.

I climb steadily, taking a breath in and out again with each step.

The sheer walls of the stairs rise up on either side of me, confining and claustrophobic. They are dotted with framed photographs of the children, of me and Blake. I don't look at them. I focus on moving towards the window on the landing that gives a partial view of the bottom of Violet Road.

From here I can see the rear corner of the roof of Bev

and Mike's house. Grace was in there a couple of hours ago, safe and sound. If one of us had gone to collect her, she'd be home with us now.

The door to her bedroom is slightly ajar. The police searched in here earlier, looking for her as if she might be playing some silly game of hide-and-seek. They'll have opened drawers and her wardrobe, looking for evidence that she'd perhaps packed a bag, executing a plan to run away from home. They'll have found nothing of the sort. Like I told them from the off, Grace is not hiding and she hasn't run away.

I push the door open fully and step inside. It's been a fairly bright day outside today, but of course, now it's starting to get dark. So there's no sunlight flooding in through her window to bathe me in a sense of hope.

The police have been sensitive in their search, I can see that. No drawers left pulled out, nor possessions strewn around the floor. Still, I can instantly see the order has been disturbed.

Her dressed Spanish dolls on top of the chest of drawers are no longer equidistant from each other, as Grace prefers to display them. The stacked annuals at the side of her bed have been disturbed. The army of soft toys that sit on her windowsill are higgledy-piggledy, falling into each other's laps.

I look around, trying to see the room from a stranger's point of view. This is the bedroom of a child who is well looked after and loved. The Little Mix posters on the wall, the CD player and collection of pop music CDs show her love of music. The essence of Grace is here, and yet something is missing.

I'm so desperate for a sense of her, but it feels barren in here, devoid of Grace's tinkling laughter and indomitable spirit.

In my own bedroom, with the door closed, the silence echoes in my ears.

The only time the house is this quiet is when Grace is out, and that's not very often. Noise accompanies her when she is here: she sings, watches television, listens to music, and sometimes plays games on my iPad.

I stand behind the curtain to watch the growing group of people outside. I recognise a few locals, some of whom are talking to the press.

I turn away and lie down on the bed. My body feels taut and bruised, tender wherever my clothes touch it. I take a few deep breaths in and blow long, extended breaths out, but it doesn't seem to change anything.

If wishing hard could turn back time, I'd be transported back to this morning, when Grace sat on the edge of this very bed with her bowl of cereal. I keep constantly wishing—*willing*—for the chance to make different decisions and of course it doesn't work. I should've learned by now.

In this life, we're all encouraged to support other people. We tell them they deserve another chance if they make a mess of things. It only seems fair, and yet when life itself deals a blow, it often has unchangeable consequences.

This morning, my daughter sat right here, munching her breakfast, too excited to finish it. Now she is missing.

So far, nobody seems to know anything. Violet Road is not the busiest street, but it is lined with houses.

Surely someone saw *something*?

My mind is constantly searching for a reason this has happened to us. Surely the stuff of nightmares always happens to someone else, on the TV?

I really, really need a reason. I simply can't accept that it's arbitrary, that some random child disappears off the face of the earth, and it happens to be my daughter.

I need to put a frame around it, give it some kind of context.

An uncomfortable ache starts up in my solar plexus. It's the place I often feel the first rumblings of anxiety when something is wrong.

I will it to go away, but there's no chance of that.

I wiggle my jaw from side to side when I realise I've clamped down so hard on my back teeth it's making my headache even worse. But I have a reoccurring thought rattling around my head that I can't get rid of.

I think this might be my fault.

I've tried to be a good person all my life. I made one mistake, many years ago, but it wasn't my fault. Truly, I would never wish to harm another person.

Sometimes people find themselves in impossible situations. Sometimes you have to decide in a split second whether to do the right thing and go under, or fight to survive.

That's what I did. I made a decision to survive.

The ache in my belly grows stronger still.

What happens to the bad things people have done? Does that negative energy just dissipate, never to be seen again, or does it rack up and follow you around until you're forced to face it?

I've spent the last sixteen years refusing to acknowledge what happened when I was younger, but I've always known it's still there, lurking in the ether. Waiting to make a comeback.

Living my life in the shadows seems to have worked so far. Until now.

Now, I can't help wondering if the moment has finally arrived. Has some greater power finally decided that the price I must pay is losing my daughter...my entire world?

CHAPTER 15

There's no way I'm going to be able to rest up here. I honestly doubt I will sleep again until we get Grace back. *Until* we get her back, not *if*. The word "if" leads to madness; I instinctively know that and refuse to even think it.

I run through the detectives' questions again in my mind. The way Blake seemed adamant he didn't want to go to the station and then appeared to do a 360-degree turn and asked them to take him in.

At first I felt annoyed he seemed to be more concerned with his professional image and the perception of the local community and press. But now I remind myself just how much he—and we as a family—has sacrificed to build his successful political career. He's making a fantastic success of being a councillor and attracting the attention of all the right people.

"I'm just a step away from going to Westminster, Luce. I can feel it here," he's said more than once, tapping his chest. "If I can pull it off, it will transform our lives."

Anyone who reads newspapers or takes a passing interest

in the popular news sites online will know how the slightest seed of doubt or whiff of scandal can ruin a career, regardless of actual guilt being proven.

This was the reason Blake was reluctant to go to the police station. I shared his trepidation that pictures of him being led out of our house to a marked police car would instantly be splashed all over the local newspapers and online. No doubt to be snapped up by the nationals within the hour. So to hear him volunteering to go in made no sense to me at all.

Blake is one of the most moral, principled people I know and I trust him implicitly. Why, then, is this worm of suspicion burrowing into my imagination? What could Blake possibly need to talk to the police about that he can't say in front of me?

His assertion that it was to keep the focus off me and away from the house didn't really wash. Anyway, the press haven't followed him to the police station; they're all still out there, watching the house like vultures.

I close my eyes and try to relax, naming each part of my body as I learned to do in the days when I still attended yoga classes. I might not be able to sleep, but if only I can ease the physical pain I feel in every single inch of my flesh, I'll be able to think more clearly. I can't—and won't—stay stuck in the house waiting passively for them to bring me news. Grace is out there somewhere. The thought both tortures me, because I'm lying here doing nothing to find her, and comforts me, because while she's out there and hasn't turned up injured or worse, she may still be safely found.

I'm tight as a drum from the top of my head to my toes. I can't seem to keep my mind on track in the relaxation exercise of naming the parts; *fingers, thumbs, palms, wrists, forearms…*

I lose my way time and time again, and my mind starts to

drift further and further away until I'm disoriented, trapped in a bubble of anxiety that starts my heart banging, making sleep impossible.

I reach for my phone on the bedside table.

It only rings twice before Dad answers.

"Lucie? Blake called earlier. Is Grace back home?"

"No, Dad," I say, squeezing down my emotion. "They're... still looking. They've taken Blake to the police station."

"What?" He's dumbstruck for a moment or two. "Why? I mean, they don't think..."

"They just want to ask him some questions, Dad, it's a formality. He volunteered to go, to try and keep the press away from the house." I glance out of the window, at the shoddy band of local newspaper reporters and photographers. "It hasn't worked, I'm afraid. Looks like they're going nowhere any time soon."

Dad sighs. "I'm so sorry this has happened, love. I wish I—oh God, I feel like somehow I'm to blame and—"

His voice cracks and for an awful moment, I think he's going to burst into tears.

"It's not your fault, Dad!" I can't bear hearing him like this, my rock for so many years. Then I realise I interrupted him. "You were saying, you feel like you should've... what?"

There's a beat of silence and when he speaks again, he seems to have collected himself.

"I just meant I wish I could get out there to help look for her. It's so frustrating, stuck in here like an invalid."

"You're doing us a massive favour looking after Oscar, Dad. That's why I'm ringing, to see how he is. It shouldn't be too long before Blake can fetch him."

I force myself to imagine Grace home and the four of us being reunited tonight.

"He's fine, aren't you, lad?" I hear Oscar chuckling in the background. "He can stay here as long as you like, you know that." He hesitates. "But I'd much rather be there with you, love."

"Thanks, Dad, but there's nothing you can do at the moment. I'm just sat here twiddling my thumbs and going quietly crazy waiting for news." I feel unable to keep the flat, dark feelings out of my voice.

"But I can support you and Blake, can't I? I feel cut off here, I'd like to come over. Be together as a family."

A tingling pinch starts up between my eyes.

"OK, thanks, Dad. I'll send Blake across to pick you up soon as he gets back from the station," I manage.

"Gracie's bound to be back soon." He jollies up his voice but it can't disguise the weight of his worry. "I mean, she'll have wandered off somewhere, that's all. Nosy little thing that she is."

"I know. I hope so." I take a breath. "Got to go, Dad, see what's happening. I'll tell Blake to call you when he comes home."

"Let me know when Gracie's back," he says as I end the call.

I let out a sob.

I hope with all my heart Dad is right and Grace has wandered off somewhere. But how can it take hours for her to resurface again? West Bridgford is a friendly place. A small place. She'd only have to ask someone if she somehow got disorientated and needed to get back to Violet Road.

Deep down, although nobody is actually saying it, we all know that Grace hasn't wandered off at all. The only logical conclusion, the thing that makes most sense, is that someone has taken her.

I can feel the truth of that unbearable possibility growing

with every fibre of my being. Even as I pray it's not the case, I can feel my own stability beginning to slip.

As each hour passes without Grace, I know it's only a matter of time before events of the past begin to inch closer. If I allow those pernicious memories to get too close, it could quickly turn into a landslide I won't be able to escape from.

And I haven't a chance in hell of helping my daughter if I become ill again.

CHAPTER 16

Sixteen years earlier

Lucie stared at the letter in her hand, read it for the umpteenth time.

"I'm so proud of you, love," her dad said again. "The first one in our family to go to university!"

Lucie smiled, and her dad's usually tired, strained face broke into a wide grin. He had worked so hard for as long as Lucie could remember. Often worked double shifts at the chemical factory to give them both a good life after Lucie's mum, Susan, left them when her daughter was just three years old.

Susan emigrated to Germany with her new man, Klaus, a wealthy financier.

Susan had divorced Pete and married widower Klaus within a year. She'd kept in touch with her old family for a while, promising to fly back to the UK three or four times a year to see her daughter, but the visits had never materialised.

Lucie was far too young to remember, but Pete told her that Susan was a successful saleswoman for a major UK telecommunications company. She'd been very forward-thinking when it came to travelling to Europe when overseas business was a much smaller market than it was now.

"She earned three times my salary and I fully supported her. I knew her career was very important to her," Pete had explained to Lucie when she was old enough to properly understand the dynamics of relationships. "I trusted her completely, and that was my downfall. She was mixing with people who had very different lifestyles to the one Sue had been used to."

Susan's business trips to Germany had become more frequent, increasing from every two or three months to two or even three times each month.

"Still I didn't suspect," Pete said. "I was an idiot. Maybe I could've changed her mind if I'd known she'd already met Klaus and fallen in love with him."

Pete had found out from a chance meeting with one of Susan's old work colleagues that she had died of a heart attack just two weeks after Lucie had turned eight years old.

Her colleague told a devastated Pete that Klaus was a high-functioning drug addict who lived the party lifestyle. Susan quickly got pulled in to the cocaine-fuelled weekend yacht trips and hedonistic parties at their palatial home on the outskirts of Frankfurt. And it had ended in tragedy.

It was only as Lucie got much older that she realised how difficult it must have been for her dad, losing everything. Everything but her.

He'd always worked at the factory, for as long as she could remember. As she grew up, he made no secret of his ambitions for her.

"Being stuck in a dead-end job isn't what I want for you, love," he told her repeatedly over the years. "The world is your oyster if you get a good education. You're bright, just like your mum."

So when she received the offer of a place at university, she knew just how much it meant to her dad, and that in turn meant everything to Lucie. It was like she'd spent her life trying to make her dad proud of her, to somehow pay him back for being such a rock, and now she truly felt she'd achieved the ultimate goal. As far as her father was concerned, anyway.

But the best feeling of all, she had discovered, was her own sense of pride in accomplishing something she'd thought would probably be out of her reach. She had got the required A-level grades and would begin a four-year accountancy degree at Newcastle University in the autumn.

She folded up the letter and handed it back to Pete, smiling as he tucked it back inside the official envelope, stamped with the university's name and distinctive logo. She knew that it would look rather more dog-eared after he'd proudly shown it to friends and family many, many times. Not in a boastful way—well, maybe, she grinned to herself—but almost in an attempt to validate his own performance as a single father. To him, the letter meant he had achieved a very important goal of his own, in raising a daughter who had risen to a level of academic excellence.

"So as we agreed, if you can begin sorting through your wardrobe, I can get the first batch of clothing laundered and we'll be nice and prepared," Pete suggested.

Lucie sighed inwardly, resigning herself to the fact that this was how it would be until the day she left for university, in five weeks' time.

She loved her father more than anything, but he could be a bit of a martinet. A strict roster of tasks was how he'd survived in the years bringing her up alone. So part of Lucie couldn't wait to finally be in charge of her own life. If she wanted to leave her laundry until she actually felt like doing it, if she wanted to eat crap and watch TV all night long, then so it would be done.

The thought of it filled her with relief.

*   *   *

With just a week to go, everything was organised. Lucie would travel up to Newcastle on the train with just hand luggage and the rest of her belongings would follow, transported by a man-with-a-van her father had found in the local paper.

The day before she was due to travel, Lucie realised with some sadness that she had next to no one to say goodbye to. There was really only her dad.

Lucie didn't have a solid group of girlfriends who she'd known since her schooldays, like lots of people did.

Maybe it was something to do with growing up so close to her dad. Girls her own age always seemed so silly and giggly, and she quickly tired of their company. Losing her mum so young had taught Lucie that sometimes, terrible things happened in life, and she found she felt safest and most secure at home, in the company of her father.

She'd got on well with a couple of girls at college, but they'd both moved away from the area now, and despite emotional promises from all concerned, they hadn't kept in touch.

During the two years she'd studied for A levels, Lucie had held down a part-time job three evenings a week and at least one weekend shift at a local coffee shop. She'd become a qualified barista there and enjoyed getting out from under Pete's feet and being amongst people without getting involved with any of them.

Still, she reminded herself, although it would be nice to make new friends, her real aim was to bag herself an accountancy qualification that would win her employment at a prestigious company back in Nottingham. Ultimately, the plan was to open her own accountancy practice, thus securing her financial independence and a bright future.

The trouble was, Lucie had heard her father suggest that

career path so many times, she was no longer sure whether the dream was his or her own. In the event, it didn't really matter.

Neither of them could possibly have envisaged the terrible consequences that would follow within a year of Lucie leaving home for Newcastle.

CHAPTER 17

Lucie

Sunday evening

I snap awake at a light tapping noise on the bedroom door. I can't believe I drifted off.

In the second before the brain fog clears, I remember. *Grace.* Pure, undiluted fear grips my heart like an iron vice as one thought presents itself:

It's now dark outside.

The tapping noise sounds at the door again.

"Come in," I call out, sitting bolt upright in bed.

The door creaks open and DS Bean's pale, well-meaning face appears.

"Have they . . . Is Grace back?"

She presses her lips together and shakes her head. "They've let me know that Blake will be leaving the station in the next half an hour."

I can't think about Blake right now; all I can think of is the square of dark at the window. The heating is on but the room feels chilly. I shiver.

"It's already dark." My voice cracks. "What will . . . Oh my God, what will happen if . . ."

Fiona walks quickly over to the bed and sits on the edge, near the bottom. Part of me recoils at the presence of a stranger in my bedroom, but part of me welcomes the support.

The kindness in her voice when she speaks is enough to break me.

"We won't stop searching for Grace, Lucie. All night if we need to. The dark will make no difference."

But it *does* make a difference. A big difference. It feels like the light of the day is fading in direct parallel to the hope burning inside me. If I dwell on it too long, I'll crumble.

"Her medication. What if she's lost it, or... can't use it for some reason?" I block out what this reason might be. I can't face even the suggestion of it. I feel like my insides are gradually tightening like a fist.

Fiona nods. "I know this is a real concern. Someone on the team is contacting your GP, so hopefully we'll know more about the implications very soon."

"I can tell you myself how serious it could be." I can hear the desperation in my own voice. "All sorts of complications can arise if she—"

"It's in hand, Lucie," she says calmly. "We've asked your GP to come here, to speak to you and to... offer help if you need it."

Help? I know what that means: they want to medicate me. Sedate the panic out of me. But I'm not having it. I've lived in that bubble before and it's not an existence I want to go back to. I can't help my daughter if I'm drugged senseless.

"I'm not taking anything. I want to feel the pain, the panic. It's what's going to motivate me to find my daughter." I swing my legs over the side of the bed and stand up. My legs feel wobbly and I sit down again and speak through locked teeth. "I'm not sitting here waiting. I want to be outside, helping to look for Grace. I've already been resting far too long as it is."

"You've been up here for about an hour." Fiona waves away my concern. "It's a good thing you managed to get some rest. You won't be able to help look for Grace without it, Lucie, think of it that way."

I wouldn't call it rest, exactly. More like purgatory, caught between the life I had when I woke up today and the hellish existence I've plunged into without Grace.

Nevertheless, I'm shocked how long it's been. I feel exhausted, but I've no right trying to rest when my daughter is out there, alone. I push up off the bed and slowly stand again.

"I'll come down."

Fiona walks over to the door. "I'll wait for you downstairs."

When she's left the room, I sink to the floor, wrapping my arms around my knees.

I can't breathe. I drag in air, but it's not enough.

I can't do this, I just *can't*. I can't sit around the house doing nothing, despite what Fiona says.

I am Grace's mother. If I go out there, search for her, I might get some kind of telepathic vibes, an invisible maternal thread of communication that only we two can feel.

It sounds mad, I know, but I don't care. Anything that can guide me closer to my daughter is worth considering.

The one thing I'm certain of is that sitting here drinking endless cups of tea with DS Bean is not going to contribute to finding Grace. And I hate being cooped up in the house with a stranger watching my every move and reaction; it's ramping up my anxiety to levels that are bordering on unbearable.

In the bathroom, I splash some water on my face. I scoop out the tweezers I discarded there only a couple of hours ago and glance in the mirror. The last time I looked in here earlier today, I was scanning my face for new wrinkles. Now, the dark circles under my eyes are a physical mark of the terrible events of the past hours.

I dab my face dry with a hand towel and steel myself to go back downstairs, my heart growing heavier by the second. I feel like I can't go on. Something has to change, because I honestly feel I'm on the verge of losing my mind.

At the same time, I know it's a waste of energy even thinking such a thing. What I want has no relevance to what will happen, because other people are in charge of my life now. Not least the person—or persons—who knows where Grace is.

I step out of the bathroom and am about to walk to the top of the stairs when I look up and see Blake's office door facing me.

Office is a bit of a fancy word really; it's the fourth and smallest bedroom, just about big enough for a single bed but no wardrobe. Our plans to make it a kitsch little guest room faded into oblivion when, by default, it became the dumping ground the week we moved into the house. It stayed that way until just over a year ago, when Blake decided he'd run to be a local councillor.

He needed a quiet space away from the television and Grace's constant chatter. And from me too, I suppose.

So we spent a gruelling weekend bottoming the room. Seeing as we'd barely touched anything in there for the best part of four years, we ended up throwing most of the stuff out and relocating what was left to the garage.

Blake's mother insisted on ordering some Scandinavian-style bleached-wood furniture that looked a bit incongruous in such a cramped space; she refused to listen to Blake's protests about not needing anything new. He'd planned to recycle some furniture he'd been offered from the nearby vicarage.

"I'm not having my son, possibly the future prime minister, working on a scruffy desk that somebody else threw out," Nadine announced haughtily. "It simply won't do."

Blake laughed and tried to protest he'd never get so high up in the government, but I could tell he was flattered underneath.

Grace knows not to disturb her daddy when he's working up here, and I hardly ever cross the threshold, mostly because the space is so small. If I need to speak to him, I can do it from the doorway. I can even pass him a cup of tea from there.

I walk past the stairs and open the office door.

Blake doesn't keep it locked; there's no need. He takes care of the cleaning in here, insisting I have enough to do in the rest of the house. So it's rare for me to enter the room.

I glance around. It's surprisingly tidy for a man who doesn't even think about picking up his dirty socks until he starts to trip over them.

I sit down on the plush padded swivel chair and lay my flat palms on the cool blonde wood. I saw the price of the new furniture on the delivery note and it was enough to make my eyes water. We could furnish two rooms with what Nadine paid for it.

There's nothing on the desktop apart from a wire rack with a few loose papers on each shelf and a green plastic desk tidy with various tubes for storing pens, pencils, and paper clips.

I look up at the wall in front of me and my heart squeezes in on itself. Blake has fixed one of Grace's pictures up there. The kitchen walls are covered in her artwork, but I remember him claiming this picture. He particularly loved it because Grace had drawn all three of us standing in front of the house and had put newborn baby Oscar in a wheelbarrow, which Blake thought was hilarious.

This is a pedestal desk, so it has drawers built in either side. I open the top one on my right. At least I try to open it, but it's locked, and the other drawers are the same.

I stand up and pull at the free-standing filing cabinet behind me, only to find that that's locked too.

It's a bit over the top, I think. Neither Grace nor I are likely to come in here messing anything up, but maybe he's worried about intruders. I know some of the stuff he deals with is confidential.

I shrug to myself and turn to go. Blake's left his casual sports jacket on the back of the chair. He usually lives in it at weekends, but this is no ordinary weekend. All our routines have disappeared. Nothing is important any more apart from finding our daughter. Nothing.

There's a mark on the back of the jacket near the hem. Looks like he might have leaned against a wall, or perhaps it's from the gate.

I'm desperate to do something normal, something that takes up no thinking time, to alleviate the terrible ache in my head, even though I know that's impossible. I slide the shoulders of my husband's jacket from the chair. I'll take it down to the kitchen, see if I can get the mark out. It's the sort of meaningless little task I'd be doing if Grace was downstairs watching television and Oscar was taking a nap.

I check the two pockets and take out an unused folded handkerchief, which I place on the desk. When I fold the jacket over my arm, I notice there's one of those deep inside pockets too.

I plunge my fingers in there and wriggle them around, and they close on something small and cold and clinky. I pull it out to find I'm holding three tiny keys hanging from a single thin metal ring.

I put the keys on the desk with the handkerchief and take a step towards the door. And then I stop and turn around again.

Blake will be back from the police station soon. Doubts

flood my mind again about the reason for his sudden change of heart in leaving the house. It feels disloyal even to admit to myself that I don't trust my husband. Blake's a good man, I know that. Everybody says so. Except Barbara Charterhouse; she doesn't seem too impressed with him.

I pick up the keys and look at them nestled in the centre of my palm. This is probably my only chance to glance inside the desk drawers and the filing cabinet.

I dangle the keys over the desk again and then snatch them back into the palm of my hand and insert one into the filing cabinet. Second try, it twists and I open the top drawer.

Blake has organised the contents of the cabinet in suspended files, each one bearing a little white tab with neat printed letters to mark out the contents. "Monthly Surgery," "Statutory Docs," "Minutes & Agendas."

I'm surprised at his efficiency. In everything else he's so laid-back, haphazard...the moss on the path, the dirty washing by the bed.

In the bottom drawer is more of the same, largely containing details about various planning applications in the local area.

I close the drawer and lock the cabinet again, shaking my head at myself. Of course there's nothing there to show I have reason to mistrust Blake. What did I expect? The names and addresses of a dozen women he's seeing behind my back? I have to wake him most nights where he's fallen asleep on the couch. I hardly think he'd have the energy to entertain other women.

I move over to the desk, the suspicious side of me reasoning I might as well look in there now I'm here.

Nothing in the left pedestal is of any interest. Half-filled notebooks, more stationery, pens and the like. I lock that side and move on to the right.

The top drawer is super-shallow and contains only a ruler, writing implements, a couple of erasers and a book of stamps. There's only a single drawer underneath, but it's a deep one.

I'm surprised to see this drawer is in disarray compared to the others. It's filled to the brim with magazines, balls of string, even a couple of screwed-up plastic shopping bags. I rummage through what seems to be rubbish dumped on top of a pile of brown folders. Inside them is old documentation about consultations for building a new cycleway in the city. I push the folders back and dig my hand underneath them.

My fingers hit the bottom of the drawer and butt up against something straight and firm that's packed down the side.

I stop rummaging for a second and listen. All is quiet downstairs, no sign that Blake has returned. I'd easily hear the front door open and close from this room, anyway.

Confident that I have a few more minutes, I remove all the random items and place them on the desk. Then I grasp the pile of brown folders and pull them out too.

When I peer down into the nearly empty drawer, I instantly freeze.

Lining the bottom of the drawer are bundles and bundles of cash. *Fifty-pound notes.*

I'm no expert, but I reckon there must be at least two and a half thousand pounds in each of the bundles, and I count twenty-two of them.

That's over fifty thousand pounds. In cash.

We are basically on our uppers, financially, so where on earth can it be from?

CHAPTER 18

DS Bean looks up from reading through some paperwork as I enter the living room.

"Lucie! You look pale, love. Come and sit down."

I remain standing.

"Earlier, you told me I can ask you anything." I move in front of her and watch the well-rehearsed sympathetic smile slide from her face.

"And I meant it. Of course you can."

"Then tell me the real reason the detectives asked Blake to go down to the station," I say, trying to keep the desperation out of my voice. "Why would they do that, unless they think he's got something to hide?"

Fiona sighs and sits further back in her seat, as if she's subconsciously trying to increase the distance between us.

"It's not that they think he's hiding anything, it's just that . . ." She hesitates. "It's just that when we walk into these situations—where a family is in peril—we have to be sure to give people the space to be brutally honest with us about their circumstances."

I let that sink in for a moment.

"So why ask Blake to go with them and not me?"

Fiona's right foot begins to tap on the floor.

"Well, again it's all to do with circumstances. Obviously our priority is to determine the relevant events around Grace not returning home when she was expected. You've told us you were here, in the house, all the time and we've got no reason to disbelieve you. Blake on the other hand has stated he was out and about, and we just need to be crystal clear on everyone's exact movements."

Of course; it was when they asked exactly where he went and who he saw while I slept that he became jumpy and offered to go to the station. They think he might be having an affair and wouldn't want to say in front of me. I can't deny that that thought had crossed my mind too, until I found all that cash. And yet even now, I feel guilty, both for snooping and for thinking the worst of my husband.

What if there's a perfectly reasonable explanation for the cash, like... I don't know... he's looking after it for a community group or something?

Over fifty grand?

That amount of money is a serious sum, too dangerous and risky to be stuffed in a drawer. Why not put it in the bank, like a normal person?

Maybe Blake planned to speak to me in private about it, explain what it's doing there. If the police find out, they might suspect he's embezzling funds or something.

And then I remember again that he volunteered to go with the police.

Why would he do that if he's got nothing to hide from me?

"Looks like you have a visitor," Fiona says distractedly, looking out of the window.

I spring up from the sofa and peer at the black cab that's

parked at the end of the driveway. The door opens and a man gets out and the press swarm around him. When he turns around, his face a mask of alarm, I rush to the door.

"It's my dad, he's got Oscar with him." I begin to push my feet into the old trainers I keep in the hall.

Fiona appears at my side and lays a hand on my arm. "Let me go, Lucie."

Something about the look on her face stops me in my tracks and I step back as she opens the front door.

The press are wild, like a bunch of animals. Dad says a few words to them but it only seems to make them hungry for more. Fortunately, they step back when Fiona arrives, taking Oscar from Dad's arms, together with his changing bag.

"Is this Grace's brother? Has he hurt his head?"

"Did your granddaughter often walk home alone?"

"Did you have any concerns over the care of your grandchildren?"

The short, accusing questions don't stop during Dad's slow progress up the path. Fiona follows him, offering a buffer from the unwelcome attention.

When Dad steps inside the hall and holds out his arms to me, his face is grey. I bury my face in his shoulder and he wraps me up tight like he'd do when I was a kid and would get upset that other kids had a mum and I didn't.

I listen to the rasp of his laboured breathing and I start to sob.

CHAPTER 19

When I met Blake, I was already over the full-blown agora-phobia I'd been suffering from, thanks to two years of therapy that had helped me immensely.

I was no longer housebound, and although I still preferred not to go out alone, I could function; make the journey to and from work and other necessary trips.

It was only a part-time position as an events coordinator for a big hotel on the outskirts of town, but it got me interacting with people again. It was a struggle at first, and I used to dread going in each day, but gradually it started to get a little easier.

I learned that although my body was displaying all the signs of genuine panic—increased heart rate, burning cheeks, dry mouth—if I pushed through that and told myself the fear wasn't real, it was just anxiety, I could still do my job and do it well.

Still, although it might get easier, it never fully leaves you. The fear, I mean. To this day, my first reaction is to avoid very crowded or busy spaces if I can. I still feel a little anxious when I have to go out alone, even walking Grace to and from school. Just the thought of seeing the other parents at the school gate fills me with an illogical kind of dread.

If I'm honest, it's a big reason behind me agreeing to let Grace walk home alone from Olivia's house. I don't want her to end up like me, living under the shadow of what *might* happen. Plus, if I'm honest, I revelled in getting up Nadine's nose when she ruled it was too soon for Grace to make the walk alone.

God, how I wish I'd listened to my mother-in-law. Just this once.

I wish, I wish...I don't know why I'm torturing myself, because it's too late for wishing and it's impossible to turn the clock back.

I take Oscar from Fiona's arms and clasp his warm, plump body close to mine, relishing his faint vanilla smell. The mark on his temple has turned a vivid dark red.

"Looks sore. What happened?"

"He took a tumble off the bed," I murmur into Oscar's sparse fine hair when I see Fiona studying his head.

She nods. Presses her lips together.

With Dad and my baby close by, I feel more reassured and I'm beyond thankful to have them here.

Even though Dad assures me he changed Oscar before he left home, I do it anyway and then prepare to feed him. There's an element of reassurance in this ordinary day-in, day-out routine and I crave to have it back in my life again.

"Thanks for coming over, Dad. I know it must've been a massive effort to come here." His chest problems make all physical movement twice as taxing. "Blake would've picked you up, you know."

"I couldn't just sit in the house, wondering how you were,

worrying about where Grace has got to," Dad explains in the kitchen, sipping the tea Fiona gave him before making herself scarce. "I hate that house anyway."

I pause opening Oscar's food jar. "I thought you loved living there? You've always said you never want to move."

Dad shrugs and purses his lips. "I've changed my mind," he says blankly. "Stuff like this happening, I suppose it makes you realise the importance of being near family."

Dad's hardly a million miles away. He lives in Colwick, which is just a ten-minute drive from our house on a good journey.

I realise he looks really low and I reach over and squeeze his hand.

"Don't you start fretting about me, love. You've enough on your plate as it is." He presses his lips together. "When will Blake be back from the cop shop?"

"Any time now," I say and glance at the doorway, making sure Fiona isn't lurking. "I'm worried he's keeping something from me, Dad."

As soon as I've said it, I regret it. Dad's face pales.

"What do you mean? Something like what?"

"Oh, I don't know. Maybe he's got another woman." My effort of sounding tongue-in-cheek falls flat.

"I've never heard such a load of rubbish." Dad huffs. "Blake plainly adores you."

I loosen the lid on the food jar and stick it in the microwave for thirty seconds.

"Even so, he obviously didn't want to talk in front of me. That tells me there's something he's keeping quiet about."

Dad puts down his mug and taps his fingertips on the worktop. "Why give yourself even more to worry about, love? You've got to focus on keeping yourself well, so you're fit when little Gracie gets home, eh?"

I nod but I can tell Dad's worried sick about Grace just like I am. He's pale and nervy and acting out of character, like saying he hates his house.

We're just trying to survive the great gaping hole that's been burned out of the middle of all our lives.

Was Grace abducted? Lost and picked up by an opportune pervert? At this very second, as I heat up baby food and Dad drinks his tea, is she alone and terrified somewhere close by in a dark, locked room?

All the dark stuff nobody's saying is stacking up in the silences between our words. It lives and breathes in the space around us where we can't touch it, see it, or escape it.

CHAPTER 20

Sixteen years earlier

The day she finally left Nottingham for Newcastle proved to be traumatic for Lucie.

For the past twenty-four hours, her father had seemingly morphed from a proud, beaming parent who told everyone he met about his daughter's academic prowess into a blubbering wreck who held her in an iron grasp so long on the platform, Lucie feared she might actually miss the train.

"Promise you'll text the second you arrive?"

"I promise, Dad. I told you, I'll even text on my way there. I'll let you know what's happening every step of the way."

"The rest of your stuff should be there later today, including the cleaning products. Now don't forget, make sure you..."

"...bleach the floor, the loo, and the worktop before I move my stuff in. Yes, Dad, I know all of it off by heart. Please don't worry, I'll be fine."

Her father would never have meant to, but he was really unnerving Lucie by reminding her of a thousand possible perils she might encounter on her arrival. She was already managing very nicely on her own to ruin any optimism with a heavy lacing of dread, and she didn't need his anxiety as well.

Her dad worried about germs and nutritious meals; Lucie fretted constantly about making new friends and fitting in. Between them, they'd managed to turn what should have been an amazing experience into a probable nightmare.

Lucie finally managed to extract herself from Pete's vice-like grip and board the train. She put the small suitcase on the shelf above her head and her bulging rucksack on the empty seat next to her.

The carriage was quite busy, although there were still plenty of unoccupied seats. Lucie noticed there were several other young people with parents standing plaintively on the platform. The other students had a look of anticipation with a touch of nervousness; like herself, she thought. Perhaps she wasn't so different after all.

As her father took a few steps forward and stood on his tiptoes next to the window, Lucie willed the train to get going. She was genuinely in fear of him jumping aboard and begging her not to go. She'd never live down the shame amongst all these other people.

She waved, her eyes prickling with emotion as she viewed her dad from this new angle of independent university student. She saw his tired eyes and drawn expression. She saw the worn trousers and the shoes he had owned for years, and realised she couldn't remember the last time he'd bought himself anything new.

And yet her two large suitcases, soon to be on their way up to Newcastle, were packed with new garments, courtesy of a recent shopping trip with her father.

Pete had done so much for her; Lucie couldn't even count the ways.

She pressed her face and hands closer to the glass and blew him a kiss.

"Love you," she mouthed silently.

The train gathered speed and soon the platform fell away. She watched until her father was nothing more than a waving shape amongst the other people left behind. Then she settled back into her seat, took a deep breath, and closed her eyes.

"New life, here I come," she murmured softly.

CHAPTER 21

Lucie

Sunday evening

When Blake finally gets back from the police station, he looks tired. Haggard.

"What happened?" I rush into the hallway, still clutching a sleepy Oscar in my arms as the shouting from the media shuts off abruptly when the front door closes. "What did they say?"

"They just asked me a load of questions." He shrugs. "I answered them the best I could."

"Come in here." I lead him into the living room and notice with a flash of irritation that Fiona is drifting across the hallway too. Before Blake walked in, she was talking to Dad in the kitchen but now decides to loiter near the lounge doorway. I lower my voice. "What exactly did they ask you?"

"What time did your wife go to sleep, what time did you leave the house, where exactly did you go, who did you see. Blah, blah, blah." He clenches his jaw. "Like I told them, while they're spending their time interrogating me about things that aren't relevant, they're not out there looking for Grace."

"Blake, you…" I falter. "You haven't got anything to tell me, have you? I mean, I'd rather know … if there's something."

"Something like what?" He stares at me.

"Like if you were … I don't know, *hiding* something from me." The wads of cash in his desk drawer fill my mind's eye.

"Christ!" He claps a hand to his forehead. "Is that what you really think of me, Luce?"

Oscar grumbles and I jiggle him in my arms.

"No! I … It's just with you changing your mind, offering to go to the station with them, I just—"

"I wanted to take the pressure off you a bit, that's all. You look exhausted. I know you're fragile, Lucie, and if truth be known, I'm scared you'll go under again."

"I'm already under!" I snap. "Finding out you've been lying to me is only going to make things a hundred times worse, if that's even possible."

I feel like screaming at him, like I'm about to lose it. I clamp my back teeth together and look away.

"Lucie, I don't know why you're going on about this, but it's not helping. I'm not hiding anything."

His outright lie fills me with fury, but I'm mindful that Fiona is lurking. Blowing his secret wide open could damage us irreparably and take focus from the investigation into what has happened to Grace.

With great effort, I try and reason with him.

"Nobody changes their mind in the space of a few minutes like you did. One minute you're refusing to go to the station, the next, you're volunteering. I'm not an idiot, Blake. I'm asking you, giving you a chance to explain why—"

"I've told you. I just wanted to protect you from their probing questions, that's all." He sighs and looks at his hands.

Out in the hall, Fiona's phone rings. She's definitely still out there, hanging on our conversation. A bolt of fury zips through me.

"It's driving me crazy, *her* hanging around all the time. I think she's here to spy on us. She's not actually adding anything to finding out where Grace is."

"Fiona's a valuable link to what's happening out there, Luce. If they find Grace, then we'll know immediately rather than having to wait for—"

He takes sleeping Oscar gently from my arms and holds him. My arm aches from holding him so close but I immediately miss his soothing warmth and presence.

"She could be out there searching with the other coppers, instead of just sitting in here making fucking tea."

"Sorry to interrupt," Fiona says from the doorway.

Our heads both jerk up, sudden hope bright in our eyes. "Your GP is on his way; he'll be here in five minutes." She presses her lips together and, finally, heads to the kitchen.

I slump down into a chair. I realise Fiona probably heard what I said, but who cares? It doesn't matter.

Nothing in this world matters except finding Grace.

I stare out of the window, wondering how the light had faded so fast.

"Grace doesn't like the dark," I say faintly.

Even though, on the one hand, she tells us how grown-up she is now she is nine, our daughter still insists on having the night light on, bathing her bedroom in a dim starlit glow.

"Don't think about it, Luce." Blake supports Oscar in one arm and reaches for my hand, and I see that regardless of the fact that it's futile, he too has closed his eyes against any thoughts of Grace being in a place where she is suffering and afraid.

Somehow, we both understand that we can't voice these things.

Just in case it makes it so.

I try to pull my hand away but he holds it tight. Despite my suspicions and my discovery of the money upstairs, I let him.

Tensions are high. We're both dying inside; we're right on the edge. We just need our baby back.

There's no sense in us tearing each other apart.

CHAPTER 22

Fiona shows Dr. Mahmoud into the living room. Dad takes Oscar into the other room and nods his own greeting as he passes.

The doctor is a small, squat man with a perennial smile. He's been my children's GP for the whole of their lives and he knows Grace particularly well, as she's a regular visitor to the health centre due to her diabetes.

"I am very sorry to meet here with you both under such terrible circumstances," he says gravely before sitting down in Blake's proffered chair. "Myself and my wife, we are both praying for the safe return of Grace." His toothy smile is tinged with sadness and compassion.

"Thank you, Doctor," I say gratefully. "It's a terrible situation only made worse by Grace's condition."

"Of course, this is certainly a worry. I have spoken to the detective leading the investigation and explained my concerns regarding Grace's diabetes. I understand she has her blood sugar monitor and insulin on her person?"

Blake nods. "She was at her friend's house and they made sure she had her medication with her when she left there."

"But what if she can't use it? What if someone's taken it or..." The words choke in my throat, and in the end, I find I can't voice the dreadful possibility. I bite the inside of my lip viciously in an effort to keep the tears at bay.

"Please be honest with us," Blake says, so pleadingly I want to hug him despite his deceit. "What are the *real* risks if Grace can't access her medication?"

Dr. Mahmoud glances at me warily.

"We want to know all possible eventualities," I confirm. "We *need* to know."

He nods. Clears his throat.

"Very well. Truthfully, if Grace is found soon, there should not be a problem. As you know, her body cannot regulate blood sugar itself, so the injected insulin does this job. If she does eat but does not inject, it's possible her blood sugar levels could increase, but in the short term, this would not be dangerous."

Dr. Mahmoud must know that we know all this. I think he's skirting around the issue.

"Obviously, we don't know where Grace is yet," I say, striving to speak calmly. "We don't know when she'll be found. I suppose what we're asking is what happens if...if the situation continues for some time? What happens if the police can't find Grace and, for whatever reason, she can't access her medication for a length of time?"

Dr. Mahmoud's brow furrows.

"Well, as a worst-case scenario, untreated diabetes can commonly lead to diabetic ketoacidosis. The common name for this is diabetic coma."

"That sound pretty serious," Blake says grimly.

"Indeed. But if Grace is found within the next forty-eight hours, then it will not be a worry."

That blasted statistic again: *forty-eight hours.*

Not so long ago, forty-eight hours sounded like a good chunk of time; now it seems like the blink of an eye.

"Is a diabetic coma the worst that can happen?" Blake presses him.

"It can lead to cerebral oedema, an accumulation of liquid in the brain." Dr. Mahmoud hesitates before continuing. "It's very serious, and sadly, children are at higher risk of this condition."

A cloak of silence descends on us as we all consider this. I feel like I'm watching from a distance, like I'm standing outside of myself.

"Luce?" Blake's voice cuts through the strange disassociation. "Dr. Mahmoud is talking to you."

"Sorry?" I say vaguely.

"I have prepared a prescription for you, Mrs. Sullivan." The doctor holds out the white printed slip.

"No thanks." I feel my expression harden. "I need to be aware of everything that's happening. I need to get out there and help to search for Grace, and I can't do that if I'm in a self-medicated bubble."

"Ah, you misunderstand." He smiles. "This prescription is not for sedation purposes; it is simply some mild medication to calm the nerves." He looks meaningfully at me. Nods encouragingly.

He's been my GP for the last ten years. He's aware of my medical history, of the anxiety-related conditions that have blighted half my life.

I look at the small white note in his outstretched fingers.

"Lucie," Blake says gently. "Please. Take the prescription."

And so I do.

CHAPTER 23

Sunday evening

It's officially dark when DI Pearlman and DS Paige return to the house. They speak in low, indecipherable tones to Fiona in the hallway.

Dad has taken Oscar upstairs and is having a lie-down himself, so that leaves Blake and me staring wordlessly at each other with wide eyes. But it's soon clear that there's no positive news.

I feel the light that I'm trying so hard to keep burning brightly inside myself dim a little more.

The detectives appear in the doorway.

"We've come to give you an update on what's happening out there," DI Pearlman says, stepping into the room. "But before we do, we've got the leader of the community search here. He wonders if he could have a quick word...Is that OK?"

He addresses Blake but glances nervously in my direction. They're treading on eggshells around me. I'm falling apart inside, but I thought I was giving the impression I'm just about holding it together. Judging by their reaction now, though, I'm not so sure.

"I have to say he's doing a great job," DS Paige adds. "The community search is really adding value to our operation, releasing officers for other important duties in the investigation."

"Of course, we'd love to meet him," Blake says. "Please, bring him in."

DS Paige disappears into the hallway. I hear the front door open and close and lowered voices conversing.

"Incredible that someone would take it upon themselves to get involved and organise a search like that," Blake remarks, and I nod in agreement.

A few seconds later, the detective comes back into the room, followed by . . . our neighbour, Jeffery Bonser.

"Jeffery is leading the community search," DS Paige says, "and he's only just told me you already know each other."

I stare at Jeffery, who, under my enquiring gaze, shuffles his weight awkwardly, one foot to the other.

"I'll leave you all to have a quick chat." Paige walks out of the room, already looking at his phone.

"Jeff! You absolute hero." Blake jumps up and embraces our neighbour. "We can't thank you enough for what you're doing. Right, Luce?"

"Yes. Thank you," I say, my arms and legs suddenly feeling cold.

Blake is saying something about community spirit and support and putting his arm around Jeffery's shoulders in a brotherly manner.

I stare blankly at the two of them, trying to reconcile the usually insular and socially awkward man with this new self-appointed organiser of the community search.

Jeffery soaks up Blake's thanks and compliments and accepts them easily. He seems to hold himself taller and with a new dignity. It's quite a transformation.

Unexpectedly, he steps away from Blake and advances towards me. I shrink back into my seat.

"Lucie, I wanted to express to you my sadness that Grace has gone. I'm so, so sorry." He crouches down by the side of my seat, close enough that I can see a slick of grease on the skin either side of his nose.

"Grace is missing," I say, a little curtly. "She isn't *gone*. Gone is forever. Gone is for good."

"Lucie!" Blake frowns at me.

"What?" I snap. "People need to think about what they're saying before they blurt out thoughtless stuff."

Jeffery stands up, clearly mortified.

"Of...of course, you're right," he stammers. "I'm so sorry, I didn't mean..."

"We have to keep hold of hope any way we can," I say, ignoring Blake's efforts to catch my eye. "We have to believe with all our hearts that Grace will be back home soon. It's only been a few hours."

"I understand." Jeffery knots his fingers together. "She's such a lovely little girl. I'll miss seeing her leave for school each morning, and playing in the garden on her trampoline. I like to see her jumping and twirling out there."

I shiver and pull my cardigan closer to me. The thought of him peering out of his windows watching Grace like that gives me the heebie-jeebies.

Blake steps forwards, lays his hand on Jeffery's upper arm.

"We really appreciate everything you're doing, mate," he reiterates. "It takes a lot to get involved in something like this when it's not your problem."

"You're my friends." Jeffery shrugs. "And friends do stuff for each other, right?"

"Right." Blake nods, tears of gratitude shining in his eyes.

Jeffery looks at his shuffling feet. "I couldn't just sit by when Grace is . . . missing."

I don't see why not. He has nothing whatsoever to do with Grace; doesn't say two words to her from one week to the next.

I'm being unnecessarily mean, I know. I should be feeling enormously grateful, like Blake is. But something about him doing this just doesn't sit right with me.

"Thank you, Jeffery," I manage, before addressing my husband. "DI Pearlman's waiting to speak to us," I remind him.

More hugs and effusive thanks from Blake, and finally Jeffery leaves the house.

"I can't believe you were like that with him," Blake remarks as the detectives come back into the room. "You heard what DS Paige said. Jeff's help has been invaluable."

I don't respond. I refuse to waste any more energy arguing about our bloody neighbour.

"Have you checked him out?" I say pointedly to DI Pearlman. "Jeffery Bonser, I mean."

The detective looks confused.

"Lucie. You're not thinking straight," Blake says in what I recognise as his warning tone.

"He watches Grace when she's playing in the garden," I snap at him. "He just admitted it . . . you heard him!"

"He didn't mean it like *that*," Blake says to the detective, ignoring me. "Lucie's never liked him."

"He's a weirdo. Lived with his mother for years, and now he's a loner. I've heard about cases before where the abductor gets a kick out of helping in a search or investigation."

DS Paige gets out his notebook.

"What exactly did he say?"

Blake answers before I can respond.

"He said he felt very sad about what had happened. That he'll miss seeing Grace leave for school in the morning . . ."

"...and miss watching her twirling on her trampoline in the garden." I shudder. "It's like he knows she won't be coming home." My voice breaks and tears tip down my cheeks. I wipe them angrily away and glare at DI Pearlman.

"Rest assured, Lucie, we'll be looking at everyone who knows Grace," he says calmly as DI Paige scribbles something down. "In the first few hours, we're concentrating all efforts on the immediacy of a search operation."

"And what have you found so far? Because now it's dark and Grace is out there somewhere, terrified."

I'm so sick and tired of not knowing anything because I'm cooped up in here.

"You should've searched all the houses on the street." My voice rises an octave and Blake looks across at me, concerned.

"They can't just barge in and ransack people's houses without good reason, Luce. You know that!"

"I wouldn't mind if someone else's child was missing. The police could come in here and—"

DI Pearlman raises his hand to quieten me. "All in good time, Lucie. It's essential we get things in the right order. We want Grace safely home as soon as humanly possible, but there's a process to follow and..."

His voice fades out as I stop listening.

I just want my little girl home. I want her back in my arms, safe and sound. Is that too much for any mother to ask?

CHAPTER 24

Four hours. That's how long Grace has been missing. Four hours ago, our friend Mike saw her off on her five-minute journey home.

The detectives have left the house again, Dad must've fallen asleep upstairs with Oscar, and Blake is talking to Fiona in the kitchen.

I stare out of the window, but I'm not really watching anything. The group of press are still at the gate, and various people come and go, chatting to each other and looking at the house. There's a uniformed officer down there making sure nobody ventures up the path.

Blake wanted me to take one of Dr. Mahmoud's tablets right away when he brought my prescription back from the chemist.

"It'll help, Luce. Take the edge off your nerves."

But I refused. I need to stay lucid so I'm aware of what's happening in the search for Grace. Good or bad, I have to know.

It's dark out now; it would be pitch black if it wasn't for

the street lights, and the press seem to have their own lighting out there, sourced from large white vans.

I wonder if it's pitch dark where Grace is. My mind offers scenarios, too rapidly for me to stop them. Terrible visions of her struggling to unlock the door of a speeding car, sobbing and imprisoned in some cold, damp place or lying lifeless in a ditch somewhere.

I know I shouldn't, Blake and DS Bean have both warned me, but I can't put it off any longer. I pick up my iPad, which I slipped down the side of the sofa before Blake could censor it, and I open up the BBC news page.

There's nothing on here about Grace yet, but when I click on the local news tab, there's a paragraph and a small photograph of a panoramic view of Violet Road.

LOCAL SEARCH FOR MISSING CHILD

Police are becoming increasingly concerned for a nine-year-old girl who went missing earlier today from Violet Road in West Bridgford, Nottingham. A search is currently under way, organised by local residents.

Grace Sullivan left a friend's house alone but never arrived home. Grace is around 135–140 cm (just over 4 ft) tall with dark brown hair in a ponytail. She was dressed in bright colours, including a pink coat and a red knitted hat.

Police say Grace is diabetic and requires regular medication to manage her condition.

The last confirmed sighting of her was at the bottom end of Violet Road leading on to Abbey Road.

If you saw Grace on Sunday afternoon between 4:30 and 4:45, or have any information, please contact Nottinghamshire Police.

COMMENTS:
Carolann66 What the hell was a 9-yr-old doing walking home on her own anyway???
Stardust-Girl This is a safe area, maybe the kid's run away from home for some reason.
Boxing99Fan Why speculate until you know all the facts? Her parents must be desperately worried!
Carolann66 Just saying. My kid didn't go missing, cos at 9 yo I collected her from her mates' houses.

I stare at the article and my hands start to shake as if they belong to someone else.

The news report itself is a simple statement of facts, but seeing it on the BBC website makes it feel like someone took a magnifying glass to my pain.

"Lucie, did you want me to make you…" Fiona's eyes alight on the iPad and she steps forward and takes it gently from my hands. "Don't. Don't do this to yourself."

"I should have never let her walk home. I should have—"

"What happened to Grace is not your fault, Lucie," she says softly.

"That's not what they're saying. They're saying…"

Fiona shakes her head.

"*They*, whoever they are, don't know anything about you or your family. It's just trolls, trying to extract a reaction. They don't deserve to take up a second of your time."

I get to my feet. "I'm just popping upstairs to freshen up."

It doesn't matter how many times she tells me it's not my fault, I know I had the final decision about whether Grace was allowed to walk home. Blake might have pushed for it, but he also deferred to me each time it came up.

My own insecurities from the period when I hardly dared

to go out definitely played their part in me agreeing to it. I never wanted my daughter to feel like that.

Now she may never get the chance.

I shake my head against the horror. Four hours she's been gone, just four hours. If forty-eight hours is the key deadline, then we still have time, don't we? Time to find Grace.

Everybody—the police and the local community—is working to cover all the obvious things that need to be taken care of, like door-to-door inquiries and a local search. But *surely* I can add value by focusing on thinking outside the box. We spend so much time together; I know my daughter best of anyone. Better than Blake, even.

I can make a difference, I know it. I just have to *do* something, instead of sitting around waiting for others to make a breakthrough.

I climb the stairs quietly so as not to disturb Dad and Oscar, and enter Grace's bedroom, renewed hope sparking in my heart.

Running along the back gardens of the houses on Violet Road is a narrow track. It's a sort of no-man's-land between our homes and the back gardens of the houses on the next street. Nobody even seems sure who the strip belongs to.

The only people who really use it are kids playing chase, or dog walkers after a shortcut back home from the park. In any case, unless you're local, you wouldn't know about it.

I stand at Grace's window now, staring down there. I can't see the actual pathway in the dark, and there are no lights illuminating it except for the odd few seconds when someone's outdoor sensor light flickers on.

Still, it's the perfect way to get out of the house without the press knowing.

I start at the sound of footsteps on the stairs, and a few seconds later, Blake walks into the room and stands behind me at the window, his hands on my shoulders.

"You can't torture yourself like this, Luce. Come downstairs. Please."

He's hurting just like I am, I know he is. But he sounds so calm and logical. I could easily lose it and turn on him right now, accusing him of lying to me and not caring enough about Grace.

I know this is not a game of one-upmanship, and yet I'm really struggling to comprehend how he can remain so calm. Surely, if he's so calm, he can't be feeling as bad as I do; as if part of me has been ripped away.

"I asked you a question before, Blake," I say, keeping my voice level and low to evade Fiona's ever-listening ears. "I asked you if you were keeping anything from me, and you said no."

"Not this again," he groans. "I told you, didn't I? There's nothing—"

"I know," I say simply. "About all that cash in your desk."

"What?"

I turn to face him. I can see the colour draining from his cheeks even in this dim light.

"Why did you go in my . . . It's not what you think."

"Then what is it? Why is there fifty grand or more hidden in your office? What if we'd been burgled? Whose is it?"

"I can't discuss it now." His voice drops to a whisper. "I'll explain everything to you. I will."

"When, exactly?"

"Soon. It would be gone already if . . . if Grace hadn't gone missing. I can't do much with the police watching my every move."

A weight settles on my chest as my suspicions are confirmed.

"Obviously it's not kosher, then. If you don't want the police to know, that says it all."

"Shh!" He looks around furtively at the door. "Give me the benefit of the doubt this once, Lucie, please. I *will* explain, I promise."

"Does Barbara Charterhouse know about this?"

"What?" He frowns and shakes his head. "No, of course not. Why do you say that?"

"Because this morning she said you operate behind a facade that some people can't see through."

He looks at me as if I'm crazy.

"If you start to believe anything *she* tells you, then we really are done for."

I'm furious he won't tell me, and also terrified why that might be.

"Could this...the money...have anything to do with someone taking Grace?" I fix my gaze on his. "Is someone blackmailing you, or out for revenge? Some people would do anything to get their hands on a sum like that."

He gives a mirthless laugh. "No, is the short answer. Look, Lucie, this is ridiculous, can we just stop—"

"Because if there's the slightest, tiniest chance that might be the case, then you need to tell the police, regardless of your reputation."

"I said no," he says stubbornly. "I can't believe you're even thinking this stuff."

"I'm going out," I say, making a massive effort to keep my voice level. "You can come with me, or not. Up to you."

"What?" He stares at me as if I've lost my marbles. "Out *where*, exactly?"

"I'm going to sneak out of the back garden and use the track to get down to Bev and Mike's house."

Blake swallows. "But why? What good will that do?"

"It can't do any harm. I feel I know nothing about today, about exactly what happened. I want them to talk me through every single minute of the day from when Mike picked Grace up to go to Alton Towers right up until the moment she opened their front door and he watched her walk up the street."

Blake sighs and runs his fingers through his hair.

"The detectives will already have asked them all that stuff, Luce. We're better off staying here, surely. For when there's any news."

"The police will know where to find us. I can't sit here and do nothing any more, Blake. I just can't."

I know my husband well, but the expression on his face right now is hard to identify.

"Leave it, Lucie. Please. Don't go round there."

"Why on earth not? They were the last people to see Grace."

"I just don't think you should—"

"I don't need your permission to talk to Bev and Mike!" I snap at him. "Why are you so adamant they can't add anything to what we know?"

His cheeks flush slightly but he holds his ground.

"You're trying to control everything and you'll just end up making it worse, can't you see that? We have to let the police drive the investigation."

I can't stop my voice rising. "No! They're so tied up in red tape with all their boxes to tick, but we're not. Can't you see that?"

He looks at me blankly, and I turn away from him.

"Fine. Well I'm doing this with or without you, so please yourself."

I march from the room.

"You might make everything worse," I hear him cry out, but I don't stop walking.

CHAPTER 25

I grab my coat from the hall cupboard and push my feet into my flat ankle boots.

Fiona looks up from her laptop screen. She's taken over the breakfast bar; paperwork is strewn across the whole surface. I spot a *Hello!* magazine poking out from under a sheaf of documentation.

"Everything all right?" she asks lightly.

I pause a second, giving her stupid question some space.

"Fine." She's probably been skulking around at the bottom of the stairs, listening to our disagreement. "I'm popping down to Bev and Mike's house. I'll go the back way, so I don't have to speak to the press. If Dad asks, can you tell him where I've gone?"

I walk across the room and reach for the door handle.

"If you don't mind me asking, is there any particular reason why you're going down there?" She slides from the bar stool and laces her fingers in front of her.

I feel like a pressure cooker about to blow. I'd like to yell that yes, I bloody well do mind her asking. I know she's just doing her job, but I can't shake the feeling she's here to spy more than support us.

Still, I also feel it's in my interests to maintain a stable demeanour, no matter how pent-up I feel inside. Otherwise nobody will take me seriously and Blake will start trying to push Dr. Mahmoud's medication on me again. So I tell her the truth.

"It's just I feel like I don't know everything about what happened today. I didn't get a chance to talk about their trip to Alton Towers, or how Grace seemed to them today."

"I think the detectives have already covered that," Fiona offers. "I could ask DI Pearlman to go through what was said, if you like?"

"Thanks, but I'd rather hear it for myself. We're all good friends and I'd feel better for seeing them," I say tightly. "Obviously we haven't had a chance to talk properly at all about what happened yet."

A noise at the doorway makes me turn.

"Don't worry, I'll go with her." Blake exchanges a look with Fiona.

Why do I feel like the outsider here? Surely it should be Blake and I who are tight together, and yet all of a sudden he seems to be the police's best mate.

"I'm perfectly fine speaking to our friends on my own." I turn the door handle and step out into the chilly night air.

The cloud cover is too thick to see any stars tonight. Grace loves to stand at her window before bedtime to spot the North Star, since my dad told her it watches over her every night to keep her safe. Where is the North Star now? I wonder. I hope wherever Grace is, she can see it.

I hear Blake step out of the house behind me and close the back door.

"Why don't you stay here," I say without turning around. "In case there's news."

He wraps his arms around me and places his chin on the top of my head. I stand stock still.

"I know you're hurting, Luce. We all are."

Hurting? I'm dying. Dying inside.

"I don't want you getting yourself in a state, that's all," Blake continues. "I can speak to Mike and Bev, ask them to—"

"I can't stop you coming, but I have to do this myself," I say curtly. "I can't sit in the house a moment longer, just waiting and waiting for news that never comes."

"I hear you," he says, sounding beaten.

We walk down our long, narrow garden. Even though it's a few days since we had rain, the ground feels marshy under my feet. When we get to the bottom, we both turn on the torch function on our phones and inch sideways, past Grace's trampoline and through the slim space where our hedge meets Jeffery's fence next door.

I glance back at Jeffery's house. There's a light on in his kitchen. I can't see anything clearly because the blind is pulled down but a shadowy figure is moving around in there.

Out on the track, the hard earth is muddy in places. I lead the way and Blake follows. It's quiet out here, with nobody in their gardens now that dark has fallen. It's eerie, even though the light from my phone illuminates a good chunk of ground in front of me.

"This all feels a bit cloak-and-dagger," Blake grumbles behind me.

I ignore him, but it does feel spooky. Wherever Grace is, I hope she's not alone in the dark.

Five minutes later, we arrive at the end of Bev and Mike's back garden.

"Perhaps we should have warned them we were coming," Blake whispers as I push open the wooden gate in their fence.

Bev and I are always popping into each other's houses at the weekend. I don't see why this should be any different.

Their garden is the same length as ours, and we gingerly pick our way up the path strewn with overgrown weeds. Like our own, the lawn, when my feet catch it, feels unpleasantly marshy. I wait for an outside light sensor to kick in, but the garden remains dark, so I keep my phone torch lit up.

Ahead of us, the kitchen unit lights are on and the room is bathed in a soft light. At the other side of the house, large French doors in the dark open-plan dining area provide a view through to the illuminated lounge at the front.

As we near the house, I see that Bev and Mike are in the kitchen. The door is closed, and they're standing facing each other, side-on to the window. Something in the way they are standing—too close and with concerned expressions—makes me feel uncomfortable.

I stop walking and whisper to Blake, "They look worried about something, don't you think?"

"I'm sure they're worried about Grace's whereabouts, Lucie, like everyone is."

"Yes, but . . ." I let my words trail away. I feel like Blake is ready to shoot down anything I say.

They look angry at each other, is what I want to say. They do. I recognise it in Bev especially. She's frowning and seems to be the one saying the most.

I start walking again. We're only a few paces away from the kitchen window now, and the back door.

Bev is a good friend, a good mother to Olivia. It's her arms I want to feel around me; she will at least understand on some level how Grace's absence is truly killing me.

I'm still staring when, without warning, her hand suddenly shoots out and she slaps Mike across the face.

"Shit!" Blake hisses behind me. "Lucie...come on, we can't go in there now. Let's go back home."

Mike's own hand flies to his stung cheek and he steps towards Bev, his face assuming a mask of fury that makes my knees feel wobbly. In all the time we've known him, I've never seen him so angry. He's like a completely different person.

I make a half-turn, ready to leave. But then Bev and Mike must see the flashlights from our phones, because Bev's mouth falls open and her hand moves up to cover it.

I'm standing still in shock, not sure what to do, when the back door flies open and Mike is there.

CHAPTER 26

"Lucie, Blake...is everything OK?" He clears his throat and looks from Blake to me. "Have they found her? Is Grace back home?"

"No, not yet," I say quietly. "Look, Mike, I'm sorry to just turn up like this out of the blue. I just needed to speak to you and Bev. I..."

The tears take me by surprise. My cheeks are wet and my nose is running.

"Come in. Come on." He steps outside in his slippers and puts his arm around my shoulders.

When I go inside, Bev is waiting there for me.

"I'm sorry," I sniff. "Disturbing you like this."

"Don't be silly. We wanted to come over but didn't want to intrude when it's all so raw. Come through to the living room." She glares at Mike. "Do you think you could make some tea?"

"Course," he replies, his tone thick with sarcasm.

To my surprise, Blake doesn't stay with Mike in the kitchen, but comes into the lounge with us. Olivia is sitting on the settee in her pyjamas, watching television. I want to question her, ask if Grace said anything about calling somewhere on the way home. She looks at me warily. I think I'm staring.

"Listen, Bev," I hear Blake say. "We shouldn't have just turned up like this. I should've called you first. I'm sorry, we can come back another time."

"Nonsense!" Bev insists. "It's fine. Sit yourself down, Lucie. I simply can't imagine what you're going through." She looks at Olivia. "Darling, can you watch the rest of the programme in your bedroom?"

Olivia slides wordlessly out of her seat. She slows down as she passes my chair, and for a second, I think she's going to say something.

"Are you OK, Livvy?" I ask. She nods warily.

"Up to your bedroom then, poppet," Bev says.

Olivia breaks eye contact and scurries away.

"She's taken it really hard," Bev whispers. "She's desperately worried about Grace. As we all are."

"Have you asked her if Grace said anything about calling somewhere before coming home, or—"

"We've talked to her several times," Bev confirms a little tersely, I think. "The police have had a quick chat with her too."

Something in her voice tells me that that's as far as she wants Olivia questioned.

Mike comes in and sits on the arm of the sofa next to me, as far away from Bev as he can get, I notice.

"Anything we can do, you only have to say. I hope you know that," he says.

"Thanks, mate, appreciate that," Blake tells him.

I look up and catch Mike aiming what I'm sure is a glare at my husband. I feel shocked but immediately think I must've read something into it that's not there.

Blake doesn't seem to have noticed, but when I look at him properly, for what feels like the first time in a long time, his stubbled face is pale and weary.

"There's no news at all yet?" Mike says awkwardly, breaking the silence.

"I'm sure they'd have said right away if they'd heard anything, Mike." Bev's nostrils flare.

Blake shifts in his seat. It's all so uncomfortable, as if there's stuff happening that I'm not aware of. But then I haven't come around here for a cosy, relaxing chat.

"We've heard nothing at all," I say. "It's getting on for five hours now that Grace has been missing. Five hours!" Just saying the words out loud is devastating.

My daughter has been somewhere else for nearly *five whole hours*.

The top of my nose starts to prickle, but I force the tears back. Snivelling isn't going to help find Grace, so I press on.

"I wanted to come because I want you to take me through the whole day, if you would. Everything happened so quickly and the police just commandeered us, so I feel like I'm in the dark about how everything unfolded."

Bev sighs. "Well, when we got back from Alton—"

"No, Bev, tell me from when you picked Grace up from the house this morning."

She nods and proceeds to catalogue everything that happened.

"The girls were nattering in the back and Mike and I were talking about parking and getting into the theme park. It took us just over an hour to get there and it was full on from the minute we were inside."

She describes the rides, the girls' delight on being allowed on the scariest ones. I recall Grace's face, so alive and excited in the Smiler photo that Mike texted while they were there. It feels like a long time ago now.

"The girls had a slice of pizza each for lunch and we just had a sandwich." She glances at Mike, but there seems to be an invisible screen in place between them.

"How did Grace seem?" I say. "I mean, was she her usual self or did she seem a bit subdued?"

"Definitely not subdued," Mike responds quickly. "I'd say she was her normal self but in extra-excitement mode. They were both bubbling over."

"They ran ahead almost the whole time," Bev agrees. "We kept them in sight, but we gave them a little space and they loved it."

I nod, my heart growing heavier by the second. There's nothing new here. Nothing that could help.

"It seemed to drop cold really quickly, so we left the park a bit earlier than we'd initially planned," Mike says.

I immediately wonder what would have happened if they'd been a bit later. Would Grace have arrived home safely? Would she have missed a dreadful window of opportunity when someone decided to take her away?

I dig my fingernails into my palms, realising what I've just admitted to myself. After five hours of Grace being missing, it seems I'm arriving at an abduction conclusion, despite keeping the hope alive that she called somewhere else before home; got distracted and delayed.

"On the journey back, the girls were less talkative because they were tired," Bev remarks. "We were all a bit quiet, but Grace said she was looking forward to getting her pyjamas on and watching a film with you both later."

I press my fingers to my lips and feel a spring of hot tears.

"I'm sorry, Lucie." Bev looks at her hands. "I can't imagine how hard this is for you."

"It's fine. Honestly, carry on." The last thing I want is for Bev to clam up and stop telling me about the day. I need to know everything, every last detail.

"When we got back, the girls played upstairs in Olivia's bedroom for around twenty minutes, and then Mike called Grace down."

"She was bouncing again, excited to be walking home alone. Livvy came down to wave her off and she was excited for Grace, too. It was a big deal to them both," Mike says softly.

"Can you tell me exactly what happened next?" I say, trying to take a step back from my emotions and failing as my heart hammers relentlessly at my chest.

Mike draws in a big breath.

"She put her trainers, coat, hat and gloves on and I tucked her insulin case in her pocket and took her to the gate. Once she'd set off, I texted Blake to say she'd just left and then stepped back inside the gate and watched her covertly so she wouldn't see me if she looked back."

"Did she seem nervous at all?" I ask him.

"Not in the slightest." Mike shook his head. "She marched up the road with purpose, and when she got near to the bend, I came inside."

I silently repeat back to myself what he just said.

"Did you watch her until she disappeared around the bend?" I ask.

"Yes...well, almost." Mike frowns, thinking. "She was nearly there and I heard Bev calling me. As Grace was almost at the bend and I knew Blake was waiting, I came back inside."

His cheeks are colouring up as quickly as the colour drains from my own. I can't believe what he just said.

"Where exactly—*exactly*—did she get up to on the road

before you came back inside, Mike?" The effort needed to stay calm is immense.

"I watched her cross over Abbey Road and then I came back inside." His voice sounds weaker and he looks at Bev, who hasn't said a word yet.

Abbey Road leads off Violet Road. It's quiet, never much traffic, but there's one thing about it that makes my blood run cold.

It's thirty yards or so from the start of the bend. Grace would have been completely alone, invisible to Blake, for at least twenty seconds.

CHAPTER 27

We hurry home in silence, back along the dark track.

"Did you have to lose it in there?" Blake says accusingly behind me. "They must feel bad enough Grace going missing on their watch, Lucie. It's just not helpful to—"

"I don't give a shit whether it's helpful or not." The tears are clogging up my throat and threatening to choke me. "Why would Mike even do that? Why would he leave our daughter at a crucial moment when a few more seconds would have seen her well past the bend and safely in your care?"

Silence.

I asked Mike that very same thing and his only answer was, "Bev called me inside."

But Bev *knew* he was watching Grace halfway home. Why would she call him back into the house at such an important time when she knew he'd only be a couple of minutes at the most?

"What was so important that you needed him back inside, Bev?" I asked her.

"I ... I can't recall now. I didn't think he'd come back until he'd watched Grace as far as he could." That had earned her a withering glare from Mike.

"We need to speak to the police." I drive my feet into the mud, desperate to cover ground quickly. "They need to know about the crucial time lapse and we need to tell them about the money upstairs before they find it for themselves. It can only be a matter of time before they do a more thorough search."

"Lucie, please. Let me deal with the cash issue. I can explain everything to you, but let's not get involved in that discussion while Grace is still missing. Please."

"For all I know, you might be in trouble. You've kept a massive amount of cash from me; what if you're keeping other secrets? What if you've double-crossed someone who's out for revenge and has abducted Grace?"

"Lucie, you're being ridiculous. This isn't a TV crime drama."

"Oh, I'm painfully aware of that," I say acidly. "But it follows that if nothing is amiss, then you shouldn't mind the police knowing."

And then something repeats in my head and it feels like a light bulb pinging on.

Why would Mike leave our daughter at a crucial moment when a few more seconds would have seen her well past the bend and safely in your care?

But Blake *wasn't* watching at the gate because his phone distracted him and he slipped on the mossy path.

"Why did you check your phone, just before you slipped?" I ask him.

"A text came through," he says in a tone that indicates he's tiring of me going over old ground. "I thought it might be council business."

"And was it? Was it council business?"

"No, as it happens, it wasn't," he retorts. "Give it a rest, can't you? I'm tired, you're tired. There's no point blaming—"

"So who was it from, this message?"

He waits just a beat too long before he answers. "Oh, just a colleague about a meeting. Nothing important. Look, I've been thinking. You really need to take the tablets Dr. Mahmoud prescribed; there's only so long you can run on adrenaline, and when she's back home, Grace will need our support twenty-four-seven."

Very clever. Using the prospect of Grace's return to keep me drugged up and out of his hair.

He carries on listing reasons why I need to stop my "crazy theories," as he puts it, but I just fade him out. I wouldn't admit it to him, but I do feel exhausted. I feel ill.

The more I poke around, the more I feel like there's a lot of stuff going on I'm unaware of. Have I really become so detached from everything outside of the children and the house that I haven't registered what's happening right under my nose?

And now . . . what if Blake is in some kind of trouble he's tried to keep from me? He might have got into something well over his head and not know what to do about it.

I like to think he'd confide in me about anything, but I know he worries about my state of mind. Although he doesn't know what happened in Newcastle all those years ago, he knows about the anxiety that has plagued me, the panic attacks, the agoraphobia.

He's never pressured me to talk about possible reasons; has always just accepted that's the way I am and tried to support me.

He might not feel he can burden me with the truth.

As I run through possible scenarios explaining why he

has got so much cash in the house, cash he has kept a secret, the irony is not lost on me.

I'm enraged at the thought of him keeping secrets, and yet what about my own past, my mistakes, my buried truths?

What if... what if Grace going missing is nothing to do with Bev, or Mike, or Blake's secret stash of money? What if her disappearance is some kind of karma—to make me pay for what I did?

CHAPTER 28

Sixteen years earlier

On arrival at the university, Lucie was allocated a very small, very basic room that overlooked a scrap of ill-maintained garden with a scratched, graffiti-marked wooden bench.

All first-year students were entitled to live on the university campus, and Lucie didn't mind that the room was shoddy, but she did mind the single bed, which not only resembled what she imagined you'd get in a prison cell, but also felt like a bad camping mattress. It was incredibly uncomfortable, not helped by the polythene cover that the list of rules pinned to the door instructed her not to remove before adding her own bedding.

The house manager showed Lucie and a small group of other students around. Next to Lucie's room, there was a large communal kitchen with a wooden table and eight plastic chairs.

"You should label all your own food and obviously not use anyone else's stuff," the manager recited from a printed list she held.

The others had already started joking with each other,

whispering smart replies to the house manager's comments. Lucie had quickly gathered, from what people had said while they waited for their tour, that the others didn't know each other. But light-hearted chat seemed to come naturally to them. They were interacting and behaving like old friends from the off.

There were five boys and three girls on her landing. One of them, a short, thin girl with glasses and shoulder-length mousy hair, had smiled awkwardly at Lucie once or twice, and she'd smiled back. But that had been the extent of their communication. Lucie didn't want to be friends with someone as shy and inadequate as herself. If possible, she wanted a new set of friends who'd show her how to start enjoying life at last.

Some hope there was of that, she thought glumly as they all trooped after the wittering house manager.

There were still a couple more days until lectures began.

Lucie found it was worryingly easy to sit in her room, draw the thin curtains and turn on the small flat-screen television. Here, she was free to hibernate, away from uncomfortable interactions with others.

The location of her room, right next to the kitchen, was both a blessing and bad fortune. When the boys, who had immediately bonded as firm friends, came home in the early hours, the first place they congregated was the kitchen.

Kebabs were upended on plates extracted noisily from the cupboards. The fridge was raided, crockery dropped, glasses clinked against a backdrop of screeching laughter and yelled conversations.

When they were finally tucked up in bed and snoozing like babies, Lucie would wake and listen, one ear pressed against the wall. Although she was sorely tempted to bang on all their doors to get her own back, she instead capitalised on the good fortune of being able to identify, through the wall, whether anybody was in the kitchen before she ventured in there.

When she was satisfied the coast was clear, she'd dash in and quickly prepare some breakfast. But not before she'd cleared at least *some* of the detritus left over from the boys' midnight feast.

She scraped coagulated kebab meat into the bin and often had to wash up a plate and cup for herself before she could begin to prepare her own meal.

One morning, the house manager stuck her head around the door.

"Everything OK here?"

"Not really." Lucie frowned, nodding to the table, covered in empty beer cans and takeaway pizza boxes. "Nobody seems to be taking any notice of the rules, and it's the second morning someone's used nearly all my milk."

"Annoying, isn't it?" The manager rolled her eyes. "Boys will be boys, eh?"

"That's not really good enough, though, is it? The rules are there for a reason."

The manager checked her watch. "I've got to dash now, but don't feel it's your job to clean up after the mucky so-and-so's. Tell them to sort themselves out!"

Lucie was beginning to appreciate the structure she'd enjoyed at home. She'd always taken it for granted, been irritated by her dad's love of routine at times. But now she could see first-hand the chaos that ensued when it was missing.

One of Pete's favourite phrases came to mind: "Rules are there for a reason: because they work."

It was a sobering thought for Lucie to realise, in this new oasis of freedom, that he had been right all along.

*   *   *

After a few days had passed surprisingly quickly, she realised she would have to force herself to leave the building.

She had exhausted all the acceptable reasons for staying in, having unpacked most of her stuff, which had arrived on time as planned. She'd texted and called her father regularly, assuring him everything was super and not mentioning any of the stark realities of university life. And most importantly, she'd now run out of food, helped to some extent by the pilfering boys she had the misfortune to share the accommodation with.

She pulled on an old grey sweatshirt over her fashionably ripped jeans and stuck her wallet in her back pocket. Before leaving, she glanced in the mirror at her pale face and took another couple of minutes to brush on a little bronzer, mascara and a slick of pale pink lip gloss.

She tied her dark blonde hair up into a messy topknot and headed outside.

The campus was busy with students walking in different directions, some with books tucked under their arm, some strolling more leisurely, talking on phones or clutching paper coffee cups.

A group of girls sauntered in front of Lucie in a line, arms hooked into each other's as if they were inseparable friends. Was this yet another case of people playing the role of life-long buddies in order to cement their place in the social fabric? It seemed so false and, frankly, embarrassing to her.

She slowed down her pace, not wanting to catch up with them and have to overtake their stringy, giggling line, which blocked the whole path leading to the main building. The air was fresh, bordering on chilly, and she wished she'd had the sense to put on her coat instead of just a fleece.

She'd spotted on her tour that there was a small supermarket on site, about a five-minute walk from her room, and that was where she was headed.

She passed the building where her first lecture would take place and felt the warm glow of being prepared. She already had the set texts she'd need for the first year of the course, and half a dozen large lined notepads and a set of coloured pens to boot.

She couldn't wait for the course to start, so she could fill her day with purpose. Up ahead, the library loomed. She had seen it on the initial tour but hadn't spent any time in there yet. It was another place she could go to while away the hours at the end of the day, if necessary.

The noise level from the girls in front ramped up suddenly and they made a right turn, on to a short path that lead to a building signposted as a café.

Impulsively, Lucie found herself following.

Her stomach was growling. She hadn't had breakfast this morning as someone had used the last few slices of her bread and she'd drunk the last of her orange juice.

Inside was a bright, modern space, but she realised with a start that there were no small tables free where she could tuck herself away as she'd hoped. Most people seemed to be sitting together in larger groups. Chatting, laughing, generally behaving like the sociable students she'd anticipated—and half dreaded—being amongst.

She felt sure people were turning to stare at her, this nervy-looking girl, still obviously alone with no new friends at the start of her course.

She looked longingly back at the door, but another large group of students were already approaching, blocking the exit. She shuffled in closer behind the girls she'd followed into the café, in the hope that it might look as though she was with them. Before she knew it, she was in the queue for food.

A few minutes later, she carried a tray over to a large table to the right of the emergency exit doors. A group of around seven students, male and female, sat at one end of it. She placed the tray down at the other end, far enough away from them for it not to be rude not to ask if the seat was free.

She removed her plate with the jacket potato and tuna and the small bottle of fresh orange juice, and then propped the tray against her chair. She cursed herself for not bringing a book with her, but she'd only intended going to the shop, hadn't she? Coming here was never part of the plan.

If she kept her eyes on her plate, she wouldn't see people gawping at her: the pathetic lone student in a whole room of groups. *The imposter.*

"Lucie!"

A clear voice cut through her thoughts. It came from the other end of the table.

Lucie's head jerked up to see who had called out, her potato-loaded fork hovering in mid-air.

It was the mousy-haired girl who lived on her landing. Lucie wished she'd paid more attention to what her name was, as the girl obviously had to hers.

"Don't sit there on your own; come and join us!"

"It's fine." Lucie smiled shyly. "Thanks, though."

She ate the forkful of food and looked back down at her plate. Even the little mouse had found herself a group of friends! But Lucie wouldn't have people feeling sorry for her. If she had to get through the next four years with no one to hang around with, then so be it, she resolved.

She didn't need other people. She just needed her qualification, and then she'd go back to Nottingham, back to her dad and everything in her life that was familiar.

How ironic that the very things she'd initially set out to

escape from now felt like a sanctuary she'd happily return to in a heartbeat.

"Lucie, isn't it? I'm Stefan."

She jumped slightly and her fork clattered down on to her plate. A tall, muscular guy who looked to be in his late twenties stood over her. She felt her skin heat as he smiled, showing even white teeth and a strong, square jawline.

"Sorry, didn't want to startle you. Come and join us; we won't bite, you know."

Lucie found herself smiling mutely, then picking up her tray and loading her plate and drink back on to it to move to the other end of the table.

She would never forget the decision she made to join the other students that day, because it was the first time she ever laid eyes on Stefan O'Hara.

CHAPTER 29

I'm the invisible person around here, the person nobody is interested in.

There's only one thing worse than being ignored, and that is being overlooked.

But I'm not stupid, I've learned you can make people notice you. With the right planning and the right research, most people have things in their past they'd rather stay hidden away.

Yet some things need to be revealed. People who have been silenced should be given a voice and not forgotten.

And that's where I come in.

CHAPTER 30

Lucie

Sunday evening

When we get back to our own garden from Bev and Mike's house, I can hear the faint buzz of the press talking from the front of the house.

We've barely taken our shoes and coat off and moved into the sitting room when there's a commotion out in the hallway. A blast of crowd noise and then the door closing. Muffled, concerned voices.

Blake peers around the door, then turns back to me.

"My parents are here," he says.

A shiver of nervous energy zips up my spine. Nadine always makes me feel so inadequate, sometimes without even saying a great deal. God only knows what she'll have to say about Grace.

I wish Oscar was down here, nuzzled close to me. And I could do with Dad's support, too. I glance out of the window and see Jeffery from next door standing near the gaggle of press and staring straight at the house. I shiver and push the thoughts that present themselves out of my head.

I'm about to ask Blake to call Dad and Oscar downstairs

when the living room door opens and there she is in all her coiffured glory. Nadine.

"Darling." She sweeps past me and embraces Blake. "I have no words. We have no words, do we, Colm?"

"Dear Lucie." Colm follows his wife in and walks straight over to me, sitting down and grasping my hands in both of his warm, dry ones. "I'm so, so sorry you're having to go through this."

Nadine leaves Blake and walks over to me, lays a cool hand on my shoulder.

"Where's the baby, dear?" she asks.

"He's asleep. My dad is upstairs with him."

"Why don't you let me take Oscar, just for a few days, until this is all resolved?"

"It's an idea, Luce," Blake says gently. "It will let you get some much-needed rest."

Nadine's compassionate smile dissolves instantly when I shake my head.

"I want him to stay here with me."

"But he isn't here with you, is he? You clearly can't cope if your father is having to lend a hand and with his own health so questionable . . . I—"

Colm touches her arm. "Leave it, Nadine. Lucie's made her feelings clear."

She snatches her hand from my shoulder. Ever since Oscar was born she's been desperate to get her hands on him. I was barely out of hospital when she tried to discuss which exclusive independent pre-school they'd like to fund for him.

It infuriated me that no such interest was shown for Grace. Both Nadine and Colm had such old-fashioned, out-dated ideas about the first boy in the family. Even darling Liberty, Blake's brother's daughter, couldn't live up to *that*.

Then they'd bought the cottage in rural Nottingham-shire precisely so they could see more of Oscar but I'd shot down Nadine's plans on keeping him for the entire weekend right away.

"He's our son, not hers." I'd instantly made my feelings crystal clear to Blake when he tried to argue his mother's corner. But judging by her increased frostiness these past few months, I think she's finally got the message.

It hasn't stopped her trying to capitalise on our tragedy, though.

"Never in my worst nightmares did I think we'd have a situation like this in the family. Our personal business plas-tered all over the Internet."

I can't recall in seeing or hearing her name mentioned at all yet, but still...

Nadine shakes her head, looking at the floor before turning back to Blake. "Tell me what happened. From the beginning."

As Blake reminds her about Grace's insistent request at the party to walk home from Olivia's house, Nadine slips off her dusty-pink cashmere coat, laying it across the arm of the chair.

"And so you just caved in and decided that she could?" She looks at me aghast, as something clicks. "Come to think of it, I heard you say she could. At the party."

I nod, mute in my misery. I remember how I impulsively said yes, just to get up Nadine's nose.

"I told you, didn't I? I said that in my opinion, she was still far too young. I know Aisha wouldn't dream of letting—"

"Mum, please," Blake pleads with her.

"Liberty tried to push the boundaries too. Heaven knows, they all do! But Aisha wouldn't hear of it, told her she'd have to wait until she got to senior school. Eleven, she'd have been, is that right? A full two years older than Grace."

"But Aisha isn't Grace's mother, Nadine. I am."

The air is thick with blame, with suppressed tension.

"No use in revisiting all that now, Nadine," Colm offers. "What's done is done. The point is—"

"The point *is* that Grace should never have been out there on her own," Nadine asserts frostily.

I'm biting the inside of my cheek. I can feel my teeth shearing off tiny threads of wet flesh.

"Whatever possessed you? Both of you?" She looks at Blake and then at me. But her eyes stay fixed on me, and I can feel the scorching blame radiating from her, solely in my direction.

"Grace went on and on, Mum." Blake's eyes flicker nervously towards me. "She mithered both of us to death about it."

"Who's the child and who's the parent here?" Nadine snorted. "That's what I'd like to know."

"She just walked up Violet Road, the same road we live on, for goodness' sake," Blake snaps. "It's a five-minute walk. We agreed that Mike would watch her up to the bend and that I'd watch her home from there."

"But you slipped, didn't you, Blake?" There's no emotion in my voice. "He slipped on the wet moss while he was looking at a message on his phone."

Blake lowers his eyes.

"And where were you, Lucie, whilst Grace was walking home alone at dusk?"

I stare at her, not dignifying her spite with a reply.

"It was just after four thirty in the afternoon, Mum. Hardly dusk."

"That's not what people are saying online," Nadine snaps. Colm coughs. "Nadine, that's—"

"I don't *care* what people are saying online." Blake's cheeks are ruddy. "All I care about is getting Grace back home safe."

Nadine ignores him and asks me again, "So where *were* you when Grace was walking home?"

"I'd just woken up from a nap."

"I see. You were sleeping." Her words are loaded with unspoken disapproval.

"Look, it's no good sniping at each other like this," Colm remarks. "The important thing, and what we came to find out, is what exactly are they doing to find Grace?"

Blake runs through what we know so far.

"I know the chief constable of the South Yorkshire police," Colm declares. "I could give him a call."

"We're fifty miles away from his jurisdiction, Dad. I hardly think that'll help."

"It will if there's something they're not telling you," Nadine says. "He'll be able to find out if they know something awful . . ." Her voice peters out.

I study her for a moment. She hasn't shed a tear since she arrived. She's not pale, her dyed curled hair is as immaculate as ever and her lips are a harsh red slash on heavily rouged skin.

"Something awful like what? What might they not be telling us?" I challenge her. "Do you think they've found Grace lying in a ditch somewhere? Is that what you mean?"

"Lucie, for God's sake!" Blake shakes his head at me, warning me to pipe down.

"Really!" Nadine reaches for her coat. "I haven't come here to be spoken to like this."

"Sit down, Nadine." Colm's stern voice cuts through our bickering. "This has got to stop. We came here to support, not antagonise."

Nadine's eyes well up now as if someone has flicked a switch inside her bony chest.

"This was supposed to be a wonderful day. Your father just heard—"

"Not now," Colm says wearily.

"What is it?" Blake asks.

"Your father just found out that he's to become a magistrate," Nadine says, her face lighting up with pride. "It's been months of the bar scrutinising his suitability, and now, he's finally been approved. It's such an honour."

Blake told me about the rigorous process his father had been subjected to. They'd even asked for family members' dates of birth and any previous names.

"To make sure none of us have criminal records," he explained, which made my heart hammer.

"That's...great news, Dad," he says flatly now. "Congratulations."

The praise sounds hollow, because this is all a load of crap. Nadine and her driving ambition for social advancement make me sick to my stomach. I don't want her here. I feel desperate for the two of them to leave.

"All we need now is for Grace to walk through that door," Colm says brightly. "She'll be back before long, I just know it."

"And how do you think that's going to happen?" I say quietly.

"She might've got lost, or simply been delayed talking to someone," Nadine says.

"For over *five* hours?"

They're adding nothing to our dire situation, just inflaming it. I feel worse, if that were possible, since they arrived.

"*Anything* is possible," Nadine bristles. "When young children are left to their own devices, anything is possible."

The living room door opens and DI Pearlman steps into the room.

"There's been a sighting," he says, his voice urgent. "Someone who lives locally claims they saw Grace as she walked home this afternoon."

CHAPTER 31

Everyone crowds around the detectives. Blake, Nadine, Colm. Even our FLO, Fiona.

But I find I can't move from my seat. And I can't say a word.

Is this it? Is *this* the moment when we find out what happened to Grace?

If Grace isn't home safe, then she's missing. But while she's missing, there's a chance she's safe. Does it even make sense that I'm thinking that? What if it's bad news? I don't think I can bear to know...

I swallow down the bitter taste that floods my mouth.

Where, who, when?

I sit there, staring up at my husband and his parents. They spit out their one-word questions and the detectives stand silently with their hands in the air, waiting for them to quieten down.

Finally they fall away and give DI Pearlman some space.

"A lady called in at the police station in response to the local poster campaign, to say she'd seen Grace walking alone. Apparently she watched her turn into Abbey Road which leads off Violet Road. The witness was a passenger in the car her husband was driving."

"Mike said he'd watched her across Abbey Road," I blurt out. "He didn't watch her right to the bend because Bev called him inside the house."

After referring back to pages in his notebook, it was DS Paige who spoke next.

"Mike Parker did confirm that to us. The witness didn't see anyone else; she said Grace didn't stop walking. Unfortunately, their car then passed by and Grace fell out of her sight."

"How did she know it was definitely Grace?" Blake asks. "Was it by her clothes?"

"The poster gives a good description, but the witness is likely to prove reliable because she confirmed she actually knows Grace, knows your family. It was exactly the right time of day for it to be your daughter, too."

"Lots of people know us around here because of my job." Blake nods. "Who is it?"

DS Paige consults his notebook. "It's...a Mrs. Barbara Charterhouse."

"Jesus." Blake sits down heavily and covers his face with his hands.

"What is it, sir?" DI Pearlman is immediately on alert.

"Do you know of this woman?" Nadine says fearfully.

"You could say that," Blake groans.

I look down into my lap, remember the soggy, sour smell of the tomato juice soaking through my clothes. The way it reminded me of what happened when I was younger.

Blake quickly recounts this morning's altercation. It sounds less dramatic than it actually was.

"She's an unpleasant woman, out to cause trouble in

whatever way she can," he explains. "I wouldn't put it past her to fabricate seeing Grace just to scupper the investigation."

"Lying to the police is a serious offence, sir," DS Paige remarks.

"So is assaulting someone in a café, which is what she effectively did when she threw tomato juice over my wife." Blake shakes his head and sighs in frustration. "Everyone around here knows that Barbara Charterhouse is unstable. She'd have no problem saying she saw Grace and then claiming she must've been mistaken."

"Lucie had some kind of *skirmish* in a café?" Nadine says incredulously.

DI Pearlman frowns. "Blake, can I ask why you didn't mention your altercation with this woman in our earlier conversation?"

"Didn't seem relevant." Blake shrugs. "Grace wasn't even with us when it happened."

"*She* mentioned Grace and Oscar in her ranting, though," I say quietly, and they all turn to look at me.

"I think," DI Pearlman says, sitting down, "we need to revisit our question about what you did once Grace left for the theme park. Let's start again from the beginning. And this time, leave nothing out. Nothing at all."

The house is quiet. They've all gone at last and left us alone.

Dad is in the single bed in Oscar's room and Blake is sleeping next to me.

Sleeping! I feel a surge of negative emotion rush through me. It's made up of all sorts of feelings: anger, sadness, envy that he seems to be taking it all in his stride and remains positive that Grace will return.

I know I'm not being fair, but it doesn't stop the way I feel.

After Blake insisting, and then pleading, I ended up taking one of Dr. Mahmoud's tablets before bed. They're not sedatives, apparently, but I can feel the effect on me, like it's taken the sharp edge off the physical pain.

I'm aching, head to foot. It's a deep, bruising ache that has infiltrated my flesh and bones. I am aching for the missing piece of me: for my Grace.

The pain is so bad I almost wish I'd asked the doctor for the strongest sedatives he's able to prescribe. I don't know how long I can stand the torture of not knowing. Of waiting.

Yet I know oblivion will not provide respite or answers.

Nothing can stop the terrible feelings from rising up. I learned that lesson a long time ago.

CHAPTER 32

Sixteen years earlier

The boy sitting next to Stefan picked up his sandwich wrapper and moved to another seat without being asked. Stefan indicated for Lucie to sit down.

Their group of seven was made up of two male and five female students. They all looked up to smile or say hi to Lucie, but to her relief, nobody stared long enough to make her feel uncomfortable.

"So, Angela tells me you're new here and you live on her landing?" Stefan rested his elbows on the table and cradled his chin in his hands as he watched her.

So *that* was the mousy-haired girl's name.

Lucie mashed a little of her potato into a soft, neat pile, but she couldn't eat it. Not while he was watching her like this, and besides, her appetite had completely disappeared.

"That's right." She was surprised to hear her voice sounding upbeat and rather more confident than she felt. "I'm studying accountancy."

"My deepest condolences," Stefan murmured, lowering his eyes. When she looked startled, his face sprang alive again as he laughed. "Only joking, Lucie! You'll get used to me, I like winding people up."

"Too right." The bespectacled red-haired boy next to him grimaced.

Stefan elbowed him in jest, but Lucie noticed his smile dim as he did so.

"So." He angled himself so he was turned a little more towards Lucie. "Tell me a bit about yourself. Is Lucie your full name?"

Lucie pushed her plate away. She glanced around self-consciously, but the others appeared to be chatting amongst themselves, apart from one girl. She appeared to be in conversation, but instead of looking at the person she was talking to, she stared unblinkingly at Stefan.

"My full name's Lucinda, but nobody calls me that."

"Why not? It's a gorgeous name. Sounds aristocratic and mysterious." Stefan laughed as Lucie blushed. "What else?"

"Nothing much else to tell, really."

"Now I *know* that's not true. Someone like you...beautiful, a little secretive...I'm intrigued. Tell me anything at all about yourself, but be truthful. I can spot a liar from ten paces."

A heat flushed through her. His candour was disarming, as were his compliments. It was just bullshit, she knew that, but still. She couldn't help a part of her responding to him.

"I'm nineteen, from Nottingham, and if I'm truthful, I was full of excitement at coming to Newcastle and now I'm wondering if I've done the right thing."

"Completely natural," Stefan declared, taking a swig from his can of Coca-Cola. "I felt the same way myself when I did my first degree."

"*First* degree?"

She'd spotted he was older than everyone else at the table.

Maybe he was a lecturer? She glanced over at the staring girl again and saw her seat was now empty.

"I'm what polite people call a lifelong student and what everyone else calls a bit of a waster, I suppose." He laughed heartily. "I didn't feel ready for a job when I completed my BA in English, a good few years ago now. So I did a history degree, and after that, I still felt exactly the same, so now I'm studying for an MA in history of art."

Lucie started a little mental arithmetic.

"I'm nearly thirty, if you were wondering." He grinned.

"No! I mean, I wasn't..."

"See, I'm a good person to hang around with. There's nothing I don't know about this place, nothing I haven't seen. If you've got a problem, don't bother with your useless house manager or your tutors, just come and see your uncle Stefan."

She nodded, felt her shoulders relax a little.

Stefan seemed really nice, as did everyone else in the group. Lucie noticed there was another guy sitting a little further down the table who also looked older, but the rest of them seemed to be freshers like herself.

On the one hand, everyone seemed so relaxed but she thought she could sense something else, something strange and unidentifiable, running underneath like a current that belied the apparent calmness of the surface.

Stefan's voice broke through her thoughts.

"So, have you got any brothers or sisters at home?"

"Just me and my dad," Lucie said. "He's really proud I made it to university, but he's devastated at the same time. I never really knew my mum and she died a long time ago, so it's been hard on my dad, me leaving home."

As she said the words, she felt surprised to hear herself opening up to Stefan. He just seemed to have that way about him; like he was a good listener and wouldn't judge.

"Oh, that's just the old empty-nest syndrome," he remarked, waving his hand dismissively. "Nearly kills them, but they soon get over it. This is your time to enjoy life; don't let guilt spoil it for you."

Lucie pressed her lips together, not wanting to comment. Half of her knew he was right, but the other half felt disloyal speaking about her dad like this, especially with a stranger.

She'd made a real effort to text regularly and call Pete each day, but it never seemed to be enough for him.

When she'd woken up this morning, he had already sent two texts. The first one complained that he'd expected to chat to her before nine a.m. and why was she sleeping in so late? The second one demanded exact details of what she was cooking and eating.

She missed her father dearly, she really did. But after only a few days away from home, she was realising to what extent her every move had been governed by him. She had never complained, because it was all she'd ever known and she fully understood that it came from a place of pure good intentions.

"Dad worries terribly about me," she said when she realised Stefan was still waiting for her to say something. "I'm texting and calling him lots, but I think he expects more of me."

He shook his head. "Wrong way to go about it. You need to make a real effort to contact him *less*." He shuffled his chair a tiny bit closer to hers. "Think of it this way. You'll be helping him get a life, too. He's probably given up so much, looking after you the best he could, and now he has more time to enjoy the stuff *he* wants to do. He just has to realise that."

Lucie felt as if a weight had been lifted from her shoulders. She'd never looked at it like that. What Stefan was saying made perfect sense.

"I think you're right," she said. "Thank you."

"I know I'm right." He smiled. "Like I said, I've seen it all. Ever read 'This Be the Verse' by Philip Larkin? I reckon he's spot on when he talks about your mum and dad fucking you up. Most of them do, in my experience."

Lucie gave him a weak smile, but she didn't agree with Larkin and said so. "To be fair, my dad has done his level best to make sure I have every chance in life."

Stefan's rugged features moved closer, and she saw tiny amber flecks in the depths of his chocolate-brown eyes. "Admit it, though. You're still a little bit fucked up, right?"

Lucie laughed, thinking about her loner-bordering-on-sociopath tendencies since she'd arrived in Newcastle.

"I suppose you're right," she agreed reluctantly.

"Don't worry, doll." He smiled, baring wolfish incisors that she actually found rather attractive. "We're all fucked up here."

CHAPTER 33

Olivia

When Olivia's dad had finished reading the customary two chapters of Harry Potter she was allowed before sleep, he kissed her forehead and said, like always, "Night night, don't let the bed bugs bite."

Olivia lay still, squeezing her eyelids shut. When she heard her father's slippered feet pad downstairs, she counted . . . ten, eleven, twelve . . . then rolled silently from her bed, lying down on the carpeted floor.

She stretched her arm straight and extended her small fingers as far as they would go under the bed until she touched the small pink rucksack that Grace had pushed as close as possible to the wall.

"Promise you won't tell a single person it's there?" Grace had said when they got home from their trip to Alton Towers.

"I promise," Olivia pledged solemnly. "But why aren't you taking your rucksack home?"

"Mum will want to unpack it and I don't want her to see I've been writing in my diary." Grace shrugged. "And Livvy?"

Olivia looked up from setting up a game on her computer.

"Promise you won't look in the bag either?"

"OK."

"I mean it. Say you promise."

"I *promise*!" Olivia sighed dramatically. "I don't want to read your diary anyway, Grace. I know all your secrets already, don't I?"

"Hmm." Grace nodded. "I've fastened the rucksack up in a special way, anyway. I'll be able to tell right away if someone's been meddling with it. Oh, and the diary is locked and I have the key at home."

Grace had started to annoy Olivia now. This wasn't the way best friends were supposed to act with each other.

"How long do I have to keep it under my bed for, anyway?" Olivia asked, suddenly worrying what she'd say if her mum found it.

"Just until tomorrow night after school," Grace said easily. "If I come over to yours to play Fortnite for a bit, I can get it back then."

"OK, but I don't know why you can't take it with you when you go home later," Olivia grumbled, turning on the game.

Grace sat down next to her and picked up her controller.

"I'll tell you soon, I promise," she said cryptically. "I think everybody will know about it soon."

It was nearly ten o'clock in the evening now, and Grace still hadn't turned up at home.

Grace's parents had visited tonight, and her mum, Lucie—who was always really nice to Olivia when she went over there for tea—had looked so sad and ill that Olivia almost told her about the rucksack under the bed so she'd know Grace had a secret.

But her mum would've been furious with Olivia for not telling her and Dad when they'd asked her if there was anything she could tell them about what Grace might have said or done.

Her own parents were weirdly trying to act normally in an attempt to make Olivia think nothing was wrong. Their voices sounded brighter than usual, and when she'd asked for a second helping of Ben & Jerry's after their pizza tea, her mother dished it out, no question. And that *never* happened.

Whenever they thought Olivia wasn't paying attention, her mum and dad put their heads together, whispering. And she'd heard her dad on the phone in his office with the door shut.

Olivia had tiptoed outside the room and stood there with her ear pressed to the door.

"We say nothing, do you hear me? Nobody needs to know; it'll just make everything ten times worse," she'd heard her father say. "But just so you know, if anything goes wrong, this is entirely all your fault."

Nobody needs to know what, exactly? And what might go wrong that's someone else's fault? Olivia wondered, but she didn't hang around, just in case her mum caught her eavesdropping.

Besides, the whispering seemed to have turned into proper fighting. They kept going into the kitchen and closing the door. They thought she couldn't hear, thought they were keeping their voices low. But Olivia discovered that if she hung around in the hallway a while, their voices soon grew louder, like they'd forgotten she was in the house at all.

"What is wrong with you?" she'd heard her mum half shout just before Grace's parents arrived tonight. "How could you even *think* of doing something like that?"

There had been a sharp slapping noise and Olivia guessed her mum had hit her hand angrily down on the worktop in temper, or something like that.

Olivia glanced at her bedroom window. Her dad had forgotten to pull the curtains closed and the night sky was black as ink. She wondered if Grace was scared, wherever she was.

It had only been a few hours; perhaps Grace would come back soon. She turned away from the window so the panicky feeling would stop, and instead of thinking scary thoughts, she dragged the rucksack towards her and looked quizzically at the fastenings.

Grace said she'd done it up in a special secure way, but as far as Olivia could see, they looked like the regular plastic clips that you found on any rucksack. Impulsively, she reached for them and flicked them open with ease. Then she opened the top flap of the bag and peered inside.

She saw a dog-eared copy of *Diary of a Wimpy Kid*, a large spotted handkerchief and a crumpled T-shirt. She reached in and moved the items aside. Underneath them lay a small pink diary decorated with a floral print.

Grace was weird like that. She loved notebooks, paper, and glittery pens; always made a beeline for Paperchase when they went into town with their mums.

Olivia lifted the diary out and inspected it, feeling a twinge of disappointment when she realised, exactly as Grace had told her, that it was one of those with a tiny padlock.

Olivia had one herself in her desk drawer, though she'd never used it. Her auntie had bought it her for Christmas last year, but she'd mislaid the key and hadn't got around to looking for it yet. She preferred typing on a keyboard to writing by hand, and if she was going to keep a diary, she'd rather get one of those cool electronic ones that you could put a password on.

She stuck a fingernail in the top of the closely packed pages and caught a tantalising glimpse of Grace's handwriting. She couldn't see enough to read anything, but it looked like her friend had written a lot.

She placed the diary back in the rucksack and stuffed the items on top again so it was invisible, like before. After refastening the bag, she pushed it, this time with her foot, as far as she could back under the bed.

If Grace found out she'd been snooping, she'd probably never speak to Olivia again.

But if Grace didn't return home soon, Olivia would be forced to say something, wouldn't she? And what then?

She didn't want to get into trouble with her parents, and especially not with the police.

No. It was best she said nothing at all. For now.

CHAPTER 34

Lucie

Sunday night

Blake snorts and turns over in his sleep, and I snap awake. My heart is hammering; my palms are damp.

I've tried my damnedest to bury this stuff for sixteen years, and yet here it all is; every detail, every nuance has been filed away and retrieved by my unconscious mind, as if it just happened yesterday.

These are the early chapters, the setting, the build-up. My mind is presenting the terrible story like a perfectly structured novel, but I can't stand revisiting the horror of what came later. I just can't face it.

I'm a different person now. That girl—the monstrous person I became at university—it wasn't me, not really. I was coerced and controlled until I forgot about everything that was important to me.

I wish I could go back and draw a line between the person I was and the person I became. They have blurred into the fabricated person I am today.

I was forced to make a decision back then. I *had* to. Under the circumstances, I think the outcome I chose was the one most people would've opted for.

Some might say how apt it is that I'm suffering now. They might say it's only right that I'm finding out for myself the pain of losing the thing I love the most.

"Luce?" Blake rouses from his slumber and props himself up on one elbow. "Are you OK?"

"Go back to sleep."

"I haven't been asleep, not properly. I'm just resting, just trying to—"

"You've been fast asleep. Snoring, in fact."

"Listen, Luce. I want to say something." His voice is dry and croaky. I know he's suffering like I am; we just deal with it differently. "I want to say that I love you and Grace and Oscar so much it hurts. I want you to know that."

It feels like this might be a preamble to him saying something else: a confession about the money, or that he's having an affair? Something I might not want to hear, anyway.

I turn on my side so I'm looking right at him. "I know you do. I love you too."

"I know this is the hardest thing to deal with, but I don't want us to end up hating each other. I couldn't bear it."

"That won't happen," I say.

"People can be cruel at times like this. They can stick the knife in, put doubt in our minds about each other."

"Tell me about the cash, Blake. You've brought it into our home and I've a right to know where it's from and who it belongs to."

His eyes bore into mine. He takes a breath and his fingers brush away a wisp of hair lying across my cheek.

"It's really important we're truthful with each other," I say gently. "However bad things get, I'd rather hear it from you than from someone else. We owe each other that much."

The irony of my words hits me like a truck, and I squeeze my eyes shut with the shame of what I just said. God help me if he ever finds out how I've concealed the truth of past events from him.

I wait. Two or three seconds seem like an eternity.

"It's not my money."

"How much is there, Blake?"

"Just over fifty grand. But it's not mine."

So I was right about the amount. Over fifty thousand pounds of someone else's money, salted away in a drawer. That's the definition of dodgy in anyone's book.

"You say it's not yours, but tell me why it's in our house. Is this why you suggested that we can afford a holiday all of a sudden?" I say bitterly. The idea that he'd take us, his family, on a holiday using dodgy money sickens me to my core. This is not the action of the man I love and trust.

"Are you even listening?" He's getting snappy now. "It's nothing to do with the holiday. I don't spend money that isn't mine."

"Then who the hell's is it?" I raise my voice, then immediately bite back, thinking of my dad and Oscar in the other room.

"Can you trust me without judging me, Lucie? Just for a short while longer?"

I snap on the bedside lamp and glare at him. "How can I trust you when you're scared of the police finding out? If there was nothing dodgy about that money, you wouldn't have stashed it in your office and you wouldn't be terrified of the police discovering it. How do you even come to have fifty grand in cash that doesn't belong you? Can't you understand how ridiculous it sounds?"

He turns away from me and lies on his back. When he speaks, the emotion has gone from his voice. "I've told you, I will explain everything. Just not now. Suffice to say, it's nothing to do with Grace going missing, and she has to be our priority right now."

I don't answer. I pick up the glass of water by the bed and take another of Dr. Mahmoud's pills, praying it will abate the wave of sadness I feel that my husband can't—or won't—confide in me.

Wherever there's a lot of dodgy money, there's a chance that someone is out to get it by whatever means possible. Until I know the details, he will not convince me that it has nothing to do with Grace's disappearance.

"I blame myself for her going missing, you must know that," he continues, staring at the ceiling. "I had one job and that was to watch Grace come home. I couldn't resist checking my fucking phone, I never cleared up the fucking moss, I—"

"Leave it," I say softly. "We all have regrets, Blake."

"Ain't that the truth," he says, and his voice is so full of remorse, of unspoken truths, that goose bumps prickle my forearms like tiny thorns.

CHAPTER 35

Monday morning

I sit in the living room, leaving the toast and tea that Fiona made me untouched.

The lounge picture window that overlooks the street is large, lets in lots of natural light. It's one of the many reasons we liked the house on our first viewing. But this morning, the room seems drab with shadowy corners I've never noticed that the daylight struggles to penetrate.

I can hear the hum of voices in the kitchen and the odd yelled conversation outside, amongst the press already gathering at the gate.

No breakfast to make or school blouse to hurriedly iron. No missing shoe or glove to hunt for. No frustrated sigh following a glance at the kitchen wall clock with its oversized numbers that Grace and Blake stuck on so carefully together one Saturday afternoon.

All the things that irritated me last Monday, I desperately wish I had back in my life today.

A whole night without Grace. A whole night Grace has suffered without *us*. Without her family.

Dad sits in the chair, shaking Oscar's rattle to keep him amused. He keeps glancing at me, as if there's something he wants to say. But when I catch his eye, he looks away again.

"Your friends Bev and Mike are here," Fiona says brightly from the doorway. She's doing her best, but I'm starting to feel a little irritated at her efforts to keep upbeat in our increasingly dire and heartbreaking situation.

I lost it a bit with Bev and Mike last night, but I'm past caring about that. I'm totally consumed by the horror of Grace being gone for an entire night. Everything else seems irrelevant.

Bev walks in first. She says nothing at all, but offers me her outstretched arms. I stand up and rush towards her. It's a relief to fall into them.

"It's so shit. So utterly shit," she sobs into my hair. "I can't believe she's all but vanished into thin air. She has to be somewhere. She *has* to be."

"She could be miles away by now," I say flatly. "She could be anywhere at all. It's completely hopeless...I just don't know what to do any more."

"Come on, love, don't think like that," Dad says softly.

I don't cry. I feel dry as a bone inside, as if there are simply no tears left. And what use are they anyway, tears? They do nothing to help; just hinder. I feel like I've left tears behind.

"Pete's right, it's *not* hopeless." Mike's tone is strident, insistent. "We *will* find her, Lucie. We have to. No one will rest until Grace is back home."

His words are sincere, but they don't mean anything, not really. It doesn't matter how forcefully he says that Grace will be found, we all know this can't be achieved by the strength of our intention alone.

Eighteen hours she's been gone. Door-to-door inquiries,

searches, contacting hospitals, alerting all transportation leaving the country...and nothing. No whisper of my beautiful, innocent girl.

Someone has her, I'm almost certain of it now. Someone has taken our baby.

"Let's go and sit upstairs, just the two of us," Bev says softly in my ear. "I don't know about you, but I feel like I'm under so much scrutiny. Everything I say, everything I do."

I nod.

"We're just going for five minutes' quiet time upstairs," she tells Blake, and he accepts it immediately.

"Leave Oscar with me," Dad says. "He's happy enough."

As we leave the room, I notice that he and Mike have not yet spoken to each other but I hear my dad's voice speaking to them both. He sounds so worried, despite him putting on a show for me.

I climb the stairs and Bev follows.

"Dad's been great with Oscar," I tell her. "I need to do more, though. I'm just sitting around and it's not fair on Dad."

Bev makes a little noise of understanding behind me.

I'm distracted by Grace's bedroom door to the left, but instead of lingering there, I turn right, walking into our bedroom. I seem to be finding it hard to concentrate.

I register the mess in there—clothes strewn on the floor, a cold cup of coffee on the chest of drawers, plates holding untouched sandwiches on the bedside tables—but I don't offer any explanation. I know none is needed. I feel at ease with Bev.

I wait for her to bring out the stock phrases about keeping up hope, that Grace will come home...but she doesn't say any of those things.

I perch on the side of the bed and Bev pulls across the tasselled velvet dressing table stool. She sits on it opposite me, resting her elbows on her knees.

"Lucie, I need to ask you something," she says, linking her fingers together and looking at them rather than me. "I need you to give me a truthful answer."

"OK," I say, wishing I could just lie down on the bed and drift off to another place. Anywhere that's not here.

Finally, she looks at me.

"Is there anything—anything at all—you want to tell me?"

I scowl at her. I don't reply, because I haven't got a clue what she's getting at. Then I remember the money in Blake's office. But I can't tell her about *that*; Blake would never forgive me.

She gives me a long look, then delves into her coat pocket and pulls something out.

"This was shoved through our letter box at some point during the night. I was first up this morning and I found it when I went downstairs."

She hands me a small white envelope. I pull out the lined sheet of paper torn from a spiral-bound notebook and unfold it.

> *You think you know Lucie Sullivan, but you don't.*
> *Nobody knows who she really is. Except me. I know*
> *the person behind the respectable mask. Be warned.*

I feel a chill at the base of my spine. It reminds me of what Barbara Charterhouse said about Blake in the café yesterday. His *facade*, as she referred to it. But it's my husband she has the knives out for, not me.

I give a brisk laugh and stuff the note back into the envelope.

"Probably just some crank getting off on the drama," I say bitterly.

"You're saying there's nothing in this?"

"Like what? What were you expecting me to say?"

"I don't know." Bev sighs. "I was just shocked to get it, you know? I'd usually be inclined to give something like that straight to the police, but you're my friend. I don't want to get you into trouble, if there's something..." Her words tail off.

"Go on."

"I dunno... I suppose I mean if someone *has* got something on you." She sighs in frustration. "Look, I don't even know what I'm trying to say. It was just a feeling I had when I got the note... a feeling that something might not be right and... I just wanted to give you the chance to tell me, to share the burden if..." She takes in my incredulous expression. "I'm waffling. I'm sorry."

"I can't believe you're taking any notice of this bit of paper, but seeing as you ask: no, there's nothing I need to tell you." I speak evenly, trying to cover up my irritation with her. "Anyone can shove an inane scrap of a note through the door like this. It has no substance. Surely you can see that, Bev."

"I had to ask. I haven't even shown it to Mike."

That surprises me. "Why wouldn't you show it to him?"

She shrugs. "We're not getting on too well at the moment. Let's just say there have been some... problems." She gives me a thin smile. "It's decent of you not to mention it, but I know you must've seen us arguing last night. In the kitchen."

The stinging slap she delivered to Mike's face when we were walking up the garden.

"None of our business." I can't think of anything else to say. "Anyway, you might as well chuck that note away, because it's a hoax."

"If you say so." She stuffs the envelope back into her bag, and as her hand emerges again, I see she's clutching something else. "But there was this, too, you see." She passes me a photograph. "It must be someone who knows you, or used to know you. Wouldn't you agree?"

The image is slightly out of focus, the colours and clarity marking it as a dated Polaroid.

I'm dressed in jeans and a long-sleeved black polo-necked sweater that ends above the waist of my jeans, revealing an inch of pale, toned midriff.

I'm turning as though someone has just shouted my name, and smiling, my eyes alight with something that resembles mischievous anticipation.

I can remember the exact day this photograph was taken, sixteen years ago.

I know exactly who the photographer was and what happened the day after he took the shot.

I open my mouth to speak, but find I can utter no words. I stand up, and my legs wobble.

"Lucie!" Bev shrieks as my knees fold. I fall heavily to the floor, and as I do, my fingers clench convulsively to crumple the photograph into a small, screwed-up ball in the palm of my hand.

CHAPTER 36

Sixteen years earlier

Once she had met Stefan and his friends in the university café, Lucie's life seemed transformed.

There was no longer time to sit around in her soulless little room watching daytime television and existing on tea and toast.

She was part of Stefan's friendship circle now, and on top of that, her course had started with a full roster of lectures and she was loving it.

It sounded a bit weird, she supposed, loving the processes of accounting. It was the reliability of numbers that she liked. The way that everything could be ticked off via a logical and tested process. Formulae could be applied to ensure that you ended up with an accurate, satisfactory result. If only life could be like that, too.

The course was going to be academically challenging, there was no doubt about that. But whenever she began working on an accounting problem that seemed almost impossible to resolve, she kept a single thought in mind that always inspired her and got her through: the answer was there, it was just a matter of finding it.

The other students on her course all seemed very studious and committed. They reminded her a bit of herself before she became involved with Stefan and his friends. It didn't bear thinking about how lonely she would have been if she'd started the course without already having met people, because this lot were very obviously natural loner types who headed straight to the library to swot after each and every lecture.

None of them made the effort to befriend each other or sit together during study periods, but that didn't bother Lucie now. She'd found her own sort of people to hang around with out of class, though she spent a lot of time in the library too. The tutors had made it abundantly clear that self-study was crucial to getting the required marks, and she was determined to make the most of the well-resourced area.

So much so that she'd actually turned down Angela's offer to go down to the Quayside area of the city later for a bite to eat followed by drinks with "the gang," as Angela referred to their mutual friendship circle.

Lucie had a full day of lectures, and the following morning first thing there was to be a question-and-answer session. She wanted to use the evening ahead to prepare some intelligent questions. It was important the tutors realised she was committed and keen, and she could only show that by putting the study time in.

She headed across the campus, intending to spend the next two hours in the library.

"Hey, gorgeous, how's it going?"

She glanced at the figure advancing on her from the left.

"Stefan!" She felt her cheeks heating up. It was so annoying how she was forced to reveal her feelings, courtesy of her inherited high colouring. Her dad was just the same. "I'm good. How are you?"

"I'm fine, Lucinda. Better now I've seen you. A little bird tells me you're not coming out tonight?"

He insisted on using her full name, even though she'd asked him not to. It made her sound a bit stuck-up but she'd learned to ignore it.

"Sadly I can't make it. Maybe next time, though."

"Seize the day!" Stefan punched the air. "That's always been my maxim and it's stood me in good stead so far. What's so important that you're turning down having fun?"

Lucie explained about the Q-and-A session preparation. "Also, I've told my dad I'm staying in to study and we've arranged a call at eight o'clock."

"Tut tut. Still tied to Daddy's apron strings? That will never do."

Lucie shrugged. "It's just...he sounded a bit down when I spoke to him this morning, and he really perked up when I said we could chat later."

"What did I tell you? You've got to be cruel to be kind. If he's not waiting in for your call, he might just make the effort to get out himself and start to build his own life."

Stefan had a point, but her dad wasn't really the sort to join a class or take up a hobby. Bob down the road was his only friend, and apart from the odd bet on the horses, all his hobbies—reading, gardening, watching movies—were home-based.

But Stefan would not be dissuaded.

"It's only a few drinks. You'll probably be tucked up in bed no later than ten, and you can get up super-early and squeeze a bit of studying in if you're really keen."

She looked up at him, feeling small and protected in his company.

"What do you say?"

She hesitated.

"That's agreed then. Meet you at the campus bus stop at seven, yeah?"

And with that, he turned and melted into the crowd of students who'd just piled out of the lecture theatre opposite.

Lucie sighed and headed over to the library. She didn't mind being jostled by the crowd; it felt good to be amongst people who were here to study and make a better life, like herself.

She knew she'd allowed Stefan to press-gang her into going out, although she felt certain he meant well. And most of what he'd said made perfect sense, to be fair.

There was something else, too, although she'd never admit it to anyone else. Stefan liked her. She could tell.

She'd noticed the other girls in the group look longingly when he saved her a seat next to him or slung his arm casually around her as they left the café together.

He'd also insisted on walking her and Angela home one night when they'd had drinks in the student union bar.

"He's never offered to walk me home before when I've been alone," Angela had remarked sourly.

Lucie tried to tell herself there was nothing in it. He was a full ten years older than her, after all, and more like an older brother. She ignored the silly butterflies in her stomach, and the fact that she now took much greater care with her appearance.

Stefan had already told her he felt protective towards her. That he'd lost his sister while he was still at high school.

"She had leukaemia," he said sadly, his brown eyes seeming to darken with grief. "She'd had it for some time, battled through the treatment, and we all thought she'd beaten it. Then suddenly the bastard thing killed her. One day she was there, the next she'd gone."

They'd sat in silence for a moment, Stefan remembering his sister, Lucie thinking about her mum.

"I'm so sorry you had to go through that," she'd said softly.

He slid his arm around her shoulders and pulled her close. The heat of his body both stimulated and soothed her, and she nestled into his strength.

She'd looked up then and seen several of the other girls watching with poorly disguised envy. She pulled away from his embrace and sat up straight. She could see what it looked like, but it had been a pure, natural emotion between them. Nothing more.

Now she broke away from the flow of students and took the path across the grass that led directly to the entrance of the library.

She did feel guilty about abandoning her study plans that evening, and even worse about the fact that she wouldn't be able to speak to her dad. But she also felt a building excitement about her evening out. She had a proper student lifestyle now!

She really liked Stefan and she valued his friendship, but that was all it was.

She wanted to give this degree her best shot, and that meant keeping life simple. She didn't want the complication of getting into a relationship with an older man, who, although well-meaning, had the potential to really throw her off track when it came to her study plans.

There were plenty of girls who'd do anything to date Stefan O'Hara.

Lucie told herself she wasn't one of them.

CHAPTER 37

Lucie

Monday morning

Blake and I sit and stare at an uncomfortable-looking DI Pearlman.

"So you're telling us there's nothing at all? You're no further forward in finding Grace," Blake states bluntly.

"It feels as though she's just disappeared off the face of the earth," I say faintly, still feeling a little vague from having taken one of my tablets after Bev left.

"As I said, we've interviewed Mrs. Charterhouse, who is adamant she did see Grace. Unfortunately, she has nothing to add to the information already given. Grace was in her sight for a matter of seconds."

I can't bear to think that if the Charterhouses had stopped the car and asked Grace if she was all right, this whole terrible situation could have been avoided.

"We launched another door-to-door on Abbey Road, where Grace was sighted, but all inquiries in the area have drawn a blank so far," the detective continues. "One or two people think they may have seen her walking up Violet Road, but they can't swear to it. Infuriatingly, it just seems to be a small pocket of time when everyone was busy doing something else."

From where I sit, I can see Grace's slippers, tucked under the sideboard next to the television. They're too small for her now, but she loves the sparkly pink and silver design so much she's just flattened down the fabric heels and continues to wear them like mules.

"CCTV, hospitals, train stations, airports...nothing?" Blake says, incredulously.

DI Pearlman shakes his head. He looks pale and tired around the eyes. He's wearing the same suit and shirt as yesterday and I suspect he's been working around the clock to find Grace one way or another.

"We've circulated a full description around all points of exit from the country. There's no CCTV anywhere near Violet Road or the surrounding area, and we're currently in the process of checking with nearby houses if anything has been caught on a residential security camera. A further complication is that we don't know what car we're looking for—if indeed a car is involved—making it extremely difficult to trace a vehicle at this stage."

"We're also putting out an urgent plea for drivers in the area to check their dash-cam footage," DS Paige adds.

"We're very grateful for everything you're doing," I say. "I'm sorry if we come across as the opposite."

"No need to apologise, Lucie. I simply can't imagine what you're both going through," the detective says. "Believe me, we're doing everything we can to find Grace, and we will continue to do so. In cases like these, a breakthrough can literally come at any moment, so we must all stay positive. We just need one person to come forward with something solid we can follow up on and we'll be straight on it."

There are a couple of moments of silence, then DI Pearlman speaks again.

"There is something we'd like to run by you, something powerful that you could both do to give a real boost to the investigation."

"Anything," Blake says quickly. "We'll do anything at all."

"A live television appeal. Tomorrow morning?" The detective looks at each of us in turn. "Hopefully Grace will be back and we won't need to go through with it, but if you're willing, we could get the wheels turning right away."

The note Bev received flashes into my mind. What if the person who sent it watches the appeal? Gets off on me looking desperate and upset? I push the thought aside.

"Of course we'll do it," I say as Blake eagerly nods his agreement. "We'll do anything and everything in our power, to bring Grace back home."

CHAPTER 38

Sixteen years earlier

The night at the Quayside with Stefan and the others was without doubt the best night out of her life so far. They had so much fun and best of all, she didn't have to spend a penny of her own money!

Lucie was gratified that they stuck together as one big group as they visited pub after pub. Each establishment they stopped at seemed to have a happy hour, when drinks were ridiculously cheap, and what was more, each discounted beverage came with a free shot.

Stefan refused to let anyone pay for their own drinks all night. He was obviously the sort of person who was incredibly generous to his friends.

She got to know everyone a little better and warmed to one or two people in particular. Gregg, the red-headed guy who'd been sitting next to Stefan the day she'd first met them in the café, was funny, and Lucie found he had a self-deprecating sense of humour that she couldn't fail to warm to.

"Has Stefan got a good job?" she asked Gregg, the alcohol warming her blood.

He blinked. "Why do you ask that?"

"He's paying for everyone's drinks and I thought students were all supposed to be skint."

"Oh, right. See what you mean." Gregg laughed. "Let's just say he makes enough to live a comfortable life."

He nudged her playfully and she grinned.

Lucie squinted and tried to focus on a figure to her right. She'd noticed it before, someone standing in the shadows of the bar, seemingly merging back into the crowd when she tried to get a better look.

A flash of cropped blonde hair and high heels confirmed that it was Rhonda. The girl who'd been staring at Stefan the first time she'd met the group.

Lucie's housemate, Angela, came over and Rhonda followed her.

"Remember Rhonda?" Angela introduced her. "She's studying business and finance, so you two should have stuff in common." Angela stood on her tiptoes and looked across the room, her eyes searching something or someone out. "Stuff to do. Catch you later."

Lucie and Rhonda sat together for a while, chatting inanely about their respective courses in a hesitant, polite way at first. Rhonda reached for her handbag and Lucie recognised it as a Gucci latest design from a fashion magazine she'd picked up in the library.

"So, did you know Stefan before university?" Rhonda ventured. It was pretty obvious to Lucie the other girl had waited until she could bring the conversation around to Stefan.

"No, not at all. You?"

"Oh, me and Stefan, we go back a long way." She smirked cryptically. She raised a hand to flick her hair back and a large ruby flashed under the lights in a ring on her right hand. "You and him are just friends, yeah?"

"Of course!" Lucie was beginning to resent Rhonda's rather bold questioning. Despite her annoying manner, Lucie had to admit she was very attractive in a gamine, understated kind of way.

"I just wondered if he'd asked you yet..." She shook her head and laughed. "Ignore me. None of my business."

Lucie didn't respond. She thought Rhonda wanted to know if Stefan had asked Lucie out on a date or something. He hadn't but that was none of *her* business.

"You're not talking shop, surely?" Stefan appeared, bearing fresh drinks for both girls. "There's really no hope for you. Enough, I say!"

A look passed between Stefan and Rhonda, so quickly, Lucie thought she might have imagined it.

He sat down with them, and before Lucie knew it, she was holding court, telling Stefan and Rhonda about her dream of starting her own accountancy practice in Nottingham after graduating. They hadn't eaten yet, and her head seemed to swim with the lights of the bar and Stefan's loud laughter as he gently poked fun at her in that harmless way he had. She put down her drink and he pushed another shot towards her.

"Come on, drink up." Rhonda threw back her head and laughed. "We don't allow lightweights in our inner circle, you know."

A shiver of warning travelled down Lucie's spine. Something inside was trying to tell her she'd had way too much to drink already, but she wanted to show Stefan she was more than just a naïve little daddy's girl, and she picked up the shot and knocked it back in one.

A flurry of applause rose up around her. It sounded like a slowed-down record in Lucie's ears. She felt clever, powerful even, when she realised the others were watching her impressive display.

Yes, she was a bit queasy, but that was to be expected, as she wasn't used to drinking. But she pushed the feeling away and, to the cheers of what seemed to her to be the entire bar, banged on the table for yet another shot.

She woke to a tap-tapping on her bedroom door.

She forced her crusty eyelids open and groaned as a jackhammer started up in her head.

Snatches of last night's drinking marathon flashed in and out of her mind in glorious, fractured Technicolor. Knocking back shots, singing, and a wisp of an unwelcome memory of clambering on a nearby table to dance, aided and abetted by the whooping laughter around her.

She swallowed and wished she hadn't. Her throat felt like sandpaper.

That tapping noise again…it could only be Angela enquiring how she was, but her efforts were making Lucie's headache worse.

"Go away," she groaned, turning her head to the wall and closing her eyes again.

Tap, tap, tap. Now a more insistent knocking.

"Lucie? Open up, it's me."

Stefan!

She sat bolt upright in bed and held both temples in an effort to relieve the agonising pounding as her poor swollen brain registered its objections to the rapid movement.

"Lucie?"

"Coming," she called out as loudly as she could bear. Little more than a croak emerged from her mouth.

Impatient knocking at the door now.

She gingerly swung her legs out of bed, pressing the soles of her feet on to the cold tiled floor. She stood up and waited a beat, trying to decide if she was likely to be sick again.

She dreaded to estimate how long she'd sat hunched over the toilet bowl last night, vomiting up the contents of her overindulgence. It had been long enough for her to start falling asleep on the bathroom floor, only roused by her jaw hitting the loo seat. So gross.

"Lucie, come *on*! I'm getting cold out here."

She pulled on her robe and crossed shakily to the door, reaching out a trembling hand to twist the latch. The door opened.

"At last! I thought you were...Oh dear." Stefan's eyes took in the state of her. "I think it's definitely going to be a bad-hair day. I'd skip your first lecture if I were you."

He looked fresh and eager, standing there in the doorway, fit and lean in his jeans and clean white T-shirt. Lucie caught a faint strain of sandalwood soap and her stomach roiled.

He pushed a brown paper bag into her hands.

"I brought you coffee and a croissant. Are you going to invite me in, or do I have to stand out here in the corridor?"

"Sorry. Sorry, come in. I'm afraid I'm a bit disorganised." She looked around at her small space, littered as it was with last night's leggings and dress, the contents of her handbag where she'd obviously turned it upside down, and, she was mortified to see, her lacy knickers and bra.

Stefan's eyes flickered over the garments. "Hmm. You did get yourself in a bit of a state."

"I know. Sorry." She opened the brown bag, extracted the beaker of coffee and placed the croissant on her desk.

Stefan pulled out the desk chair and sat down.

"No need to apologise. We all had a good night, just like I told you we would."

"You also said we'd be back home by ten," Lucie reminded him.

She opened the lid of the cardboard cup and inspected the frothy latte within. She swallowed down a sudden sickly taste in her mouth and set the cup back on the desk, untouched.

Stefan laughed. "Oh dear, is it that bad? If coffee won't help, you must be suffering."

"I feel so, so ill," Lucie said gravely.

"You're not *ill*, you've got a hangover." Stefan shrugged. "Are you seriously telling me you've never had a hangover before?"

"Not like this." Lucie shook her head, slowly and carefully in an effort to avoid more pain.

"Aww, my little hangover virgin!" Stefan said gleefully.

Her face flushed with heat and she hung her head, mortified.

"Oh, come on, it's not that bad. You're living life at last, look at it that way."

Her father's disapproving face floated into her mind. The narrowed eyes, the lips pressing into grim disapproval. Thank God he wasn't here now, to witness her downfall.

"I can't remember much about last night, just awful flashes. I can't even recall how I got back here."

"Oh, I can help you with that, doll. I brought you back. I stopped you falling into the bushes and carried you the last few yards."

She was going to throw up again. Stefan had brought her back here? But she was naked when she woke up this morning; how had ...

"Don't look so worried. Rhonda came with us and got you safely tucked up in bed. I retreated like the perfect gentleman I am." He grinned wolfishly.

"Thanks," Lucie whispered. "For looking after me."

"Hey, no problem. Don't take it so seriously. You had too much to drink, nobody died."

Not yet, Lucie thought grimly. It felt exactly like she was on the cusp of dying. And now she was bothered by what Stefan had said about Rhonda getting her tucked up in bed. Why didn't she leave her fully clothed? That was what you'd do if someone was drunk. You'd just pull a cover over them and leave them to sleep it off.

How creepy that she'd been naked this morning.

Still, Stefan had proved himself to be a gentleman, despite her dad's colourful warnings about the drink and drugs and wild hedonistic parties one encountered at university.

Oh shit! She had completely forgotten about cancelling the call last night with her dad.

She reached for her phone to find the screen covered in missed call and text message notifications, every one of them from her father.

CHAPTER 39

Lucie

Monday morning

I feed Oscar and then Dad pulls his little coat on. "I might not be able to take him out for a walk with those wolves at the door"—he nods at the press—"but we can get some fresh air in the back garden at least."

I nod distractedly as Dad reaches for Oscar's mittens.

"Are you taking your medication, love?" He gives me a long look. "Blake tells me you're not so good."

"Is it any wonder?" I stare at him. "My daughter's still missing, so no, I'm not feeling on top of the world, Dad."

"I'm only worried about you, Lucie." He seems subdued, a little jumpy.

"Are *you* OK?"

"Don't worry about me, I'm just a silly old fool who can sort himself out." He's always struggled to accept concern from other people. "Focus on getting yourself straight."

When Dad's gone outside, I clear up Oscar's lunch tray. Our kitchen is now the Family Liaison Officer's HQ central, it seems. Of course, I can go in there any time I like, and sometimes I'm forced to. But under Fiona's watchful gaze,

I feel my anxiety ramping up twofold, so I avoid it when I can. Particularly after Bev brought around that note and photograph.

The last thing I need is them digging around in my past.

I can hear Fiona on the phone in there, but I can't wait until she's finished. I'm going to wrap up myself and have five minutes outside with Dad and Oscar. I could use a breath of fresh air.

In my old life, I used to make a weekly batch of fresh purees and freeze them in ice cube trays, rather than buy expensive and less healthy baby food from the supermarket. Or was that for Grace? When I try and think back to Oscar's early months, they feel impenetrable, like cotton wool in my head.

I need to pull myself together and get my thoughts in order.

I pull open the freezer drawer and take out a tray, noting that my reserves are depleting fast. Fiona raises her hand by way of acknowledging me when I turn around then turns back to watch Dad and Oscar in the garden.

Jeffery is out there too—in our garden! When he sees me at the window he rushes up to the kitchen door. I open it an inch.

"Lucie, can I possibly have a word? I've been watching the house and—"

"You've been what?" I look at Fiona aghast, but she is busy with her phone conversation.

"I've been keeping an eye on everything," Jeffery babbles. "I need to speak to you about a possible new strand of investigation. There's been a—"

"Please stop watching us," I tell him, forcing myself not to be really rude. "Let the police do their job, Jeffery. You are not a detective, remember that."

"But—"

I close the door against his nonsense and go back to sorting out Oscar's frozen food cubes, resolving to ask Blake to warn Jeffery off.

I look over at Fiona but she is still speaking in monosyllables to whoever is on the other end of the phone. *Yes, no, right. Hmm.* It's obvious she's trying not to give anything away to me regarding what the other person is saying.

I'm trying to juggle two ice cube trays when one crashes on to the worktop and slides over the counter to where Fiona is sitting.

Sorry, I mouth, stepping close to her to retrieve the tray. I reach across the worktop, and as I do so, I happen to glance down at the paperwork near my hand.

I see Blake's name written there together with Bev's and Mike's, and she has drawn a circle around all three of them and applied a question mark at the side.

I snatch up the tray and don't give any sign that I've seen her notes. I pop out three frozen cubes and stick them in a small dish for Oscar to have later, trying to focus on the task in hand and battling the sickly feeling that's rising in my chest.

Blake, Bev, and Mike... what is it with those three at the moment? The vibe has completely changed around them and I no longer feel it's my imagination that I'm being kept in the dark about certain things. Trouble is, I haven't got a clue what those things might be or how to even broach the subject.

Bev took the trouble to come over and show me the note and photograph she'd received. If she's on my side, then why not mention if there's something else happening behind the scenes? It was the perfect chance to confide in me... unless my friend has some kind of hidden agenda.

Fiona is still on her call and seems to be doing more listening than talking herself.

Blake is out again, canvassing the area for any information about Grace. His mother offered to come and sit with me and Oscar, apparently.

"That would tip me over the edge," I told him, and to his credit, he agreed that having Nadine around wasn't something I needed to put up with. "You could stay at home today and let me go out to speak to people," I added. "I feel so helpless, not doing anything towards finding Grace."

"It's just that folks are far more likely to want to help if they see me in person," he explained. "Put Oscar down in his cot and take some time to try and nap."

I looked at him as if he was mad. "And let Fiona report that I'm neglecting the one child I have left? Not likely. She's already questioned me about how Oscar bumped his head."

"Maybe your dad ought to go home soon," he says carefully after I mentioned he didn't seem himself. "I'm not sure it's doing you any good having him to worry about, too."

I didn't react to that. After Dad saying what he had about the house, I figured he was better off staying with us for a couple more days.

Fiona ends her call.

"Want me to do anything?" she asks, glancing pointedly at the sink. "I can tidy round a bit in here if you like, or..." She hesitates and looks at Oscar. "I could look after the baby while you take a shower, give your dad a break? Whatever will help."

Downstairs is getting into a bit of a mess, I know. But cleaning is at the rock bottom of my priorities and I've no idea what she's like with babies, so I'm not inclined to leave Oscar in her care when he's so fractious.

Still, I'll have to get myself sorted out somehow. Last time I risked looking in the mirror, I saw that the dark circles under my eyes were the worst I'd ever seen them; my skin actually looked bruised. I haven't had a shower yet this morning, but when I do, it will literally be just a quick scrub and I'll jump straight out.

My hair is lank and begging for a wash, but I just can't find the will to deal with it, although I'll have to at least try to look decent for the TV appeal tomorrow. According to the comments I've seen on Twitter, some people have already made their minds up that I'm a complete mess as a mother. My throat feels tight just thinking about it.

"No need, thanks," I mumble to Fiona, rinsing out Oscar's plastic bowl at the sink. "I'll take a shower later when Blake gets back. Oscar will only play you up."

"Oh, I meant to say . . ." She picks up a sheet of paper; underneath it is a phone. "Blake left this on the side before he went out this morning. I was on a call and he'd already gone when I went after him with it."

"Oh, right. Thanks." I take the phone and tuck it into the back pocket of my jeans. My heart is thumping and I'm instantly distracted, but I try and cover up my reaction.

Blake keeps his phone with him all the time, so I can't believe I actually have it on my person. I'm pretty certain he'll be back any minute when he realises he's left it. My plans to join Dad and Oscar in the garden are quickly shelved as I head upstairs.

Up in our bedroom, I close the door behind me. The gaggle of press at the gate seems to have grown. Grace missing overnight has certainly seemed to whet their appetite for a story to grab the readers' heartstrings. There are another couple of broadcast vans lurking around, and some of the reporters, undaunted by the lack of news, are broadcasting with the house in the background. The home of the missing girl must make a thrilling backdrop for their viewers, no doubt.

The number of times over the years I've sat eating a snack

or enjoying a glass of wine, watching a similar news report with, I suppose, a kind of morbid fascination even though I felt obvious concern, too.

I might mention it to Blake in passing; someone going missing or a tragic incident involving a local family, but then I'd get on with my day, swallowed up in my own petty worries and concerns.

Now that I'm on the other side of it, I've got a whole different outlook.

I've been tempted to put the television on, see what's being said on the news, but Blake has begged me not to.

"We don't need to know what they're thinking, Lucie," he told me this morning before he left. "They know nothing, even less than us. And *please* stay offline."

I know he's right, but being stuck here all day, the thought keeps crossing my mind.

I take Blake's phone out of my pocket and tap in his date of birth to gain access to the device. The screen wobbles. Password incorrect.

He's always used his birth date on his devices, as I have, for as long as I can remember. Admittedly, it's been a long time since I've tried to access his phone, but still, why change a tried and tested method?

I glance out of the window, panicking that he will return at any moment for his phone. Almost without thinking, I tap in Grace's date of birth.

The screen blinks and his phone icons load. I'm in.

CHAPTER 40

Sixteen years earlier

Nights out with Stefan and the gang had become a regular feature of her week.

Lucie had noticed that she barely woke up with anything worse than a thick head now. And that was usually sorted with a couple of paracetamol and a strong coffee. She must be getting used to the alcohol.

Last night she and Stefan had broken off from the group and gone to a club. Stefan knew the doorman and they were able to skip the long line and go straight inside.

Before they left the group, Lucie spotted Rhonda watching the two of them. She smiled and nodded to Stefan as they left but she didn't acknowledge Lucie. Since she'd apparently looked after Lucie on that first night out, she'd kept her distance. Although not from Stefan. She always seemed to take any chance she got to whisper something in his ear when Lucie wasn't next to him.

Wherever they went, Stefan seemed to know people. Three girls who were leaving squealed and fawned as they spotted him, tottering over on their high heels to air-kiss him in the club's small, dimly lit foyer.

Lucie felt a million dollars when he slid his arm around her shoulders and pulled her closer to him as he chatted to the girls for a few moments. She saw the envy glittering in their eyes.

One of them whispered something to him, but he shook his head and turned away.

"What did she say to you?" Lucie asked when they moved off.

"Don't you worry your pretty little head about a cheap tart like that." He said it in a tone that warned her not to pursue her line of questioning.

She was happy to let it go. *She* was the girl on Stefan's arm and that was all that mattered. But she did sometimes get the feeling he had matters to discuss with others when they were out. Whispered words, a nod here and there and then he'd disappear to the loo for a while. Maybe she was imagining it, she wasn't sure.

They stayed in the club for a couple of hours last night, spending most of their time swaying on the dance floor. Lucie stretched her arms up, linking her fingers around the back of Stefan's neck, and he wrapped his muscular arms around her waist, pressing his whole body against her as they moved as one to the seductive beats.

If she'd convinced herself she wasn't interested in a relationship with Stefan, she'd now changed her mind.

Afterwards, he came back to her room for the first time.

She could feel the effects of the alcohol she'd consumed, but she was far from drunk. She was aware of every delicious moment together.

They were woken the next morning by Lucie's phone ringing shrilly.

"Damn." She must have forgotten to turn it to silent when she got in last night.

She glanced at the screen to see it was her father ringing. Of course it was!

She was about to reject the call when she felt a sharp twist of guilt. She couldn't keep avoiding him like this, it wasn't fair.

Stefan was still dead to the world beside her, so she slipped out of bed and answered the call in the tiny bathroom.

"Lucie? At last! I was on the brink of coming up to Newcastle."

"Sorry, Dad. I...I've been really busy with mock exams and stuff."

"So busy you can't afford to take two minutes out to call your old man? And why are you whispering?"

"My...friend is here."

"Friend? What friend comes over at seven thirty in the morning?"

Lucie bit back a sigh. She was nineteen years old and was heartily sick of her father trying to rule every last detail of her life.

"We're going to our early lecture together," she said tightly. "Look, Dad, I have to finish getting ready or I'll be late. I'll call you tonight, I promise."

"Right you are, love." Pete sounded suddenly deflated. "I just worry when I don't hear from you, that's all. I'm proud of you working so hard, you know that, don't you?"

"Yes, Dad."

"Well then, I'll look forward to chatting later. I'm out with Bob this lunchtime, just a pie and pint and we'll probably watch a couple of races at the bookie's."

"Hmm. Got to go now, Dad. Speak later, love you."

She grimaced when she realised her father hadn't quite finished saying goodbye before she ended the call.

"You're going to have to do something about your bloody dad, you know."

Stefan sat up in bed, lazily smoking a cigarette. He looked like he belonged in one of those sexy Armani adverts.

"He's my father," Lucie replied tartly as she climbed back into the tiny bed. "I'm afraid I'm stuck with him."

"You said it, doll. He's your *father*, not your keeper. You've got to show him you're a big girl now."

"I know. I just feel bad, I think he's lonely and—"

"Shh." Stefan's hand disappeared under the covers and snaked down her flat stomach.

She groaned with pleasure. "Stop. I have to get up now or I'll miss my business finance lecture and I didn't turn up last week. I can't—"

Stefan's phone rang and she felt him hesitate.

"Leave it," she whispered.

A few more rings and the phone stopped.

And almost immediately rang again.

"I'll have to get this," he said regretfully and turned away from her.

"Yes?" he answered curtly.

Lucie heard a panicky-sounding voice on the end of the line. It was definitely a female voice, but she couldn't hear the details what was being said.

"When did it happen?" Stefan's face darkened as he got a reply Lucie was unable to decipher.

"Who was that?" She looked at him expectantly but he didn't meet her eyes.

"Where are you now?" The voice on the end of the phone seemed to rise up an octave.

"I'm on my way."

He sprang out of bed and pulled on his clothes.

Two minutes later, he'd kissed her on the cheek and was gone.

CHAPTER 41

Lucie

Monday afternoon

Blake has organised his icons in different places to my own iPhone, and even though we have the same model, it takes me a while to find his messages and click into them.

When they load, the screen displays the most recent texts. I fume as I scan the last few, a conversation between Blake and his mother.

Lucie seems so stressed. Is she still leaving the baby with her father all the time?

She's fine, Mum. The FLO is here to help, she knows Luce is struggling.

I can come over. Somebody needs to clean that house up and I'm concerned about Oscar's well-being.

Thanks, Mum, but it keeps her busy. And stop fretting, Oscar's fine.

How bloody dare she? What does she expect? Of course I'm worried about Oscar. He might be tiny, but he can sense when things aren't right. Nadine should also be totally stressed that her granddaughter is missing.

She seems to forget that Dad is Oscar's grandparent, just

the same as she is. She's so bloody hierarchical, can't bear to think Dad gets to see him more than she does.

I hear the back door open and slam shut. That'll be Dad and Oscar back from the garden, so I need to get on with the task in hand.

Focus, Lucie, I tell myself, clicking out of Nadine's pathetic messages and into the main listing of texts.

There are so many names of people I've never heard of here, but then for a councillor, I suppose that's entirely normal. I click into a couple and predictably they contain meeting details, links to articles online, and appointments for Blake's regular surgery.

I'm trying to work out how to find the text he received yesterday at around 4:30, when he went out to meet Grace. Then I spot that the time and date of the last text received by each person is displayed on the list of names.

I scroll down, past the texts he's received today, most still unread, to the messages logged as being received yesterday.

There are ten people Blake texted or received texts from yesterday. Straight away, my eyes gravitate to one particular name and I feel my scalp tighten.

I click on it and open the text message that my husband received from Bev at 4:32 p.m. yesterday, the exact time he was distracted by his phone and slipped on the mossy path.

Mike knows. It's time for us to come clean.

My tongue feels like a dry piece of leather in my mouth as I scroll down with trembling fingers but there is no reply sent from Blake. Probably because he slipped and fell as he read it. Now I can see why he was so distracted when he was supposed to be watching out for our daughter. *The utter bastard.*

And her, too! Having the bare-faced cheek to come over here, to embrace me this morning, to cry in pretence of feeling my pain.

Shit. Shit. Shit.

I knew it. *I knew it!*

It's all fitting together. Blake and Bev are obviously having an affair and somehow Mike has found out. No wonder he felt so uncomfortable around me.

I feel sick to my stomach. My friend...our friends. And Bev had the audacity to slap Mike's face when it's obviously *her* who's playing away.

I start as I hear Dad calling upstairs. "Got a little man here who's filled his nappy!"

"I'll be down in two minutes, Dad," I call back.

I stare again at the text message that distracted my husband from his parental duty.

The police must already be aware that something is going on between the three of them, hence Fiona drawing a circle around their names with a question mark in her notes.

I think about the note and the photograph Bev showed me. What if she's trying to push me over the edge? She could've faked the note, and she comes around here regularly. What's to stop her popping upstairs to our bedroom and rifling through my things? That photo could have been one of many I've bundled away in my wardrobe. I haven't looked at them for years.

I'm devastated. Not because they've been having an affair, although that's bad enough, but because of what the consequences were. My daughter, missing because of those two sly, underhand...

"Luce?" I jump at Blake's voice calling up to me as he climbs the stairs. "I've come back for my phone."

I stand up and tuck the phone back into my jeans pocket.

Blake pushes the bedroom door open wider.

"Fiona said she gave it to you." He doesn't sound nervous, but he probably is.

I turn around and take the phone out of my pocket.

"I just want you to listen without saying anything," I say, watching his face. It doesn't change.

I feel surprisingly calm. It's surreal. My daughter is missing and my husband is having an affair, and this is what it feels like. A nothingness inside. I'm numb, everywhere.

"I've seen Bev's text. I know you two are having an affair."

"What? No! Don't be ridiculous."

"I said listen!" I raise my voice and he closes his mouth. "I've sensed the tension between you all, between you and Mike and between Bev and Mike. How long has it been going on?"

He reaches for his phone and I snatch it behind my back.

"Lucie, you've got this all wrong. I swear to God, there's nothing happening." He's putting on a good act, I'll give him that.

"She sent you a fucking text yesterday saying that Mike knows, that it's time to come clean! I saw it with my own eyes. It's crystal clear what's happening, so don't even try and deny it." I swallow back a sob. "I don't care. Do you understand? I don't care about anything but getting Grace home again, but this text"—I jab the phone at him—"is what distracted you from watching for my daughter. It stopped you keeping her safe. You prioritised your mistress over our beautiful Grace." I spit the word "mistress" out like a rancid scrap of food.

"No. You've got it wrong." He sighs, and the corners of his mouth turn downwards. "Lucie, this is the last thing I wanted to explain to you now, in the middle of all our pain. I wanted to protect you from it as long as I could, especially with you being unwell."

"I'm not unwell, I'm just insane with worry!" I yell at him, and then lower my voice before Dad or Fiona hears.

"Why does everyone keep saying I'm not well? My daughter is missing...I'm losing the will to live, for God's sake."

I wait for a response but he just looks at me.

"Look, if you're trying to wriggle out of this by focusing on my weaknesses, it's not working," I say curtly.

"I don't know how you're going to handle what I'm about to tell you, Lucie, but you've got to promise me you won't lose it. You can't let this affect you, because you might not be able to recover."

He closes the bedroom door behind him and walks towards me.

I'm scared now, but I won't show him. What the hell could be so bad, if it's not that he's having an affair with my best friend? Nothing in this world can be worse than Grace being gone, anyway. Nothing.

Blake sits down on the bed and puts his head in his hands. When he looks up, his face is white and his voice is low. "OK, here goes. Your dad is in trouble, Luce."

"What?" I sit down next to him. "What's Dad got to do with you and Bev?"

"He's got himself into a mess. He's been gambling, betting on the horses, the dogs, the outcome of football matches...you name it, he's betting on it. He's been doing it for months. He's well and truly addicted."

I shake my head. I knew Dad liked the odd flutter at the bookie's, but he's always been restrained, careful. He's never had the money to be a high roller. And then it suddenly hits me. "Hang on, are you saying that cash in your office drawer is money that Dad's *won*?"

Blake gives a sad laugh. "If only, but no. Far from it. That's the problem: he hasn't won for a long time, and if he did happen to get a win, by his own admission he'd just put it straight back on another bet."

Now I'm puzzled. "But where has he got money from to gamble big amounts? Dad draws incapacity benefit. He can't work, for goodness' sake."

Blake nods, his expression grave. "Now you're starting to put the pieces together. He's borrowed the money, Lucie."

"The bank gave him a loan?" How irresponsible, lending money to a man who clearly can't make the repayments. It serves them right if he defaults on it.

"Not the bank, no. Loan sharks. Doorstep lenders. Your dad met some dodgy bloke in a pub his friend Bob knew, who offered him a small amount of money a few months ago. After that, Pete said he always seemed to be bumping into him and before long there was a ready supply of funds on offer. Serious money."

"How much are we talking about?" I ask faintly.

"He's borrowed nearly twenty grand over a period of six months."

I suck in air. *Twenty grand!*

"Except loan sharks have their own unregulated rate of interest," Blake continues. "The debt has now soared to fifty grand, and if he doesn't pay up in the next fourteen days, they're demanding he sell his house."

I can't speak. I can't process the horror of what my husband is telling me. Dad's worsening respiratory problems, his weight loss, his depression... it's all fitting together.

"Obviously, at your dad's age, with no income, he hasn't got a hope in hell of getting any help from the usual sources. He came to me, Luce. He was too worried about how you'd react to involve you in it."

"But how... I mean, the cash in the drawer..." I can't even feel irritated at yet another accusation of me being flaky. I'm too distracted by this mammoth development.

"Bev works in financial services, as you know." Blake looks

exhausted. "She arranged a remortgage on Pete's house to raise the money, but she said Mike would go absolutely crazy if he knew she'd got involved in something like this. It's not illegal exactly, but let's just say she bent the rules slightly to pull it off."

My insides feel like they just turned to liquid.

Blake falls silent for a moment, as if he's trying to find the right words.

"Mike saw me go into Bev's office building and, after she'd been acting so secretive, accused her of having an affair with me. So she had no choice but to tell him, and now Mike is totally pissed off at us both. I can't blame him, but I knew it would kill Pete if he lost his house because of his own stupidity, and I knew it would finish you off too."

Now I can see why there are such simmering tensions between the three of them. Why Blake tried to stop me going down to Bev and Mike's house last night, in case it all kicked off, I suppose.

My eyes brim. "You and Bev did all this to help Dad?"

He nods. "I was due to pay the money over to the loan sharks this morning, but then Grace went missing and I've had to bail for a few days. They said if I got the police involved, they'd…"

"They'd what?"

"They'd burn Pete's house down with him in it."

"Oh God!" I sob into my hands. "I'm sorry, I'm sorry I didn't believe you about Bev."

He reaches for my hand.

"I would've told you, Luce. I swear to God, I was going to tell you everything. When it had all been sorted. But then…I just couldn't put that pressure on you."

I thought I'd been successful in keeping the past from Blake and from everyone else but it clearly hasn't worked. They might not know the details of what happened back then but they're aware I'm damaged. It's been painfully obvious since Grace went missing they all feel obliged to protect my fragile mental state.

It must have been difficult for my family and my friends for all these years, protecting me from something they know nothing about.

A thought stirs me up again.

"But you let Oscar go over there, stay with Dad when he could clearly have been in danger!"

"Lucie, stop! Not now. I can't face all this on top of what we have to deal with."

"You might *have* to face it! What if those people had something to do with Grace going missing?"

"They had no need to take her, Lucie. They knew your dad fully intended paying them this week."

I love Dad with all my heart, but he's put my husband and best friend in a terrible position, and my son, and possibly my daughter, in danger.

Is there no one I can trust any more?

Downstairs, the front door opens, and I hear Fiona speaking to someone. Next minute, she calls upstairs.

"Blake, could you come here for a moment, please?"

He listens for a moment—his hearing has always been better than mine—and his expression changes. Without another word, he bounds downstairs.

There are low voices speaking and I can't discern the detail. Then I hear Blake say, "Is this about Grace? Have you got any more information?"

I stand on the landing, listening to a woman responding. She is clearly struggling to keep calm. Initially she speaks in a low murmur but within the space of a few seconds, she ramps up the volume.

"No! I don't want to speak to you, I want to speak to your wife. There are things she needs to know."

My eyes widen in alarm but my feet seem rooted to the spot. I know that voice but I can't place it.

"My wife isn't feeling well and I don't want you causing trouble again, thank you." There's a pregnant pause and then Blake speaks again, his tone firmer. "Fiona, I'd like this lady to leave, please."

I scuttle out of the bedroom but a moment later, the door slams and I hear Blake and Fiona talking in the hallway.

I run downstairs and Blake appears before I reach the bottom step.

He holds his hand up in a stop sign. "Nothing for you to worry about, Lucie," he says. "Just Barbara Charterhouse trying to cause problems again."

Fiona hovers in the kitchen doorway behind him. It feels like the two of them are in cahoots.

"What did she want?" I demand. "Why didn't you let her speak to me?"

"After what happened at the café?" Blake bites the inside of his top lip. "Not bloody likely. That woman is a troublemaker, pure and simple. Everybody around here says the same."

I glare at Fiona. "But what if she knows something about Grace's disappearance? You shouldn't have just sent her away like that."

I look at my husband, as he's the one who told Fiona to ask her to leave, but he seems distracted, chewing on his thumbnail.

"She's been interviewed at length, Lucie. The detectives would have got every last scrap of detail about Grace's sighting," Fiona says gently. She hesitates, as though she's in two minds whether to carry on. "By the sounds of it, her visit here wasn't connected to Grace." Her eyes search my face. "It sounds as if it was something concerning *you* she wanted to speak about."

CHAPTER 42

Sixteen years earlier

After Stefan left, Lucie sat on the bed. She guessed most people on her landing would be attending early lectures now and her room felt silent and cold.

The thoughts ricocheted around her head as she tried to make sense of Stefan's urgent departure.

Who was the panicky woman who'd spurred him into action? Lucie had watched as his expression changed; she'd seen a malicious focus settle over his features and it had unnerved her.

He'd never been aggressive with her and had been a considerate lover last night. But she had noticed people in the friendship group often treading on eggshells around him. There were occasions where others had seemed distinctly uncomfortable in his presence, as if they were unsure or nervous of his reaction.

She wanted to believe he really cared about her, but there was something she couldn't put her finger on, like an invisible barrier that prevented her from knowing all of him.

She shivered and her eyes searched around for her robe.

They alighted on a small, grey bundle beside her single bed-side cabinet.

Stefan's rucksack.

She glanced at the door. He'd been so focused on getting away to sort out whatever problem had come up, he'd probably not notice it was missing until much later. The latch was down and the door was locked.

It was the first time, since she'd known him, that the little grey rucksack had not been on his person. His phone always went into his pocket. What could be in there that he couldn't bear to be parted from, she wondered. She'd never seen him put anything in there or take anything out!

She picked up the bag and sat back down on the bed. Holding it on her knee, she sprang the plastic buckles and opened it up.

There was a folded T-shirt which she pulled out and laid on the bed.

What she found underneath made her gasp. Tiny bags containing powder and pills. Lying on top of what was clearly, even to her innocent eyes, packets of weed. She didn't remove the drugs but poked past them with her fingers to discover two big fat bundles of rolled notes.

She grabbed the T-shirt and stuffed it back in, before re-fastening the rucksack and tossing it back where she found it.

Her heart pounded so hard on her ribcage she actually feared it might crack. Her breathing became laboured but dragging in huge gulps of air only served to make her feel light-headed.

Scenes presented themselves in her head; a slideshow of snippets that served as evidence to make sense of what she'd found.

The brief whispered conversations in pubs and clubs,

often the precursor for his frequent, extended trips to the bathrooms in such places. His generosity in buying drinks and wearing designer labels. His obsession with keeping the rucksack—his stock—close to him. His cryptic offer of a fantastic opportunity he wanted to speak to her about. The nervousness of those around him.

Did everyone know Stefan was a drug-dealer but her? Was the whole group selling . . . or using?

Lucie felt bruised, realising how readily she had trusted him. She had blindly invested everything she had in Stefan, to the detriment of her relationship with her dad and her studies.

But her own mother had died after a drug overdose. How can it not have occurred to her that Stefan was dealing? She'd told him how she despised people who sold drugs because of what happened to her mum. The signs—with hindsight—now looked so obvious. Even her father had tried to warn her about what could happen at uni, but she had laughed off his concerns.

Lucie realised she had unconsciously settled into a routine of attending just enough lectures to scrape by and avoid her tutors raising concerns. Her assignment marks had dropped, there was no denying that, but on Stefan's suggestion, she'd used the excuse that she was finding the transition to degree-level work challenging.

"I'm determined to work hard and improve my marks," she told her course tutor when he requested a one-to-one meeting and questioned the amount of work she was putting in.

Following Stefan's instructions, she'd wept a little, mentioned how tough things had been back home with just her and her dad coping alone, and emphasised how getting her degree was the most important thing in her life. It had worked splendidly. The tutor's attitude softened almost immediately, and she left the meeting feeling quite untouchable.

Stefan was so experienced, knew just what to say. How to lie convincingly. And now, she was beginning to see how he might have garnered such skills.

What a naïve idiot she'd been to fall under his spell. But, she now told herself, no more. She should try and find out what she could and then do the right thing. That much was obvious.

Despite the severity of her hangover, the unexpected injection of adrenaline now served to motivate her to get quickly dressed in jeans and a sweatshirt. She used a face wipe to remove her smudged eye makeup and secured her lank hair up into a scruffy topknot.

She pushed her feet into trainers, shrugged on her jacket, and stared at the rucksack. Now she knew what it contained, its significance seemed to fill the room. She picked it up and tossed it into the bottom of her slender wardrobe, moving her knee-high boots in front of it.

Granted, it was hardly the best security arrangement, but if, for any reason, the house manager let herself in to check the room, at least the bag wasn't in plain sight any longer.

She headed over to the library, not quite sure who she was looking for, but knowing that this was the best place to find someone from the friendship group.

Her stomach growled and yet she couldn't entertain the thought of eating anything. She breathed in the fresh, cool air but instead of freshening her up, it made her shiver and she pulled her padded jacket closer to her.

The campus was quiet, most people either in the library or in lectures with the odd member of staff walking briskly between buildings clutching paperwork. Her heart seemed to lurch into her mouth when she spotted a marked police car crawling around the top of the drive. But it came to a stop outside the entrance to the main office and the two officers that got out didn't even look in her direction.

She used her student key card to access the library building and made her way over to the main open study area. Standing near the entrance area, her eyes began to search for anyone from their friendship circle.

A waving arm alerted her from the left. Her head snapped over to where Gregg was trying to catch her attention.

Her heart warmed at the sight of a familiar face. Gregg had always struck Lucie as sensible and genuine and, right now, in the absence of people she knew well enough to confide in, she valued his opinion.

She picked her way amongst the busy tables until she reached him. The smile slid from her face when she saw his expression.

"Have you heard the news?" he hissed when she reached his small table for two, tucked away in the corner. "The shit's about to hit the fucking fan."

She stared at him, mute for a second as she realised her reaction was important. If she appeared clueless, Gregg might clam up.

"Stefan had a call and rushed off this morning before he could explain where he was going," she said.

"I bet he did."

"What's happened?"

Gregg glanced around them before answering.

"That shit he sells? Well, it finally put some kid in hospital. Stefan is lucky they survived. Some poor kid who was visiting, too. Not even a student here but the details are sketchy."

Her scalp tightened and her mother's face, remembered only from photographs, drifted into her mind.

"He's been pressuring me to sell for him so I've tried to keep out of his way a bit and... well, I've turned a blind eye to it, I suppose. Like we all do." Gregg looked as if he'd lost weight. He'd always been pale, but now dark circles framed his green eyes. "Are you...you know, working for him yet?"

"No! We don't discuss how he earns his money, never have."

"Oh! But still, you spend so much time with him, you must know what's going on."

"Honestly, no. I can see with hindsight there have been signs but I didn't have a clue. He's so attentive to me, to us...I suppose I've been blind to anything else."

"That's what he does at first, how he gets girls hooked."

His comment stung.

"Are you saying he's done this before? Dated someone just to—"

"Yeah. Sorry. Rhonda told me that's how he gets girls' trust. And then he just sort of introduces it casually to the conversation. Before they know it, they don't really have a choice in the matter."

The *fabulous opportunity* he was going to discuss...

"Do you...work for him?" she ventured.

"Not any more but he's been threatening me, trying to make me change my mind."

"What are you going to do?"

"I'm going home," he said, his voice flat. "I can't do this shit any more. I've had enough."

"Oh no!" When she'd first arrived, everyone had said how clever Gregg was. "I'm sad to hear that, Gregg. I know you had plans to qualify as a pharmacist."

"That all seems like a long time ago now. Before meeting Stefan." He shrugged. "Maybe I'll start again somewhere else. I've wanted to have a chat with you about it for a while, but I couldn't risk you telling Stefan. He's quite a powerful figure around here."

"I've sort of felt something's wrong, I just didn't know what."

"He gets the gear from some pretty powerful people, He's got the perfect set-up here, unlimited customers and people he can control to work for him, which is why he never leaves the university."

So Stefan's excuses about having an insatiable thirst for knowledge were a load of rubbish.

"Look, Lucie, you're a nice girl." Gregg sighed. "My advice is, stay away from Stefan. He's into some dark stuff you don't want to get involved in."

"What?" Her eyes widened. "What kind of stuff?"

He readied himself to speak, then seemed to think better of it. "Just dodgy business. I can't say any more and I'd be grateful if you don't mention seeing me this morning. But he's not who you think he is and what's happened, well, it's serious and he'll be looking for people to blame. That's just the way he is." He grabbed his bag and began to walk away, turning back to her again after just a few steps. "Get out while you can, Lucie."

And then he was gone.

CHAPTER 43

Lucie rushed back to her room. She felt out of breath, as if her lungs weren't taking in enough air.

She closed and locked the door behind her. Sitting on the bed, she crossed her arms to hold herself as she rocked back and forth, raking through everything she knew to try and get some clarity.

What to do? What to do?

She wanted to ring her dad and ask for his advice but she couldn't do that. The instant she let him know what she'd found and what Gregg had told her, he'd be on the next train to Newcastle ready to square up to Stefan.

No. She didn't need her dad to tell her the right thing to do here. There were two options. Confide in her tutor about what she'd found or call the police. Maybe both.

As if on cue, her phone rang.

"Hey, doll, it's me. I left my bag at your place, so I'll—"

"I know what's happened and I know what's in the bag," Lucie said, surprised at the steely tone of her own voice.

A pause at the end of the line and then, "Don't jump to conclusions. It's not what it looks like."

She didn't say anything.

"I'll send a cab now. All you have to do is get in it and come over here." He sounded so desperate to see her, to explain. "I swear, I swear, it's not what you think. But I can't tell you on the phone. Come over and I can explain everything and then, if you still want to shop me then I won't stand in your way."

He really did seem devastated she thought so poorly of him. Despite what Gregg said about the other girls, maybe...just maybe...she was different and he really did care for her.

Stefan's road was rammed full of parked cars, so the cab dropped her off at the corner. She clutched her tote bag closer to her. Inside it, she carried Stefan's rucksack and its contents. It felt like a living thing, pulsing with threat and danger.

She'd already decided she wouldn't return it to him right away; she'd hear what he had to say, first. She would hold the threat of the authorities over him a little longer. He certainly seemed more eager to speak to her while that was the case.

She walked the few yards to the house. Stefan lived in a three-storey Victorian villa that had long since been converted into six small flats with a communal bathroom, lounge and kitchen. Lucie had been around there a handful of times but Stefan had told her he refused to sit in the lounge when the landlady was around.

"She's a nosy cow," he complained. It occurred to Lucie at that point that he seemed to have a problem with women. Anyone who didn't bow to his demands was labelled insufficient in some way.

There were four other men living there, and of course

Rhonda, who'd apparently moved in at the start of the new term when she embarked on studying for her degree. Like Stefan, that was not her first course.

Lucie had felt jealous of her at first, had felt envious and was worried that Rhonda would turn Stefan's head. But she needn't have worried.

"She's a snooty bitch who thinks she's above the rest of us," he'd fumed one day when Rhonda asked him to tidy up his DVDs, which were scattered all over the lounge floor. "Always done up like a dog's dinner too, the little whore. She could do with someone giving her a lesson in manners."

Lucie felt uncomfortable at his obvious vitriol, but relieved at the same time. Although Rhonda always seemed to be simpering around him when they were out, Stefan obviously couldn't stand her, so she pushed any thoughts of the two of them hooking up out of her mind.

Stefan seemed reluctant for her to visit often but that didn't matter because Lucie hated spending time at the house. Even though the landlord kept it fairly well-maintained inside, the ageing property was in need of some structural work doing. It was cold and had draughty rotten windows that sucked any warmth from the three-bar fire.

The landlady and her husband often visited the property, cleaning and pottering around downstairs, and although she'd seen them both from a distance, she'd never actually met them.

Stefan increasingly insisted they spend time together there, instead of in Lucie's admittedly tiny but clean room on the university campus. Once she was with him, though, and they were relaxing with a drink, she forgot all about her surroundings and focused on the man she loved.

It had seemed that life was so good. And now this.

As Lucie approached, she saw the front door was slightly

ajar. Stefan's room was on the top floor and he probably wouldn't hear her knock anyway above the music he told her he liked to constantly play in the background.

So she pushed it open. She felt disappointed that Stefan was nowhere to be seen. He'd asked her to text him as soon as she was in the taxi and she had done so. He hadn't replied but she'd expected a bit of a welcome when she got here; he'd seemed so eager to have his chance to explain.

Someone had put the chain on the front door but hadn't quite secured it properly, and when Lucie pushed it, the chain slipped off and she was able to get in.

She walked past the communal kitchen, wrinkling her nose at the food-caked crockery piled high on the side. Half-eaten kebabs and pizzas spilled out of their cartons and cardboard boxes on the table in the middle of the room.

She held her breath and walked quickly past the mess, only breathing properly when she reached the inner hallway and the stairs.

She heard Stefan's music drifting down from the top floor, and there was rather a lot of banging, too. It sounded like someone was moving furniture around.

Lucie started to climb the stairs.

CHAPTER 44

Lucie

Monday afternoon

After Barbara Charterhouse's impromptu visit, I go back upstairs, not trusting myself to avoid a scene in front of Fiona.

I hear raised voices from in the hallway: Blake and my dad. It's clear they're having some kind of disagreement but I don't go down. After what I've found out, I just don't feel strong enough to face Dad right now.

I hear the front door open and slam shut, followed by low voices speaking.

Blake seems contrite when he follows me up. "Your dad's gone home. I offered to drive him but he insisted on calling a cab." He hesitates. "Why don't you have a little lie-down, Luce, maybe take one of Dr. Mahmoud's tablets?"

"Why's that? To stop me wondering why she wanted to speak to me?" I snap. "I'm assuming that's why you got rid of her so quickly?"

"It was just a gut reaction to send her packing before she upset you again." He sighs. "She's a troublemaker. You know that."

I sit on the edge of the bed and cover my face with my

hands. I can't stop thinking about Dad's predicament and every minute that passes, my heart bleeds a little more for my daughter. Two of the people I love most in the world.

Blake sits close to me and puts his arm around my shoulders. "Come on, Lucie. It'll be all right."

"Will it?" My hands fall away and I glare at him. "Will it really all be all right?"

"Truthfully? I don't know." He hangs his head and stares at his feet. "But I have to tell myself it will be all right in the end. I have to keep faith, or . . . I won't be able to carry on."

I melt a little and reach for his hand. He's hurting terribly too and here we are bickering over Barbara bloody Charterhouse when our only concern should be Grace. Yes, I'm terribly concerned about Dad, of course I am. But he's an adult. He's made certain choices and is now dealing with the consequences.

I can't take that responsibility on my shoulders right now, however tempting, or I'll crumble. I resolve to try and put Dad's problems out of my head for now, however impossible that seems.

A thought that comforts me is that my husband and best friend are truly loyal. I feel very fortunate knowing that now.

"I have a meeting at the community hall at three." Blake squeezes my hand and stands up. "Jeffery has gathered the troops with a view to extending the search," he says. "I'll be an hour at the most and then I'll come straight back here so we can talk some more."

Five minutes after he leaves, my phone rings. I've had calls and messages from numerous people, no doubt well-meaning, but I can't face answering them. I thought I'd left the phone on silent.

I look at the screen, expecting it to be Blake, already paranoid about checking if I'm OK. But it's Nadine.

"Just ringing to see if there's anything I can do," she says flatly, fully expecting me to turn down her offer, I should think.

"Thanks, Nadine, and yes, there is. Could you possibly come over and look after Oscar for a while? Blake's out and there's somewhere I have to go."

There's a beat of surprised silence before she clears her throat. "Where are you going?"

"If you could get here as soon as you can. Thanks so much."

I end the call and gather my courage. Despite Blake reassuring me about the reasons he got rid of Mrs. Charterhouse so quickly, I just need to satisfy the niggling feeling I have. Until I find out she definitely didn't want to speak to me about something related to Grace, then there's still a loose end that needs tying up.

Even though he doesn't seem ready yet, I change Oscar. I'd hate to give Nadine another reason to find me lacking.

After that, I brush my hair, wash my face, and clean my teeth, then manage to find a clean top that doesn't reek of body odour.

Nadine arrives ten minutes later.

"Oscar's in his chair in the living room," I tell her when I beat Fiona to the door. She nods to Nadine and retreats back to the kitchen. "He'll be ready for feeding soon, you'll find his food in a bowl in the fridge."

"Where are you going, Lucie? Blake told me you'd agreed to stay put for any news."

"I refuse to be a prisoner in this house any longer, Nadine. Everyone else is doing something useful to find my daughter, and I intend to do the same. I'm not going far, I'll be about an hour."

"You can't go out there; the press will eat you alive! Have you seen the things that are being said about you?"

"I'm not scared of the press," I snap back. "And I'm not interested in their vile little stories. They haven't a clue what happened to Grace."

Nadine's face assumes a sly expression. "You do know what they're saying online, I take it? That you were negligent letting Grace walk home alone? That Oscar has had a mysterious bump to the head? Some of the local people are saying you're thought of as quite strange."

"I don't give a fuck what they say about me."

Nadine gasps at the profanity and touches her throat.

I stuff my feet clumsily into my flat ankle boots, holding her stare. "All I'm interested in is finding out as much information as I can to bring Grace home."

Nadine calls out as I head for the front door. "Where shall I tell Blake you've gone if he comes back and asks?"

That brings Fiona rushing out of the kitchen again. She hovers in the doorway, a quizzical look on her face.

"Just tell him I'm out," I say flatly. "That's all he ever tells me."

"Lucie, it's imperative we know where to get hold of you," Fiona says firmly, and Nadine nods with smug approval.

"I have my phone," I say tartly. "But if you must know, I'm driving over to Barbara Charterhouse's place. I won't be long."

"I'm happy to come with you?" Fiona offers.

"Thanks, but I'll be fine. I have my phone if you need to get in touch." I grab my jacket from the coat stand.

"The press will have a field day if you go out there," Nadine says faintly. "Have you seen the state of your hair and clothing? You look like a madwoman."

I ignore her insult and step outside the front door.

Immediately, cameras begin to click and whirr, and there's a flurry of activity as the press at the gate realise who I am. The noise level increases dramatically, everyone shouting at once, but I catch a few questions.

"Mrs. Sullivan, is there any news about Grace?"

"Can you tell us where you're going, Lucie?"

"Where's your husband? Are you two keeping strong?"

"How's the baby's head? Are you struggling to cope with him?"

They don't jostle me when I step outside the gate, but they get pretty close. I feel a bit dizzy and realise I haven't eaten anything today. I try to keep my eyes on the pavement in front of me. Ten more steps will do it and I'll be inside my little Fiat.

I'm just about five steps away from my vehicle when a woman in a houndstooth coat strides in front of me, stopping dead and forcing me to stop walking. She shoves a microphone into my face and a guy with a large camera next to her starts to film.

"We're so sorry to hear Grace is missing, Mrs. Sullivan. Is there any news?"

Other faces crowd in around her, holding microphones and cameras that point at me from different angles. I start to feel disorientated.

"What? No. No news." I step forward, but she doesn't budge.

"I know the whole community is hoping for Grace's safe return; we all pray she'll be home soon. How are you coping?"

I jiggle my car keys. "Sorry. I have to go somewhere, I can't—"

"Can I ask what possessed you to let Grace walk home alone, Mrs. Sullivan?"

"What?"

She moves closer. She's heavily made up and has perfectly sculpted brows that are at least two shades too dark for her.

"She's just nine years old. Did any part of you think it might be a bad decision? Did your husband try to change your mind about—"

"Get out of my way!" I push past her and yank the car door open, sliding inside.

I feel like I'm hyperventilating. They're crowding around the driver's-side window, peering in at me.

I have to get away from here. Just like Nadine warned, they're all blaming me for what's happened.

CHAPTER 45

Monday afternoon

"Well, this *is* a surprise," Barbara Charterhouse says when she answers the door. In her tweed skirt, twinset and slippers, she looks far less fearsome than she did in the café. She cranes her head to look past me and sees I'm alone. "What can I do for you?"

"I wondered if...Could I have a quick word?"

"You'd better come in," she says curtly. "I got the distinct impression you weren't interested in talking to me when I called at the house, earlier."

"I'm afraid I was upstairs," I offer limply. "I did come down but by then, you'd already left."

"Yes. Banished by your husband, to be precise."

Several dogs bark from somewhere in the depths of the sprawling farmhouse. When I got out of the car, I saw immediately that the exterior was in grave need of repair: peeling paintwork and weeds sprouting from the guttering. Now that I'm inside, it's the same story. I can smell food cooking, but underneath it is the unmistakable odour of damp.

"You'll have to forgive the state of the place," Barbara says, a little more cordially, as I follow her into the kitchen. "Harold isn't well at the moment, so a lot of stuff isn't getting done. You can sit there if you like." She indicates a large, scratched wooden table with a collection of mismatched chairs around it.

She plucks a black kettle from a stand at the side of the open fire and fills it at the sink.

She sits down opposite me, her face unsmiling. "I said to Harold only this morning, 'We may have our differences, but I wouldn't wish this on the Sullivans.' I wouldn't wish it on anybody."

"Thank you. It is . . . devastating, as you can imagine."

"Of course. I didn't think anything of it when I saw your little girl on Sunday afternoon. Very brightly dressed she was; you couldn't miss her. I said to Harold, 'Is that the Sullivan girl?' But he was driving and missed the whole thing. Predictably hopeless, I'm afraid."

So far, she's the last person to see my daughter, and that must have something to do with the rush of familiarity I suddenly feel in her company.

"But you're absolutely sure that it was Grace?"

"Oh yes. No doubt about it. I never gave it any significance until later, though. When we got back home from visiting my sister, there was a poster affixed to the lamp post at the bottom of our lane."

The extent of what local people have done to help us suddenly hits me, and I feel so incredibly grateful. Jeffery's face flashes into my mind and I resolve to apologise to him for my sharp manner.

"Harold had to stop to let a car through and I caught sight of the photograph, you see. I instructed him to stop and got out of the car, and that's when I realised I'd seen Grace with my own eyes." She looks down at her hands. "I wish I'd stopped, asked her if she was all right, but under the circumstances . . . I mean, with the strained relationship between myself and your husband, that was never likely to happen."

"No," I say sadly. "What exactly was Grace doing when you saw her?"

"She was walking. Just walking. Not slow, not fast, just moving perfectly normally and looking straight ahead, as you would expect." She looks perplexed. "I wish I could tell you more, but I'm afraid that's it."

Both Blake and I had doubts about this woman's intentions when we heard who the witness was, but I'm completely satisfied now that she had no hidden agenda in reporting the sighting. She *did* spot Grace and did entirely the correct thing in going to the police.

She must've come to the house, just wanting to tell me about seeing Grace in her own words when Blake so rudely sent her packing.

"Thank you for coming forward," I say as the black kettle starts to whistle.

"It never entered my head not to do so, despite our disagreement at the café." She stands, takes an oven glove and picks the kettle up. The shrill whistle stops abruptly.

I expect her to apologise for tipping tomato juice in my lap but she doesn't. Instead, she looks pointedly at me before pouring boiling water into a teapot and replacing the kettle on its stand.

Somewhere nearby, the dogs start up in a cacophony of barking again but Barbara seems quite unfazed. The kitchen might be in dire need of an upgrade but it's warm and comfortable and I feel my shoulders relax a little.

"I feel like I've known you for a long time, Lucie. Not to speak to, of course, but I've become accustomed to seeing you around the area. Particularly since your husband started his political career."

I nod as she removes the lid from the teapot and stirs the contents thoughtfully.

"But I actually noticed you long before that. When you've been around as long as I have, you sometimes you get an inkling—often more than an inkling—that a person is hiding something, presenting an acceptable face to the world that is not necessarily their true persona."

She's talking in riddles, but that's fine. I'll stick with it. Then it occurs to me; could she be gearing up to tell me something about my husband? Perhaps something I'll wish I hadn't found out from his arch enemy...

"And you think Blake is one of those people? Someone who's putting on an act?"

"I spoke out of turn at the café and I'm sorry for that. I was angry, and I cast doubt on your husband because I felt so angry and bitter. The truth is, I actually believe him to be one of the most solid and principled people I know."

She sighs and, for the first time, smiles at me.

"I confess I'm not a big fan of your husband, Lucie, as well you know, but no, I wasn't talking about Blake." She pours tea into a Royal Albert floral china cup and pushes it gently across the table to me. "I was actually referring to *you*, dear."

CHAPTER 46

Sixteen years earlier

As Lucie climbed the two flights of stairs up to Stefan's room, she noticed all the doors of the other bedsits were closed and she couldn't hear any noise coming from them.

Perhaps Stefan had fallen asleep. That would explain him not being downstairs to meet her in his desperation to explain the contents of his rucksack and, if Gregg was to be believed, his involvement in someone's death.

When she got up to the top floor of the house, Lucie hesitated outside Stefan's door.

Silence. The music track must have come to a natural end.

She thought about knocking, but if he was deep asleep he probably wouldn't hear her. But she felt justified in walking in if it was open. He'd sent a cab to collect her for goodness' sake.

She pushed the handle down and opened the door slowly. The main shadeless bulb was on and ...

Lucie's hand shot to her mouth as she let out a shriek.

Rhonda lay naked on the bed, a needle discarded at the side of her arm.

There was no sign of Stefan.

She rushed over to Rhonda, a shiver settling on her skin. Dribble ran from the corner of the girl's mouth and her eyes were closed. She looked deathly pale and although Lucie could see she was breathing, the rise and fall of her bony chest seemed very shallow and irregular.

Lucie seized a grubby sheet and pulled it across for modesty. She shook Rhonda's arm gently and called her name but there was no reaction.

"Stefan!" she screeched, her hand plunging into her handbag for her phone.

Rhonda groaned. *Thank God!*

Lucie abandoned her search, threw down her handbag and reached for the girl's hand.

"Rhonda, it's me, Lucie. What have you taken?"

Lucie's own hand shook as she squeezed Rhonda's cool, flaccid flesh. It felt so surreal. Here was Rhonda, lying naked on Stefan's bed...Lucie was supposed to be coming over for him to convince her of his innocence, not to be faced with this.

Lucie's gaze was drawn to a table in the corner. Small plastic bags full of white powder and pills similar to the gear in Stefan's rucksack were piled on top of it.

Her head whipped round at a shuffling noise at the door.

"What are you doing?" Lucie let Rhonda's hand fall away as she stood up, aghast.

Stefan didn't speak. He had a camera and was taking snaps of her.

"What the hell are you doing?"

As she moved back over to the bed, she heard footfall on the stairs. Stefan turned and shook his head. "Don't come in, we've got a problem in here. The girls can't handle the gear."

Lucie thought she heard a stifled giggle.

"Who's out there? What are you talking about?" She

reached for her bag and pulled out her phone. "I feel like I don't know you, I..."

He sprang across the room and snatched the phone and bag from her.

"Kind of you to bring my gear back." He grinned, peering in at the rucksack.

Stefan laughed as her mouth fell open.

"Get your head out of the clouds, Lucinda. How did you think I made my money?"

"Are you seeing Rhonda? Why is she here, in your bedroom?" She glanced at Rhonda's prostrate body behind her. "We need to call for an ambulance."

"Mind your own business," he snarled. "I was getting sick of you anyway."

A wave of heat blasted through Lucie.

"I'm going to report this to the police, and to the university too," she yelled.

Stefan grinned, completely unflustered. "We both know that's not going to happen." He held the camera up. "I'd bet good money these photos are going to show you were helping her shoot up."

Lucie wanted to leave, to push past him and run out of the house to ring the police. It felt as if someone had removed his mask and exposed that he was a maniac. Gregg had been right after all.

"You bastard. I trusted you, I really thought you cared about me." She let out a bitter laugh. "You're just a cheat. And worse, a criminal."

Stefan exploded. "What do you want me to do? Get rid of her once and for all?"

In three big strides, he was at Rhonda's bedside.

Lucie cried out as he wrenched the pillow from under Rhonda's head and shoved it on to her face. Rhonda's arms jerked out to the sides in reflex as she tried to escape the smothering sensation.

Lucie ran over and tried to pull Stefan away from her.

"You'll kill her! You have to stop it now!"

Stefan said nothing. He stood stock still, his eyes never leaving Rhonda as he constantly shifted his body weight over the pillow to add pressure.

Lucie ran wailing to the door. "Help! Help! Is anyone here?"

She heard him chuckle. She held on to the wall as the room started to spin. The air felt thick and unbreathable and the room seemed somehow bigger, rendering herself smaller as her grasp of time slipped. She watched as Stefan's hands bore down harder on the pillow, his face morphing into a crazed mask.

Then, through her brain haze, she saw Stefan leap towards her. He grabbed her by the hair, throwing her back on to the bed. She started to scream, terrible ear-splitting cries that echoed in her ears.

"This is what you wanted, admit it!" he yelled at Lucie. "You wanted me to prove I love you, no matter what it took. You made me do it. It's your fault."

"Stefan, no! No!"

She knocked the pillow from Rhonda's face with her arm. Horrified by Rhonda's wide, staring eyes and frozen expression, she began to whimper.

"We have to help her, Stefan. Call an ambulance, please."

"Don't look if you can't handle it. You made me do it." His voice sounded unconcerned. Monotone. How could he act so clinical, so disinterested?

"There are just two truths you need to remember. You never saw anything," he said, his voice chillingly calm and cold. "And you didn't find anything in my rucksack."

Lucie scrambled to her feet. "We've got to go to the police. There's no way something like this can be covered up. You ... you've *killed* her!"

He gave a little smile. "I had no choice, but you do. You have to choose whether to walk away or take the rap, Lucinda." He looked coolly at the dead girl and then reached over and pulled the sheet back over her body and face.

"What? *You* killed her, not me!"

"She's dead now and nothing is going to bring her back. You say you'll betray me and go to the police. But I'm telling you this..." He stepped closer to her and she shrank back against the wall. "If I go to prison, I'll make sure you do too. And when I'm out, I'll do to your interfering father the same as I've done to Rhonda today." He pressed his face closer to Lucie. "He'll die horribly and painfully. Do you love him enough to keep quiet?"

Lucie covered her face with her hands. "I can't. I just can't do it."

"Nobody knows she's here, Lucinda. Her family disowned her, wanted nothing to do with her after she got a prostitution charge, working the streets for drugs money at sixteen years of age. She ran away to Nottingham and I rescued her."

A tiny noise behind her made her jump on to the balls of her feet. She turned, thinking it may not be too late to save Rhonda, but it was just the house cat, weaving between her feet in a figure of eight.

"I'll just tell the other housemates she left. Why not join me? You could make so much money." His voice softened and he stroked her arm. His touch made her flesh crawl, and she jerked her arm away. He smiled. "You don't have to love me; just cover for me and we'll be home and dry."

She tilted her head back and stared up at the cracked, watermarked ceiling.

"Not interested." Even though her hands were shaking, she kept her voice level, just waiting for a chance to escape. She now realised that the man she thought she knew was very different to the manic, violent one in front of her and so she swallowed her threats. She had to tread carefully.

Stefan laughed and stepped aside.

"Go then, but think carefully, Lucinda. If you shop me, I'll tell them you killed Rhonda in a jealous rage."

The muscles in her guts contracted and for an awful moment she thought she'd vomit right there, in front of him.

"I won't report you but I want nothing to do with it. With any of it," she said, nearly choking on her words.

"I've got the photographs if the police are in any doubt of your involvement. Do you really want to ruin your life? Think hard about going to the police. It would kill your dad if he thought you were involved in this, even before I could get to him."

And deep inside, Lucie knew that for once, he spoke the truth.

CHAPTER 47

Back in her room on campus, Lucie packed a few things into an overnight bag. She grabbed her coat and went outside to wait for the cab she'd ordered.

She'd booked a small bed and breakfast on the edge of the city. She'd seen it from the bus, always thought it looked neat and friendly. She couldn't stay here tonight; she couldn't risk Stefan coming over to try and persuade her to work for him. She needed to think.

The taxi and the night away were costing a lot of money; more than she could afford. But that didn't matter right now. What mattered was that she had bought herself some time alone to think the whole terrible mess through properly. Once she'd considered everything and thought carefully, she wouldn't look back again. She wouldn't endlessly debate it in her head once she had made a firm decision. She'd promised herself that much.

The landlady of the establishment was brisk and efficient. Lucie told her she was visiting a friend and would only be staying the one night. The woman nodded and barely looked at her, which suited Lucie just fine.

When she got up to the small, impersonal room that smelled of stale cigarettes and damp, she climbed fully clothed under the cold, scratchy covers and gave in to the shaking she'd had to control up till now. She sobbed into the pillow, unable to shake the memory of Rhonda's staring eyes and gaping mouth from her troubled mind.

So, she had two choices.

Go to the police or forget everything she had seen.

She knew the right thing to do was report the murder she'd witnessed, but either way, Rhonda would still be dead. She couldn't put that wrong right.

Her fingers were still quivering. The look on Stefan's face had been so focused, so devoid of emotion. Thinking about that same face, staring at her, kissing her, when they'd made love…it made her stomach tighten to the point of physical pain.

Stefan was a convincing liar and Lucie was the opposite. If she went to the police to report Rhonda's murder, she believed, without doubt, that Stefan would carry out his threat and tell them that she was as guilty as he was.

In contrast to Stefan's convincing line of defence, Lucie knew herself enough to know that she'd quickly dissolve into tears and become vague of details under pressure.

She's carried Stefan's rucksack with her in the taxi…how would she explain not reporting him immediately, upon discovering the drugs?

On top of that, she'd seen Gregg in the library and told him everything. So she couldn't deny she had gone to Stefan's house!

She tried to reason, to think, through the thick fog in her head.

She'd been infatuated with Stefan, maybe even loved him, and she'd certainly trusted him completely. In the space of a few hours, that trust had been utterly destroyed. Lucie was

in shock at the sudden revelation that she had been sleeping
with a monster.

It could easily have been her, suffocated to death in Stefan's room. She would only have had to put a foot wrong, or
anger him in some way. She shuddered, unable to process
the horror of it.

Maybe, if she'd realised Rhonda's own disturbing history,
they could've been friends. Rhonda had seemed infatuated
with Stefan, but she'd owed him. And he had betrayed her,
just like her own family.

Lucie's eyes prickled in regret.

What a sad end for poor Rhonda. A waste of a young life.

She'd realised pretty quickly that the only way she was
going to get out of Stefan's house unscathed was to play
along with him, at least for the time being.

Gregg's words echoed in her head. *He's always taking
girls back there . . .*

She'd been an utter fool. Naïve and stupid. And now,
she'd even managed to put her own dear dad in danger.

Her overriding thought was that she just wanted it all to
stop, to go away.

"Please, God, please let it be OK," she whispered.

She wanted to get away from this godforsaken place and go
back home to live safely and predictably with her father again.

She pulled the quilt around her and buried her face in the
rough, starched pillow. It offered little comfort.

She wished she'd never left Nottingham. She'd never in
her entire life wanted to hear her father's voice as much as
she did right now.

An hour later, Lucie sat on the edge of the bed, staring at the
wall, a blank expanse of cream-painted woodchip wallpaper.

She'd spoken to her father, and his response had been as expected; to say he was gutted was an understatement.

Still, the upshot of the fifteen uncomfortable minutes she'd spent on the phone was that her dad had grudgingly agreed to re-engage the man-with-the-van to collect her packed belongings the day after next.

It was hard to keep her thoughts on track. The logistics of going back to Nottingham seemed so inconsequential now, although it was of utmost importance to Lucie to get back to the safety of home as soon as possible.

A girl was dead because of Stefan O'Hara, and Lucie was the only person apart from him who knew what had happened.

How could it be that only yesterday, she'd lain in his arms in her own bed and he'd been so caring, so considerate?

Lucie felt sick and ashamed, her guilt and remorse laced heavily with worry. Stefan hadn't told her what he intended doing with Rhonda's body. What if he was caught disposing of it? What if the police came looking for Rhonda and Stefan told them that Lucie had killed her?

The fact that Lucie hadn't gone to the police of her own accord made her look incredibly guilty. But if she did go to the police, Stefan would implicate her in the murder anyway and they would both go to prison.

How easy it was to judge others for the decisions they made when one wasn't inextricably linked to them. If someone had recounted her choice to her, Lucie felt certain she would have said that the right thing to do was take her chances and report the crime.

But it really wasn't as simple as that. The shock and the shame would surely kill her dad. And when it came down to it, selfish or not, Lucie didn't want to go to prison. She hadn't murdered poor Rhonda, even though Stefan would ensure all the evidence pointed to it.

She felt very sad that a young woman's life had come to such an abrupt end, but it hadn't been her fault. She hadn't killed Rhonda, and the more she thought about it, the more certain she was that this one salient fact was what she must cling on to, to preserve her sanity.

She would stay in the B&B tonight, knowing there was no risk of Stefan coming after her, and tomorrow she would go back to campus, pack up her sparse belongings, and head home to Nottingham on the train.

There, she would try and build her life again and resolve to put the terrible events behind her for good.

She closed her eyes and made a solemn pact with herself and with God, who knew the truth of what had happened.

If you let me walk away from this, I'll bury the memory of today and never dwell on it again. I'll try and make the most of my life and help others where I can.

CHAPTER 48

The years passed like bleached-out patches of time that should have been filled with everything that Lucie had dreamed she would do and be.

She was surrounded by disappointment. No matter what she did, it dripped from her like melting wax, smothering the faintest hope that her life might ever improve.

Her father made at least one comment a day, often more, about how he still found it difficult to believe she had thrown her golden chance away so readily. She never came close to telling him why. She couldn't lay that at his door.

Lucie settled into grey, colourless days where she didn't leave the house. She took on some private bookkeeping work that she did from home during the mornings, usually.

The only communication that came from Stefan was a regular warning to keep quiet.

Breathe a word of what you know and I'll tell the police you were involved in Rhonda's death.

But over time, the texts appeared less and less frequently. She had honestly thought he would hunt her down, but in reality, he seemed glad to be rid of her. She was obviously of no more use to him.

After many months of barely leaving the house, Lucie's dad sat her down for a chat.

"It's not healthy, love. A young woman with everything to live for, stuck at home day in, day out." He handed her a scrappy note. "I got a counsellor's name from the clinic. Apparently, she's good. The doctor can get you on the waiting list."

Lucie had known she was struggling. She'd even looked it up: agoraphobia, the fear of going out. She didn't feel like it was a fear, as such, more the easy choice to keep anxiety at bay.

She was surprised to find she embraced her dad's suggestion and within six weeks, her first appointment came through.

Baby steps, the counsellor said. And one of those steps— a very important one, as it turned out—was to venture to the local café once a day, if she felt she could.

The first few times were difficult. She nearly turned around and didn't go on several occasions. But then, she came to look forward to the five-minute walk for a latte or a homemade lemonade, in the better weather.

A man came into the café almost every day. He was a little older than Lucie, tall and good-looking, and he always made a point of lingering a little longer at the counter than was strictly necessary, right by her regular table.

For her part, Lucie would find an excuse to walk past his table, and they'd chat, mostly about the weather or current affairs. He was very interested in politics and the environment, and she'd talk to him about the takeaway cups the café used, and about how they could suggest to the management that they cut down on plastic wrappings for the sandwiches and suchlike.

He asked her out, to a Green Party community event, and Lucie accepted.

"I don't even know your name," she laughed.

"Blake Sullivan. Eco-warrior and all-round nice guy." He beamed. "At your service."

They quickly developed an easy friendship. Lucie made it clear she wasn't looking for a deep and meaningful relationship at that point in time, and he accepted it without question. But they went out regularly as friends, and after a couple of months, it turned into something else.

Suddenly she realised they were a couple, and it felt right. It felt like she'd been given another shot at happiness.

In the evenings, Lucie would watch a bit of television with her dad, and then, if she wasn't seeing Blake, she'd retire to her bedroom to read or watch a film.

When it rained, she liked to lie in the dark, safe and secure under the covers, and listen to the water tapping on the roof. It comforted her, made her feel like the outside world was far away, and that if she chose, she could stay in this little room for the rest of her life and never see another soul.

It was true to say that very little changed in her life day to day. Practically every single thing was predictable, reliable . . . and Lucie liked it that way.

She felt herself very slowly settling down. The turmoil in her head receded a tiny bit more each week. Her daily scheduled tasks soothed the festering wound inside like a healing balm.

What everyone else took to be a menial, boring existence, Lucie craved and soaked up. That was just the way it was.

But she had changed irrevocably. Inside, where nobody could see.

The slightest upset—like the morning the bus broke down and the passengers had to get off and queue in a strange part of town for another one—could unhinge her for days afterwards. She'd become restless in the night and fractious at work. Memories would stir, resurface, and it took tremendous effort to push them back again.

One afternoon, she heard two customers talking at the table next to the counter. It was a slow day and the café was quieter than usual, and her ears pricked up when she heard the name of a popular wedding venue in town, The Carlton Hotel.

"They're going to need all sorts of positions filled: hospitality, waiters, bartenders...Tell him to mark his CV for the attention of Pamela Simpson; she's the HR person there."

Suddenly she felt ready to move on with her life. Rhonda's death became something to drive her to make the most of her life. She couldn't spend the rest of her days in her childhood bedroom, living with her dad.

It felt like a good time to put everything that had happened behind her and bury her time at university for good.

CHAPTER 49

She'd been working at The Carlton for two years when Blake picked her up from work one day.

"I've got a surprise for you." He grinned, restless with excitement.

Instead of taking her home, he drove her to a nearby park she loved to visit. They sometimes came here on a weekend if the weather was fine. They'd feed the ducks and sit on one of the wooden benches around the large pond, watching the world go by.

It was a beautiful day. The sky was a deep azure blue and the temperature soared, causing the front pages of all the newspapers to feature photographs of packed beaches and little kids enjoying ice creams. You could be forgiven for thinking you were living abroad.

Blake stood up. "I have something for you," he said softly.

She expected him to go and fetch a picnic from the car—he knew how much she loved picnics—but instead, he produced a small, dark red velvet box and dropped to one knee.

"Lucie, I love you. Will you marry me?"

Her mouth dropped open as he flicked up the lid of the box and a beautiful diamond solitaire sparkled in the sunlight.

"Yes!" she whispered as Blake jumped up and kissed her on the lips.

She'd started as an events planner when she first joined The Carlton, and had been swiftly promoted until finally, after eighteen months, the manager offered her the highly respected position of wedding planner.

Now, Lucie spent her days at work showing soon-to-be-married couples around the venue and then attending their weddings to ensure everything ran smoothly.

She'd often wondered if she and Blake might get married one day and have a wedding of their own to organise, and now it was finally going to happen.

In true Blake style, their engagement was low-key. He slid the ring gently on to her finger and they went to a local wine bar to toast the occasion with a glass of champagne.

That suited Lucie down to the ground. The thought of a big, glitzy party made her feel queasy. She had no friends to speak of, anyway. Blake knew hundreds of people as part of his involvement with the local political scene, but as a couple, they kept themselves to themselves.

They were very close, but of course, there was a part of her life that Lucie knew she could never share. For a time, she thought it wouldn't make a difference, but she came to realise that it did encroach on their intimacy. It was always there.

Still, she felt grateful and blessed to have found happiness at all. Considering.

And foolishly, she really believed that in time, she would forget all about Stefan O'Hara.

*   *   *

In contrast, a year later, it was a cold, miserable day when she left work. The television weather forecasters had been grim in their estimation of the prospects for summer that year. Yes, it was June, but that day it had felt more like a cool October afternoon.

Lucie wrapped her insubstantial mac tighter and tied the belt as she walked, lost in a reverie about her forthcoming wedding and the comprehensive advertising campaign The Carlton had run for their upcoming wedding fairs.

"Oh!" She almost collided with a man who suddenly appeared in her path. "I'm so sorry, I didn't see you..."

Her voice tapered off and she stepped aside and backed up against the wall of a nearby newsagent's shop.

Her legs began to shake, her lips trembled.

The man stepped back. Raised his hands in an unthreatening manner.

"I'm sorry. I know it's a shock, but I don't want to alarm you, or hurt you, Lucinda. That person you knew all those years ago is dead. Gone."

She stared into Stefan's face. He'd put on weight. He wasn't fat, but there was now a soft padding on what used to be taut, defined muscles and sharp features.

He looked back at her. The intensity had gone from his eyes; she could find no trace of the old pent-up aggression.

Still, she was unable to speak.

"Couldn't believe my luck when I saw your photo in the paper... you're the wedding planner here," he said by way of explanation. "I'm working locally, just for a few weeks, and I...I felt compelled to seek you out, Lucinda. To say that I am truly, truly sorry for what happened."

She nodded, hoped he'd turn around and go away. Her mouth and throat felt so dry, she felt like she might choke if she uttered a sound. Damn that bloody newspaper advert.

"Look, can we grab a quick coffee? No strings attached." He looked nervous, concerned, but the mask of hatred on his face was still as fresh in her mind as the day she witnessed it. "Just so I can explain," he continued. "So I can say sorry properly and make peace with you. What do you say?"

She couldn't afford a scene, not here outside her workplace. No one must ever know about Stefan O'Hara and what had happened in his bedsit.

"I could have come here and caused trouble at any time, Lucinda. But I'm here today not to confront you, but to offer an olive branch."

He seemed reasonable, regretful even, but she still felt he wouldn't like it if he thought she'd snubbed him. There was a small, grubby café just a couple of streets away that nobody she worked with would entertain using. She supposed they could go there.

"I've only got twenty minutes until I have to go for my bus," she said, as confidently as she could manage. Her voice sounded raw, as if she'd been screaming, but she hoped he wouldn't notice. "There's a café I know…"

"Lead the way." He smiled, stepping closer to her but taking care not to touch her. "Am I OK to leave the van parked here?"

He indicated a small, white van in the hotel car park and she nodded, hoping Vincent, the overzealous parking attendant, had already left.

As they walked, Stefan spoke about why he was in Nottingham.

"I've worked with young offenders for the past few years," he said. "Unbelievably, I've never had a criminal record myself, but I felt… well, under the circumstances, I thought I ought to try and give something back, you know?"

He glanced at her and she nodded curtly. She did know. Only too well.

"They're setting up a facility in Nottingham and asked me to oversee certain processes, and I thought it would be the perfect opportunity to try to put something else straight too. If I could find you."

He was talking in riddles and Lucie felt glad of it. She didn't want to face hearing the truth she'd denied and hidden for so long. It seemed Stefan didn't either.

They arrived at the café.

"Oh dear." He looked at the peeling paint and scuffed door. "Can't imagine you frequent this place much, but there'll be nobody you know in here, right?"

She bit her tongue and pushed open the door. He was still good at seeing right through her, even after so many years.

Stefan insisted on getting the coffees, and smiled as he put down two mugs on the sticky Formica tabletop.

"At least they make the choice easy here. No debating over lattes or cappuccinos; it's with milk or without milk and that's about your lot."

"As basic as it gets," she agreed, keeping her eyes on the steaming mug.

"Still. I haven't come for the coffee; I've come to make peace with you." He picked up his own drink and took a hesitant slurp. "I left university that year, you know. I just went. Slept rough, hitchhiked around the country, lived in Edinburgh, Falmouth, Stoke. Alcohol got me through, but it was a blessing in disguise, because that's why I'm here."

Lucie looked at him, waiting for more. She saw him glance at her engagement ring and was thankful when he didn't comment.

"I'm a recovering alcoholic, Lucinda. At my lowest point, I joined Alcoholics Anonymous and they saved my life. As part of my treatment I've had to contact the people I've hurt either intentionally or otherwise and apologise to them. There's just one person left I need to speak to, and that's you."

He reached for her hand, but she pulled it back.

"What about Rhonda's family? Have you apologised to them? All these years of not knowing what happened to their daughter..."

He looked down at the table and sighed.

"That's not been possible. I told you at the time she was estranged from her family. I still suffer from PTSD because of it. I think about it... about her every day. I think about you and how you've never said a word. You stayed true to me."

"Not because I didn't want to, but because I couldn't. Because of your threats."

"I'm so, so sorry, Lucinda, for what I did. I am truly ashamed. I'll never get over it, and I doubt you will either." This time he grabbed her hand and held it fast. "Do you hear me? I *am* sorry, for what I did and for how you suffered. Will you accept my apology?"

Tears stung at the back of her eyes but she refused to let them show. She pressed her toes into her shoes and thought about the solid floor beneath them. She could and would get through this and hope never to set eyes on Stefan O'Hara again.

"Yes," she whispered. "I forgive you."

"You don't know how happy that makes me feel." To her surprise, tears fell freely from his eyes and splashed into his coffee. "Thank you. Thank you for finding it in your heart."

She pushed her chair back and stood up.

"I'm really sorry, Stefan, but I have to go. It must have been difficult for you to come here, and I appreciate it. I do. But I can't handle going back there, you see. I just can't."

He stood up too. "I understand. Truly I do."

They left the café together and he said he'd walk with her to the bus station. She felt hot and panicky inside. She just wanted him to go away.

Questions began popping up in her mind. What had happened to Rhonda's body? Had her family eventually come looking for her?

Lucie had searched online, even called the local newspapers in Newcastle to ask if there'd been reports of a missing female student, but there had been nothing.

She wanted him to answer all the questions she still had but she couldn't handle talking about it with him. The questions remained unvoiced.

"Have you got your own place now then?" he asked her.

"No, I'm still at Dad's, but not for long." She wanted to kick herself when she said that and his eyes settled on her engagement ring.

"Looks like someone's got lucky. When are you tying the knot?"

"We haven't actually set a date yet," she said. It seemed natural to lie. To keep him at arm's length.

"Don't worry, I won't turn up at the wedding." He grinned. "Doing the job you do, you'll surely have everything planned out to the nth degree. So, when *is* the big day?"

"Next month," she said in a small voice and immediately felt angry with herself that she'd caved in.

He stopped walking and stared at her.

She felt herself tense up. Was he going to turn nasty when he realised she'd found happiness?

He looked up and swallowed. "I never loved anyone like you, Lucinda, I want you to know that. But I'm so happy for you. You deserve all the love and happiness in the world."

She took a sharp breath in; his kind words had come as a real shock.

"Thank you," she managed to say.

And that was it. Five minutes later, she got on her bus, and Stefan waved and walked out of her life for good.

Or so she thought.

CHAPTER 50

The days that followed were full of wedding plans, but this time it was so exciting because they were her own.

Since seeing Stefan, Lucie had thought about him every day. The change in him had been so pronounced, it had totally messed her up. On the one hand, she felt inexplicably lighter inside, as if his apology had untethered the burden of her guilt and it had finally begun to dissipate. On the other hand, her natural mistrust of him stirred uncomfortably in her guts, and the terror of the day he killed Rhonda seemed fresh in her mind.

She felt run-down and had picked up a nasty cold. She felt sure the constant unsettled feeling in her stomach was something to do with the downturn in her well-being. Yet she felt as if facing Stefan again, looking him in the eyes, had given her permission to be happy with Blake. She appreciated her fiancé's qualities of honesty and kindness more than ever.

Four days after she'd met up with Stefan, Blake came over to the house. Her dad was working the late shift at the factory, and she'd cooked Blake his favourite meal. Nothing fancy, just a quality rib-eye steak, hand-cut chips, and a bottle of a particular Shiraz he was rather partial to.

"To what do I owe this honour?" His mouth fell open in surprise when he arrived and she ushered him over to the beautifully set table. Usually they'd order takeout during the week, as Lucie always felt too tired to cook.

"Can't a girl treat her man now and again?" She grinned, carrying through his plate. "Just appreciating you, that's all. Excited that I'm going to be your wife very soon."

"You can't possibly be as excited as I am," he said, sitting down at the table and feasting his eyes on the meal in front of him. "I can't wait to be your husband."

At Pete's suggestion, they'd decided they'd live with him in the two-bed terrace for a year while they saved for a deposit for somewhere of their own. Blake had a small flat on the wrong side of town, and he was due to exchange contracts on its sale the following week.

Lucie set some background jazz to play and sat down at the table, occasionally sneezing into her tissue.

"Cheers." They clinked glasses. "To us."

"To us," Blake agreed.

If she was completely honest, Lucie had to admit that part of the reason for the slap-up meal was to allay the guilt she felt for not telling Blake she'd gone for a coffee with another man.

But how could she possibly do that without opening a can of worms? If she'd told him an old university friend had tracked her down, he'd have asked how they knew where to find her, and why they wanted to speak to her, and...Blake was no fool, and she'd get all flustered and then he'd know there was something she wasn't telling him.

Besides, when she'd first got to know him, she'd already passed off her short time at university as a disaster, where virtually nobody spoke to her from one day to the next.

He wasn't going to believe that someone had gone to the trouble to meet up with her just for a coffee, was he?

So she'd said nothing at all. Hadn't mentioned it. It would become just another thing to pop in the terrible memory box and push as far away as she could manage into the archives of her mind.

Blake wasn't late leaving; he had an early breakfast meeting with the council about something or other. He had his sights set on working as a local councillor one day and he'd explained to her that this was how he'd win the trust of local communities, who'd hopefully end up voting him in.

She set the bath running and began to clear the table, carrying the dirty plates through into the kitchen.

The handle of the back door rattled and she unlocked it, rolling her eyes.

"What have you forgotten this time—oh!"

She tried to close the door, but Stefan was too quick for her. He pushed it forcefully open, sending her skittling back on her heels into the kitchen.

He calmly closed the door behind him and locked it.

"I've just seen lover boy leave, so I thought you might appreciate a little company." A couple of strides and he was right in front of her. "Bet you could use some attention from a real man instead of your wet Green Party fella. Told him about our little tête-à-tête, have you?"

She swallowed hard and spoke firmly.

"Stefan. Remember everything you said the other day at the café. How you've regretted the things—"

He threw his head back and laughed. "That was all bollocks, you daft cow! I couldn't believe you swallowed it so easily." His reached out and touched her breast. "Now, where did we leave it, last time we slept together?"

"No!" She pushed him hard and turned to run from the

room, but his fingers tangled in her hair and jerked her head back.

She screamed as she felt hair ripping out of her scalp.

"You'd do well to remember how Rhonda died, Lucinda. I did it then and got away with it, and I could easily do it again." He pressed his body up close against her from the back. "One more time for the road, doll, what do you say?"

"Please...no...just leave, now. Don't do anything you'll regret..."

"That's not going to happen. I want you. I've thought about you for a long time, imagined the two of us having some of that wild fun we used to enjoy. Remember those days?"

She squeezed her eyes closed against the moving pictures in her mind.

"I want you one last time before you marry him. Just between us, because if you tell...well, you know what will happen." His voice dropped to a whisper. "I've still got them, you know. The photographs. My evidence against you."

Lucie groaned, the food she'd eaten earlier churning in her stomach.

He propelled her forward, out of the kitchen and into the dim lounge. She'd already pulled the curtains when she and Blake had sat down with coffee earlier.

Please come back to the house for something, Blake, she willed silently. *Please.*

Wordlessly, Stefan pushed her down on the carpeted floor and peeled off his T-shirt. His face looked wolfish, feral as he advanced on her.

And Blake didn't come back.

CHAPTER 51

When Stefan had left, Lucie lay curled up in the foetal position for a long time.

At that moment, she knew with all her heart there would be no escape from him. Even if she married Blake, there would be no new life waiting for her. Her life was simply an extension of the one she thought she'd left behind in Newcastle.

Stefan had the power to reclaim her at any time because he held the ultimate card: he could frame her for murder and she couldn't do a thing about it. He could make sure she spent the rest of her life in prison.

Every day she'd live in fresh fear Stefan would return.

There was only one outcome that would give her peace. In that moment, she didn't want to live any more. She didn't want to see the look on Blake's handsome face when he realised what she was, that she'd been lying to him all this time.

She wasn't the woman he thought he was marrying. She was a fraud, someone who would stand by and let a monster like Stefan O'Hara get away scot-free with murdering an innocent girl who'd had her whole life ahead of her.

She'd been incredibly selfish by not going to the police all those years ago. Yes, she'd been worried about her father's health, but really, if she was honest, it was worrying about herself that was the strongest motivation. She hadn't had the courage to do the right thing and hope that truth would prevail.

The die was cast the minute she walked away and did nothing. She'd handed power over her life, her freedom, to Stefan O'Hara on a plate.

And he was still using it.

Her stomach hurt, her legs and arms hurt; she felt bruised and battered inside.

She rolled over and managed to get up onto her hands and knees. Using the edge of the couch, she hoisted herself up to standing. Her head felt woozy, her knees almost too weak to bear her weight.

It took a few minutes to slowly limp into the kitchen. Her throat felt so raw, she would have a coughing fit if she didn't get some water, and that would crucify her sore stomach.

She reached the kitchen door and gasped. Water was gushing through the ceiling; the kitchen floor was swimming.

She'd completely forgotten she'd left the bath running upstairs.

Ironically, the bath flooding saved her. All thoughts of doing away with herself were forgotten and her practical side kicked in.

She locked the back door and bolted it, took a gulp of water straight from the tap and crawled upstairs on all fours, the wrenching ache in her lower abdomen worsening as she advanced.

When she reached the narrow landing at the top, something inside her seemed to take over. She turned off the bath taps, pulled out the plug and stepped across the soaked floor to take a quick shower.

After checking herself over and gingerly dabbing her body dry with the softest towel she could find, she was relieved to see that apart from the odd red carpet burn here and there, she had no other visible marks that would alert Blake that she'd been attacked.

She pulled on some elasticated leggings and a soft T-shirt and went back downstairs.

Before she could call Blake to come and help with the flood, her phone started ringing.

"Blake?"

"There's been a terrible accident at the end of your road, Lucie, and I wanted to check you were safe and sound inside the house."

Something made her drop the phone and walk ghost-like to the window.

A cluster of flashing blue lights and white emergency vehicles blocked the road to her right. She walked outside in bare feet. Stepping out on to the pavement, she saw other residents watching from their front gardens.

A little further up the road, a police officer stood talking on her radio.

Lucie padded towards her, focused on the vehicles.

"Can I help you, love?" the officer said, looking down at Lucie's feet. "You really need to put something on your feet; broken glass flies out miles from collisions."

"What happened?" Lucie said faintly, her heartbeat racing as she gained a better view of the smashed vehicles.

"A three-way collision," the police officer said gravely, stepping in front of Lucie as she started to move again.

"There are fatalities and life-changing injuries. Please stay where you are, madam. It's not very pleasant up there."

Lucie craned her neck around the officer and squinted at the tangled metal. She couldn't stop staring at the white van with insignia and print on the side.

Its whole body was buckled and bent; it looked to have been virtually sheared in half.

She'd seen the van before. Four days earlier, parked at The Carlton, in fact.

It belonged to Stefan O'Hara.

CHAPTER 52

Blake came over to mop up the flood. He took one look at her and put his arms around her.

"You're shaking. It's OK, only a bit of water."

She nodded, pressing her face into his warm chest.

"You look terrible, Luce. Give me your house insurance details; I'll sort it out for you. Go and sit in the lounge and I'll—"

"I can't...I don't want to sit in there," she said, calming her alarmed tone. "I'll go up to bed if that's OK. It's probably just a bug."

He made tea and brought it up to her.

"It looks a mess but it's not actually too bad. The ceiling hasn't come down and it hasn't affected the electrics."

She didn't care about the damage. She just wanted to get out of this house.

She waited for the conversation to come around to the accident. Blake made it his business to find out everything that happened in and around the community. He had good contacts in all the emergency services.

"It's terrible. Two dead and one with life-changing injuries, apparently."

Please God, she prayed inwardly. Please let Stefan be dead.

"The two dead are both female. A man has survived but is in a pretty bad way."

"Do you know what his injuries are?"

"His legs were crushed, apparently. It's bad. They've taken them all to the Queen's Medical Centre."

Damn. Damn. Damn. Her one chance to be rid of him for good, and he'd managed, as always, to escape.

*

Stefan didn't die, but Blake said the doctor had told one of the traffic officers that he would be paralysed from the neck down.

Three days after the accident, and posing as a close friend, Lucie telephoned the Queen's Medical Centre and got Stefan O'Hara's ward details from the main reception.

At visiting time that evening, while Blake was attending a meeting at the town hall about a nearby power station, she entered the ward with the group of visitors waiting to see patients.

When she explained she was a friend of Stefan's from university, a young nurse pointed out his bed. "He's not awake very much; he's been heavily sedated since his operation."

"Is it true what I heard…he's paralysed from the neck down?"

"I'm so sorry, yes. He can only move his head."

Lucie walked over and gazed down at him. His eyes were closed, his face terribly pale. His arms, covered in tubes, already looked thinner, wasted.

He didn't wake up. She'd rehearsed what she would say

to him, how she would finally have power over him, but he never even knew she was there.

It didn't matter. It felt as if she'd just emerged from a tiny locked room and walked into a wildflower meadow.

She felt vindicated. She felt free.

"Thank you, karma," she whispered into his ear.

CHAPTER 53

Lucie

Tuesday morning

I lie awake, but with my eyes closed. Once they are open, I will know it's time to face another day without Grace.

I must have got up three or four times in the night. Oscar woke, fractious and unsettled, in the early hours, no doubt picking up on the upheaval and tension in the house. I told Blake to go back to sleep and I tended to him. Relished the closeness of holding him safe in my arms. One child, I can still keep secure. Can still shower with my love.

Twice last night, I honestly thought I was going to be sick. I rushed to the bathroom and sat next to the loo for what seemed like ages.

And I *was* sick. Sick inside, sick in every cell of my body. So sick, I felt like I might just stop breathing. But I didn't stop breathing. I just kept thinking and thinking about everything. About Grace . . . and about Barbara Charterhouse and her shocking revelation.

How could I have been so stupid? Believed Stefan's lie for so long?

I open my eyes and see that Blake is lying on his side

watching me, a strange expression on his face. It's almost as if he can read my thoughts.

"What are you looking at?" I stare steadily back at him. This man I've loved and borne his children. I want to tell him what I know but I can't. Not yet.

"I'm looking at you. My beautiful wife who I love more than anything."

I sit up and swing my legs over the bed. We desperately need to talk, but it can wait until after the television appeal today. It *has* to wait.

Emotion washes over me like a tidal wave, and without warning, I start to sob. Great wet, messy sobs. Then Blake is next to me, trying to put his arm around me.

"Lucie, come on. We have to pull together on this. We have to."

Today, we're doing a live television appeal for information about our daughter. It's another step in what I can't believe is our new reality, a terribly serious development that Grace has been missing long enough that we need to do an appeal. But it could be the turning point. This could bring her home.

Is Grace coming home? Nobody can say. Only her abductor knows, and I firmly believe now that she has been taken. Hope has begun to seep away and is gathering speed. Soon there will be none left. For all my anger and disappointment with Dad and what he's done, I wish he was here with me now.

I walk into my son's room and watch him sleep. His tiny chest, rising and falling with each precious breath. He is here. He is alive. He needs me.

I shower, wash and dry my hair, and pull it up into a ponytail. I dress in a loose striped blouson top and black trousers with low-heeled black shoes.

Downstairs, the hallway is a hive of activity. Uniformed officers and the two detectives mill around endlessly making and taking telephone calls.

Nadine arrives. Blake has arranged for her to look after Oscar while we're at the television studios. He leads her to the kitchen, where I spot them through the open door, their heads together, speaking in low voices.

I walk into the living room and stand by the window. The press crowd has doubled in size.

Fiona comes in and stands next to me. I continue to stare outside.

"Morning, Lucie. I know you'll be dreading the televised appeal, but you'll get through it. This could be so powerful in progressing the investigation. Try to remember that."

I nod. I can't think what to say, so I stay quiet.

An hour later, Blake and I are in the back of an unmarked police car on our way to the BBC studios in Nottingham. We're escorted into the building and taken straight inside. When we walk into the big room filled with journalists and television cameras, silence falls.

We are the main event.

We stand behind a screen in one of the studios. When I peek around it, there's a long table with chairs and microphones. A crescent-shaped group of journalists, photographers, and film camera operators wait, buzzing with a nervous excitement.

My palms feel damp and my body is aching, as if I'm coming down with something. Blake smiles and squeezes my hand but his face looks grey and drawn.

DI Pearlman appears and I feel gratified to see a friendly face.

"OK, just like we said on the way here...be as natural as you can. Just be yourself." He looks at me. "I know it's hard, but remember you aren't on trial here, there's no script, no right or wrong things to say, so no pressure. If you can manage to say how you're feeling, both of you, how life is without Grace, then today will be a success because people will want to help. We're confident they will respond."

He says there's no pressure but I can feel it like a ten-tonne truck pushing at my back. We have to make people like us, have to let them know how we're suffering without Grace, or we might not win over public opinion.

And it's me they'll be judging. I've seen these appeals on television, watched the mother closely for signs of true grief and devastation. I've asked myself if she was in any way responsible for her child going missing. Negligent or lax.

A young woman with a BBC lanyard around her neck peers around the screen, glances at me and then addresses DI Pearlman.

"We're ready for you now," she says.

Back at the house, Nadine meets us at the door.

"How did it go? I'm sure you were brilliant, Blake, darling."

DI Pearlman is quietly optimistic as he leads us cleverly past Nadine and into the living room.

"You both came across brilliantly. Intelligent and devastated," he enthuses, as if we might be up for an award. "HQ said the phones were ringing off the desks, which is exactly what we hope for in these cases."

"I suppose you get a lot of crank calls," Blake says morosely.

"Sure. But we'll also get valuable information, if we're

lucky. You'd be surprised at the number of people who've been away, or work shifts and don't catch the news. Suddenly, something they've seen and thought nothing of can be the missing piece of our jigsaw."

"Let's pray that's the case." Nadine sighs. "It sounds like you both did a good job."

I know I must have looked like a rabbit frozen in headlights in that studio. I tried my best to express how our lives have crumbled without Grace, how we can't sleep, can't eat, how we're stuck in limbo just waiting for news. But it just seemed to come out as senseless babble. And I didn't cry. I *couldn't* cry in a sterile atmosphere that didn't even seem real.

If tears from a suffering mother move the hearts of the general public, then I failed.

Blake was eloquent. In response to a probing question from a national newspaper, he explained that yes, it was true we'd allowed Grace to make a very short walk home alone, but that we'd put monitoring plans in place that we'd genuinely thought were failsafe. We were caught out.

"I know every parent out there has made a decision in haste that they now regret. But in our case, we've paid the ultimate price. We've lost our daughter, our reason for living." He paused, reaching for my hand before carrying on, his voice breaking with emotion. "From the bottom of my heart I plead with everyone watching to please, please help us to find Grace."

Even the press fell quiet for a moment or two, such was the poignancy of my husband's words.

When the detective has left and Blake has gone off to make some calls, Fiona comes in, her arms full of mail. Different colours, sizes of envelope, all jumbled into a haphazard pile that threatens to spill over at any moment.

"From well-wishers," she says sadly as she offloads it on to the coffee table in the middle of the room. "You've got a lot of support out there, Lucie love, remember that."

My eyes prickle.

Fiona sits next to me. "I can help you look through this stuff," she says gently. "Most people are lovely and can't do enough to help, but we do occasionally get trolls, vicious types who want to make you suffer more than you are already. If that's even possible."

"It's OK," I say. "I'll just open a few, and if there are any nasty communications, I'll set them aside." Oscar is still sleeping and I can take my time looking through the mail.

The truth is, for all that Fiona is trying her best to help, I'd rather just be alone right now in my misery. I'm tired of everyone looking at me like they're so sorry for me. I don't want sympathy, I want news about Grace.

"Dr. Mahmoud has been in touch. He wants to come and see you again, see if there's anything he can do to—"

"I don't need to see him!" I feel so frustrated with all this fuss over me. It's Grace that matters. She's the *only* thing that matters to us.

Fiona nods and squeezes my arm. "I'm just in the kitchen catching up on paperwork if you need me." She gives Nadine a look and my mother-in-law sniffs and reluctantly follows her out of the room.

They close the door behind me and I feel the sore, contracted muscles in my chest and arms relax a little. You'd think that in such terrible circumstances as these, you wouldn't care what people think. That you'd just break down and not give a stuff who sees you.

But in reality, you try and keep it together, develop a shell, albeit a fragile one, where you observe generally reasonable behaviour and strive to hide your true feelings.

Now, alone again at last, I can let the pain resurface.

I rub my wet face with the backs of my hands and reach for a handful of envelopes. I can see that most of these are cards. I open a couple and they are sweet and genuine. One card with a horse on breaks my heart. It's from a girl who attends Grace's riding school.

> Dear Grace,
>   I heard you are missing and I hope you are OK. I have told your horse you will be back home soon and I will look after her for you until you ride her again.
>   Love,
>   Macy Price xx

There are other cards from people who live on Violet Road, expressing regret and wishing they could help in some way.

I shuffle through the pile and spot an envelope that looks too thin to be a card. Fiona's warning about trolls rings in my ears and gingerly I slide my finger under the flap and tear it open. Inside is a scrap of notepaper.

> Lucinda,
>   I know you'll be terribly worried right now. But I know something you don't know. So don't worry about Grace. Remember the old email? You might want to log in.

I drop the note as if it's scalding my fingers.

Nobody has called me Lucinda for years. Only one person has *ever* called me that. That tone, that style of speech; it's unmistakeable . . . to me, anyway.

But I'm getting ahead of myself. It can't be him. It just can't.

I never thought for a second that Grace going missing would have anything to do with Stefan O'Hara.

I didn't even think it was possible, given what happened to him.

CHAPTER 54

I pick up the note and read it again. The paper quivers in my hand.

That name—*Lucinda*—spoken in a voice that is forever seared into the darkest corners of my mind. Details I've tried so hard to file away forever.

I tip my head to the side, listening. I can hear Blake's deep voice coming from the closed kitchen door. Clinking crockery as someone makes tea. I think I'll be left undisturbed for a few more minutes.

I grab my phone from the bedside table and Google the contact number for the Queen's Medical Centre.

I can remember the ward. I can remember Stefan O'Hara lying there, helpless for the first time in his life. Unable to move any part of his body apart from his head.

I shudder now as I pace the length of the room, back and forth. That day I saw him in that hospital bed, I felt, for the first time, that I had a chance to seize my power back at last.

My head thumps with fresh pain and I pick up the note and screw it into a ball.

I ring the hospital and the receptionist puts me through to the ward. A hassled-sounding woman answers.

"I know it's a long shot," I say, speaking quietly but clearly, "but I wonder if anyone can help me find out about my friend who was a long-term patient on Ward 6 nine years ago?"

"Goodness, nine years! I wasn't here then, but maybe I can find someone who was. What's the patient's name?"

"Stefan O'Hara." It takes a huge effort to utter his name. It's something I'd assumed I'd never have to do again. "He was paralysed after a car accident, had to stay in the hospital for weeks. I've been out of the area for a long time and I'm trying to trace him."

"Hold the line." The call clicks on to a cranky electronic recorded track that sounds like a creepy circus ride.

My heart is racing now. I'm racking my brain to think what to say if the door opens and Blake or Fiona comes in.

After a few minutes, she's back.

"Someone does remember him vaguely, but he didn't stay here long. He was transferred to the Royal Victoria Hospital in Newcastle."

"Thank you," I say.

It's a start.

But there's something else I need to do while I can. I slide my laptop out from underneath the couch. I haven't touched it since Grace went missing.

Remember the old email? You might want to log in.

When I was at university, all students were allocated email addresses on the server. Back then, data protection was not a hot topic and there were rumours that the university snooped on the content of students' mail.

Stefan had a friend who was an IT expert, and he set the two of us up with email addresses that we only used for communicating with each other. We used to joke about it, but it felt secret and exciting to be able to send anything to each other: racy photographs, jokes and gossip about other people in our friendship circle...

It makes me feel sick now, of course, just to think of that stuff. But it was a different time back then. I didn't know who Stefan O'Hara really was.

When the laptop finally cranks into life, I open up a new window and tap in the web address to access the email. It's so long since I've done this, I'm fully prepared for the link no longer to exist.

But it is there.

Thank goodness the address and the password are so memorable, I think as I add the necessary details.

The screen whirrs and flickers, and then there it is: my old private student inbox.

There is a single email, from someone calling himself "Back from the Dead," which I assume is his idea of a joke. With shaking hands, I open it. A photo loads. As it fills the screen, I cry out.

It is a picture of a single yellow glove. Grace's glove. I can see the edge of the name label I sewed in there at the start of the school term.

Underneath the photograph is a message:

> *We come as a package. If you want her, then you must meet with me. Alone. Check back here tomorrow for instructions. Don't breathe a word, or I tell them everything. I have nothing to lose.*

I read the email again. The words explode like bombs in my head. My whole body is trembling. Half of me processes the horror of what he means; the other half pushes it away.

I listen for a moment, and when I'm satisfied that Fiona's not about to burst in, I type a hurried reply.

> *Grace is diabetic. She has insulin, please let her use it.*

I feel numb. Terrified. Most of all, I feel completely alone in facing the enormity of what has just happened.

I log out and shut the laptop quickly and push it under the sofa. I don't want to give Fiona or the detectives the idea of forensically examining its contents.

I let out a long, slow breath.

I will follow up with the hospital in Newcastle, but this is evidence enough. Stefan must somehow have recovered from his paralysis. Or maybe he got someone else to help him abduct Grace. Regardless, there's no doubt he has her. And I know, more than anyone, he's clearly unstable.

I shiver. Grace must be terrified.

Yet I can't tell another soul about his email.

Don't breathe a word, or I tell them everything.

He means business; he's already approached Bev to show me how easy it would be for him to ruin all our lives.

If I tell the police, I'll have to explain our whole history together. I'll have to convey just how dangerous he is and the extreme lengths he'd be willing to go to.

I can just imagine the protracted questioning, the investigation boxes that would need to be ticked...the valuable time that will be wasted.

If I meet with Stefan myself, I can make him see sense. I know I can.

The joy of knowing my daughter is alive is almost enough to override everything else. It gives me hope, a determination to succeed.

He holds a final secret so powerful, he could wreck my life in moments.

I have no choice but to meet him alone.

CHAPTER 55

"Are you OK, Luce?" Blake steps away so he can give me a long look of consideration. "You're so quiet and...Is anything wrong?"

"Nothing's wrong," I say. "Apart from my whole world falling to pieces."

"I know, stupid question." This man, who has so much energy and is usually so full of life, looks tired. Beaten. It's in my power to help him deal with what's happened, but I can only do that by destroying him.

I feel an utter fraud. I know our daughter is with the most loathsome man I have ever met, but she is *alive*. I believe she is alive. And if I play along with Stefan's sick little game, I can get her back.

I know I can.

I wish I could speak to Blake. I wish I could tell him everything I know.

But it is best for everyone concerned—especially Grace—that I say nothing.

I tell Blake I'm going to sleep in Oscar's room.

"It makes no sense for both of us to be exhausted if he wakes," I tell him. "I won't sleep anyway, so I might as well volunteer."

He nods without comment. Perhaps part of him senses I need some space. Perhaps he, too, is glad of the time alone with his thoughts.

I slide into the cool sheets of the little-used spare single bed and listen to my son's regular, light breathing pattern.

Getting through the television appeal and yet another day without Grace; there were times today I didn't think I'd make it. I've had to block thoughts from my mind—particularly the revelations of my visit to Barbara Charterhouse. But now I can revisit what happened, digest her words and absorb what it means to me. To my life ...

"I've known your hidden past for a long time, my dear." The sound of the tea pouring from the teapot spout echoed in my ears. "I've marvelled how you've managed to keep it all inside."

I stared blankly at the cup and saucer she places in front of me, then I looked up into the face of Barbara Charterhouse. I thought about the times she's nodded to me at some community even, her cryptic comments at the café ...

I found I couldn't actually say anything in response. I couldn't ask her what she meant by what she just said; I couldn't object, stand up or leave. I was simply struck by a mute fear of what she might know.

Surely it couldn't be anything to do with my past life in Newcastle. It *couldn't* be.

"I haven't a clue what you mean." Somehow, I managed to keep my voice level and meet her eyes.

She smiled, nodded, and ran a finger along the lip of her cup.

"You know, many moons ago, I owned my own bed and breakfast business. It was quite successful, but after a couple of years I hit a sort of ceiling. I'd grown the business as much as I was able, which was fine. I was happy there." She paused and smiled to herself. "And then I met Harold."

I breathed a small sigh of relief. It sounded as though she knew nothing of my past after all, thank goodness, and I now doubted her comment at the café, about Blake's facade, could be anything more than a spiteful slur with no substance.

"Harold, believe it or not, was hotly ambitious in those days, and he saw great opportunity in a certain area of Newcastle, where the student population was experiencing exponential growth."

Freezing cold fingers unfurled at the bottom of my spine and commenced a slow crawl up each and every vertebra.

She watched my face carefully as she continued.

"Harold had some money, compensation for a car accident he'd been involved in. I had a bit put aside too, so we sold the B&B and bought a splendid but faded Victorian villa on the outskirts of Newcastle."

Goose bumps clustered on my forearms as Barbara smiled and nodded slowly, as if she could sense everything that was happening inside me. The sick feeling, the panic, the rush of blood to my head. I was trying so hard to remain poker-faced.

"The house needed renovating top to bottom, but we did virtually nothing because the place filled with student tenants within a month. These were young people who expected very little and were perfectly happy if you let them alone."

"Why are you telling me this?" I managed, but she continued as if I hadn't spoken a word.

"Harold and I didn't interfere so long as they paid their

rent and took out their rubbish regularly. We didn't live on site, you see, and so we found it fairly easy to turn a blind eye to everything else. And I can tell you, even though I'm ashamed of our lax morals back then, that made our accommodation very popular indeed."

She couldn't possibly know. *She couldn't!* Lax morals were one thing, but if she knew a girl had died there, surely she'd have gone to the police a long time ago?

I felt like I was overheating; being so near the fire was going to literally cook me if I didn't take off my coat. I wriggled my arms out and slipped it from my shoulders.

She waited until I became still again before speaking.

"Although we didn't live there, we spent a lot of time at the house during the week. Harold would do the maintenance jobs, which were never-ending, and I'd dust and vacuum the common areas."

Stefan's voice rang in my head as if he was standing right next to me again.

We'll keep out of the lounge area; that nosy old battleaxe is cleaning in there.

"One day it came to our attention that the students were talking about some kind of incident that had happened upstairs. They were joking and laughing about it in the communal lounge, but Harold became concerned when he heard reference to an awful crime having taken place."

I tried to pick up my cup as a small barrier against her incisive glare, but my hand was shaking so much, I had to put it down again.

"Stefan killed that girl. It had nothing to do with me, I—"

"Hear me out." She put up a hand and I fell silent.

I couldn't cope with this, with her knowing. I couldn't live without my children, possibly go to prison ... It would be better for all concerned if ...

"We confronted the students, threatened them with calling the police, and that caused even more hilarity. Finally, someone explained. Apparently, Stefan, the student who'd been with us the longest—he was older than all the others and had a controlling influence in the house—had staged a mock suffocation to persuade a young student not to turn him in to the police."

I stared at her.

"The supposed victim—Rhonda, I believe her name was—was his partner in drug-dealing activities. They acted out the murder to fool the young student into believing that she had just witnessed a brutal act. Stefan took photographs of her in the room with the 'body,' and said he'd implicate her in the crime if she blew the whistle on his so-called business activities. One of the tenants even told us they'd done it before!"

"But . . . the body . . ." I said faintly.

"We went upstairs to the scene of this dreadful joke, and the room was spotless. No sign of anything amiss at all. A week or so later, Rhonda came and apologised to us. She said it had all got out of hand and she was sorry we'd had to hear about it the way we did. Of course, we put them both out anyway. It was a step too far."

A charge surged through me. The muscles between my neck and shoulders cramped, and I felt suddenly, overwhelmingly tired. Completely devoid of energy.

"The young student who'd witnessed the supposed murder ran away, they say, dropped out of university. I caught sight of her once, at the house. It would be enough to send someone crazy, believing she was party to a killing." Barbara reached for my shaking hand. "But she never was, you see. That young woman's conscience should be clear. It's the only gift I can give to you in this terrible time you're going through, dear."

I stumbled out of the house, half running, half falling into my car.

"Your coat!" Barbara shouted after me. "You forgot your coat!"

But I couldn't go back. I just couldn't.

I started the car. At the end of the lane, I pulled over and opened the window. Dragged in a lungful of cold air before making a concerted effort to push it from my mind.

I still can't process what she's told me. Can it really be true that Rhonda never died? That Stefan had invited me over not to try and explain his way out of the drug dealing, but to frame and then blackmail me into not reporting his activities to the police?

Involvement in a university drug ring is one thing, but why would Rhonda agree to be involved in such a sick stunt? And where is Rhonda now?

If it is true that she wasn't killed, then one enormous burden has been lifted from me.

But that doesn't change the fact I have another terrible secret.

CHAPTER 56

Wednesday morning

I've had an ongoing battle with myself all night long.

Yet again, life has presented me with a massive choice. If I involve the police and they conduct their investigation as cautiously and slowly as they have so far in Grace's disappearance, something awful could happen to my daughter. I know Stefan O'Hara and the police don't, plus, I'm not tied up in knots ticking procedural boxes and following a certain order of process. In my opinion that gives me an enormous advantage in dealing with the situation myself.

Conversely, I could forever regret my decision in not involving the police.

Sixteen years ago, I ran away. Ran away from responsibility and my own power. I put my fate in the hands of others.

No more. From now on, I'll run my own life and face up to the consequences.

I log back in to the email account.

10:30 a.m. today. Do not tell another soul.
I'm feeling low, Lucinda. Very low. If I decide that life isn't worth living, I may just take her with me. Tread carefully.

He names a little-used park a ten-minute drive from here. I can't think straight. Can't process the enormity of it. How am I going to get out of the house without the police asking questions? All I have to say is that I need to get away for a while. They can't blame me for that.

My fingers begin to type of their own accord.

Will Grace be with you? I need to know she is OK.

As I press send, my heart doesn't know whether to sink or soar.

I close the laptop, my heart in my mouth. My phone pings with a text message notification.

Lucie, can you come over to ours? It's urgent. Come alone. Bev x

It's 9:30 a.m. Bev has inadvertently given me an excuse to get out of the house so I can make the 10:30 a.m. meeting at the park.

As I stare out of the window, wondering what Bev could want to see me about that can't wait, Blake comes out of the shower. He has a small towel tied around his waist and he's rubbing at his wet hair. He has olive-toned skin and always looks slightly tanned and healthy even in the winter but I can see he's lost weight on his stomach and arms.

"DI Pearlman called. There have been one or two calls that could prove to be promising leads," he says. "I'm going over to the station to go through what they have." He hesitates, obviously weighing up if it's a good idea to tell me. "Want to come?"

"I'm going over to Bev's for a coffee," I say. "I want to thank her for helping Dad."

I don't know why I don't tell him about her text message. I just feel a conviction that it's best not to say anything.

Blake pulls a face. "Mike's probably still a bit sore about it. Maybe you should wait a while."

"I want this stuff out in the open between us." I pull on a jumper over my T-shirt and jeans. "They're good friends and I can be honest with them regarding my own feelings about what Dad has done."

Blake sticks out his bottom lip as if he doesn't wholly agree. But I'm relieved when he doesn't press me on the issue.

"Are you going to Bev's the back way?"

I shake my head. "I'm going to drive down the road. I'm sick of hiding away from the press, feeling like a terrible parent. They don't know anything about us, why should I hang my head in shame?"

Blake kisses the top of my head. "That's my girl. I like this new positive you." His voice softens. "I feel good, Luce. I feel like we'll get Grace back. I know it doesn't make any sense but it's a relief to hear there are new leads possibly coming in as a result of the live appeal."

"I believe we'll get her back, too," I say, pressing my cheeks to his shoulder. "I honestly do."

"If you wait five minutes I'll walk you out to your car. I'll speak to the press about going to the station regarding the appeal calls and you can slip away."

And that's what we do. I'm astonished it works so well. The press are like putty in Blake's hands when he explains I'm going to a friend's for a coffee and then follows it up with his visit to the police station.

Just before I pull my car door closed, I hear their barrage of questions begin. I'm proud of Blake, taking it all in his stride. He's so used to crowds of people and public speaking and they behave better in the face of his confidence.

I drive the short distance down Violet Road to Bev's.

Slowing down opposite Abbey Road, my eyes prickle. I can see my baby, dressed as she was when she left the house Sunday morning. Grace was here. Safe. On her way home to us, her loving family. And then something terrible happened. Stefan O'Hara happened.

I feel a rush of energy shoot through my torso. A tangle of emotions. How dare he just barge into my life again and again, causing grief and mayhem?

I will get Grace back. Whatever it takes, I will bring her home.

A minute later I park up in front of Bev and Mike's house. My stomach flutters a little and I can feel the beginnings of a headache start up at the base of my skull.

I don't know why, but something in me feels suddenly nervous as to why she has summoned me to come alone.

CHAPTER 57

Olivia

Livvy stood behind the living room door.

Grace going missing had felt like moving very slowly on one of those walking escalators at the airport and then something going badly wrong with it so that suddenly, you were running really fast and couldn't get off.

At first, Olivia's dad had told her not to worry, that Grace would probably come back very, very soon. But she hadn't come home. Then Grace's parents were on TV begging for the public to help them and had asked the person who'd taken her to bring her back home.

There had been nothing in between... slow and very fast. And Olivia had been caught out.

She'd stood behind the door as her parents watched the live appeal yesterday. Had heard her own mum crying and her dad saying soothing things to her in a low voice.

Then Grace heard the policeman on television describe what Grace was wearing and that she had been carrying a small pink rucksack, too. And that's when Olivia knew without any doubt it was important to tell her parents that Grace's bag was actually under her bed.

Her parents had gone very quiet. They'd looked at each other in the strangest way and Olivia saw the fear in their eyes. And then she'd felt afraid, too.

Now Grace's mum had arrived, and Olivia felt sick.

The living room door was slightly open and she could hear Lucie crying in there. They were talking in low voices and it seemed Lucie was thanking Olivia's mum for doing something.

"I'm so sorry it caused problems between you and Mike," Lucie said.

This must be something to do with why her parents had been arguing so much recently. Everything was suddenly such a mystery. The adults were keeping secrets from each other and it seemed that was allowed. But when children kept secrets, that was frowned upon. It was confusing and annoying, too.

They were whispering again but Olivia couldn't catch much of it. And then her mum raised her voice slightly.

"I don't know what got into her, hiding it under her bed like that. I'm so sorry, Lucie."

She hadn't hidden it under the bed. Grace had! And sworn her to secrecy, too.

Olivia had said nothing about Grace's rucksack for all the right reasons—she'd thought at the time, anyway—but now she'd managed to make Grace's mum feel even sadder and she felt very sorry about that.

She pushed open the door and both mums sat up a bit straighter in that way adults do when a kid walks in; as if they haven't been talking about anything interesting.

"Hi, Livvy," Lucie said in a funny bright voice that seemed at odds with her blotchy, wet face.

"Hello." Olivia's voice came out so quiet, so small, she felt like a bad little mouse in one of the picture books she had when she was little. There had always been a happy ending back then.

"I think you have something to say to Lucie, don't you, Olivia?" her mum said in her kind but stern voice. "I think you have something to give to her."

"Sorry I didn't tell you I had this." Olivia stepped forward and held out the rucksack. Her heart hammered inside her chest like it was desperate to escape Lucie's sad face.

"Thank you, Livvy," she said, taking the bag. "Can I ask why you didn't tell us before now that you had the bag?"

"Grace told me to keep it a secret," Olivia said quickly. "She said she didn't want anyone to read her diary."

Lucie didn't reply. She opened the rucksack and took out the things inside. She held the T-shirt up to her face and breathed in. She did it again and again. Then she took out the diary and looked at the fastening.

Olivia slid her fingers into the tiny pocket of her jeans that hardly held anything at all. She pulled out the tiny key she'd found in the corner of her desk drawer and she gave it to Lucie.

"I think Grace might've written about a secret she had," Olivia said.

CHAPTER 58

Lucie

As Livvy hands me the tiny key that will unlock Grace's diary, our hands touch and I have to fight the urge to grasp her small, cool fingers and pull her to me.

Just to feel her in my arms, so similar to my Grace...to hold her close and bury my face in her silky hair. My heart is cracking open...

I don't pull her to me, of course I don't. The last thing I want to do is scare Livvy.

She must have been nervous and confused. Not wanting to betray her best friend and yet feeling a building sense of worry about the contents of the rucksack.

I don't open the diary here. I stand up to leave, but before I go, I confide in Bev.

"Please don't mention this to anyone, at least for a couple of hours. Now I'm out of the house I'm going to drive to a quiet place to look at the diary. I need a little peace, that's all. Away from Blake, my dad...Fiona."

"I understand, course I do," Bev says. "But don't leave it too long, Luce. The police need to know you've got her bag. It could be important."

I nod, but I know what's important is to get to the park.

Back at the car, I feel sick with nerves at seeing Stefan again, but also an unmistakable excitement and relentless hope that I'll be seeing Grace. Whatever it takes, I'm bringing her back with me today. I have to.

I slide into the driver's seat and lock the doors. As I pull away from the desperate faces at the kerbside, I allow myself a sigh of relief.

It doesn't take long for the tension to return.

What will Stefan want from me in return for the safe delivery of my daughter? I know him well enough to fully expect that he'll lay out demands. And I'll agree to all of them. I will. If he's crazy enough to think we could get back together, I'll indulge him in that, too.

I'll say exactly what I need to to ensure my daughter is back in her own bed tonight and I'll deal with the aftermath when it comes.

The traffic is light and I arrive at the park ten minutes before our scheduled meeting. I park on the street, just down from the entrance, and take Grace's backpack from the passenger seat.

I hold it to my chest to try in vain to get a sense of her. I grip the straps where her fingers would have held it on Sunday afternoon.

I pull out the T-shirt and breathe the scent of my daughter in again. Then I force myself to lay it aside and I reach for the diary. I take the tiny key Livvy gave me out of my pocket and unlock it.

I flick through the pages, stunned that my Grace has been writing in it so regularly. I have never seen her do so. I'd like to read each and every entry but I scoot forward until a week before she went missing.

Her entries are neat and written in a variety of coloured

glitter gel pens I remember buying her as a stocking filler for Christmas.

I smile wistfully as I scan through the entries, each one a snapshot of a wonderful nine-year-old with a zest for life. She talks about her favourite food, the music she's listened to in her bedroom, the building excitement of her birthday party and trip to Alton Towers.

And then.

The Thursday before she went missing—just three days earlier—the tone of her writing changes.

> *It happened again at school. Just before the bell rang I heard someone shout my name. Livvy said not to go to the fence, but I had to. Then it happened again. They said not to be afraid, they only wanted to warn me that my Mum is a liar and they said the bad thing again, the horrible thing...I want to tell Mum but I'm scared it will make her poorly again.*

The diary falls from my hands as I let out an anguished yelp. He's got to Grace...at school of all places. I can't bear that my beautiful girl was afraid of speaking to me because she couldn't trust I wouldn't sink into one of my anxious, depressive states. I never realised she even noticed this stuff. I've been living in a cave.

I pull my jacket closer to me, shivering. My hands are shaking and I am terrified what's going to happen. I've underestimated Stefan. He knows everything about me...about us, our family. He was in touch with Grace and I never ever knew it.

But how? He was paralysed when I last saw him.

Tugging my beanie hat down low over my forehead and

sticking my gloved hands in the deep pockets of my quilted coat, I lock the car and walk, head down, quickly alongside the hedge that runs the length of the park. Glancing around to make sure nobody has followed me, I slip through the gap at the far end.

I stand next to an old oak tree, its enormous girth indicating that it is probably over a hundred years old, and look around. I spot two dog walkers and a man in the distance in regulation overalls picking up litter with a grab-and-grip stick.

And then I see someone over near the road but amongst the trees, looking around the park just as I am.

Time seems to slow as I take in the back of the darkly clothed, darting figure.

It's a man, but his movements are surely too quick to be Stefan.

My heart is hammering. I can't afford to put a foot wrong here. This is my chance to get my daughter back and I'm going to make it count.

I walk a little further into the park and sit on a bench. It's cool and the sky is clouded over. Little moody pockets threaten rain.

I keep running over Grace's diary in my mind. School is a place your child should be safest and yet Stefan had managed to defy even their safety processes to frighten Grace.

My skin is crawling, every inch of it. My sense of terror is a physical thing, but I have to find a way rise above it.

He's just a man, I tell myself. He's fallible, he makes mistakes. My love and determination to get Grace home safely is strong enough to face him now. It is.

Movement catches my eye again. A figure—a different one than I saw before—comes into focus and my breath catches in my throat.

It's time.

I stand up, pressing my feet down hard in an effort to ground myself and stop my knees wobbling.

But the realisation of who is in front of me nearly knocks me off my feet altogether.

It isn't Stefan at all...it's Angela. My old housemate at university.

I stand, frozen to the spot, as she walks towards me.

"Hello, Lucie," she says, her mouth twisting horribly to the side. "I've waited a long time to see you again."

I glance around. Stefan will be here somewhere, I'm certain of it.

"Who are you looking for?"

"My daughter...Grace. You know she's the reason I'm here."

"All in good time. If you want your daughter back, you have to pay the price."

"Which is?"

Her mouth twists up at one side.

"Let's just say you've a surprise coming."

"How do you know the police haven't followed me?" I say, pressing my hands into my pockets to hide the shaking.

"Because I know about Rhonda's murder. Stefan told me what you did to her and I was on the stairs that day when he told me you two were having trouble handling the drugs. I'm sure, even years later, the police would be very interested in *that*."

So it had been Angela on the stairs that day, who Stefan had spoken to.

I don't tell her I already know he staged the murder, thanks to Barbara Charterhouse. Let her think I'm afraid of it still. I know instinctively that getting Grace back will be like a game of chess. I've chosen to do this alone, without my husband, without the police to support...or hinder the process.

"Is Stefan here?" I feel sick with nerves at facing him again but I know I must. Somehow, he's recovered his health enough to be involved in this.

Her sarcastic smile melts away. "Sadly not. Stefan's dead, and you as good as killed him."

Dead? My immediate instinct is not to believe her. How can I have anything to do with his death? Unless she's referring to the car accident the night he attacked me that was nothing to do with me.

"He committed suicide six months ago. They told him he'd be paralysed for good but he was such a fighter. He worked so hard on his exercises, every day for years, and got back some movement in his hands and arms but it wasn't enough for him. Couldn't live with being a virtual vegetable any longer, he told me." She takes a step towards me and her face contorts in pure malice. "He never stopped loving you, you know. God knows why."

The relief that it might be true, that finally he might be dead, is tempered by the tangle of stuff that no longer makes sense. If Angela is here, then who has Grace?

Her eyes look deranged. I have to try and get her to talk.

"So you...and Stefan...did you get together after university?"

She gave a bitter laugh. "We were always together, you stupid cow. You always were blind as a bat, swallowed every lie he ever fed you."

"You were in a relationship with him?"

"Way before you." She nodded, stepping nearer to me. "And while he was with you, too. I devoted myself to him. He didn't always treat me well but we understood each other. He was always truthful with me about the others, put it that way. He told me he'd marry me one day."

"The others?"

"There were scores of women. That's how he recruited the people who worked for him, too. But they never meant anything to him. Until you."

I could laugh, if I didn't want to sob with desperation to see my daughter. She seriously believes he cared about me? But I have to keep my cool here.

"I don't know why he loved you. But he told me he did. Before he died."

"Loved me! Rape, murder, blackmail and lies—that's a funny way to show it. Where's Grace?"

"You're lying. He never raped you." Her eyes look wild. "But let's talk about Stefan, shall we?"

My eyes endlessly search the surrounding trees as she speaks. I don't trust a word that comes out of her mouth. She can't have done this alone. I remember her as a bit of a mouse, scared of her own shadow.

"They thought they'd found him in time after he managed to overdose, thought they could save him," Angela says vaguely. "I went to see him in hospital. He wanted to talk to me, you see. I thought that at last he would tell me he loved me, but no. He only wanted to say a few words. 'Make her pay for how she's ruined me.' That was his dying wish. It's the one last thing I can do for him."

I feel nothing for that lowlife. So far as I'm concerned, if he's dead, then the world is a better place. But I stay quiet in the light of her obvious crazy infatuation.

"Where's Grace?" No sooner have the words left my lips than a figure dashes through the sparse trees to my left. I turn towards it.

"Wait!" Angela calls, but I ignore her.

I rush towards the trees but there is no more movement. Grace isn't here.

"Did you really think it would be that easy? That I'd bring

her here?" Angela spits out the words. "If you want her back, I'm going to need money. A lot of it."

"If Stefan is dead, why carry this on?" I'm starting to unravel inside. I can feel it. I need my daughter, I want to see Grace more than I want to breathe.

"To have you suffer, like he suffered at the end. Mission accomplished. But there's more to come." She looks around the park furtively. "Walk to the car with me. Any funny business and your daughter will die. One phone call from me is all it will take."

A phone call to who, if Stefan is dead?

"I—I'll follow you in my car," I stammer. I really don't want to be in a vehicle with crazy Angela. I need to stay as much in control as I can.

"No. The deal is, you do everything I say without question. You want to see your daughter? Then you come in *my* car."

She starts to walk towards the park exit and I follow her.

"How far away is she?" I ask, dreading the answer is Newcastle.

"Not far," is all she'll say.

CHAPTER 59

"Put this over your eyes." She throws a stretchy thick black headband over to me. "And put your hood up. Head down."

I pull it over my head and position it across my eyes slightly lopsided so I still have a slice of vision. But she pushes the back of my neck so I'm forced to dip my face and all I can see is the gear stick and my left knee.

"Remember what I said. Any funny business and you'll never see your daughter again."

My heart is banging so hard against my chest and I feel hot, light-headed. But I have to keep it together.

I push away my own self-critical admonishments: *I should never have come alone, I should've told Blake, the police...*

It's too late now. I'm here. And I'm going to see my daughter. Nothing matters so long as I can find Grace.

Angela embarks on a rant as soon as the car begins to move. I try and take it all in but I can only absorb snippets because I'm focusing so hard on not having a full-blown panic attack.

"When Stefan died, his benefits stopped. His savings were swallowed up paying off debts...We...I realised you were the answer. To getting the revenge he longed for and a much-needed injection of cash."

She's clearly unhinged, babbling senselessly half the time to herself, completely incoherent. Then she starts talking about the day Grace went missing.

"I'd been watching you for a few weeks. Watching you and the house. That was my job and I did it well. You never spotted me, did you?"

She thumps my arm, hard, when I don't answer. "*Did* you?"

"No," I gasp, thinking about what Jefferey said, that he'd spotted someone skulking around.

"I've always hated being ordinary looking. Nobody ever notices me, looks at me appreciatively...I guess I finally found a use for it." She laughs. "Anyway, I got to know your routines, I even got to speak to Grace at the playground fence twice, told her that mummy was a liar and had hurt someone very badly."

The diary entry. It was Angela, not Stefan!

"So when I saw her walking home that day, she knew my face. Just hopped in the car within a second of me pulling up on the side street, happy as anything when I told her I'd call and see Mummy with her, apologise that I'd been wrong about her lying after all."

My darling, trusting Grace. No matter how much we tell our kids not to talk to strangers, not to fall for their lies...in reality, if the person is friendly and believable, they'll trust them every time.

After about ten minutes, the car makes several sharp turns—I assume we're in a warren of small streets—and it finally stops.

We sit in silence for a few seconds and then she pulls off

my hood and whips the blindfold off. We're sitting in a narrow street lined with terraced houses. Looking at the badly maintained front doors and sheets up at lots of the windows, I'm guessing we're in student territory.

We get out of the car and she leads me down one of the dingy alleyways that lead to the back yards, spaced out every three or four houses.

Then we're in the kitchen of one of them. It stinks in here, rancid food and caked-up dishes piled high in the sink and on the side.

She pushes me through a door leading to steep stairs covered in patterned, torn carpet without answering.

"And just in case you're thinking of causing trouble…" She waves a long, glinting blade in front of me. "One plunge from me and it's in your kidneys," she says and jabs me with it as I start to climb in front of her.

I can hardly breathe, terrified what I'll find as we move along the landing. She stops at one of the doors and pulls a key out of her pocket.

"Grace! Grace, are you in there?" I call.

She bares her teeth and holds the knife up at my throat.

"Shut the fuck up. Don't speak unless I tell you, or she's dead meat."

I think I hear a very faint whimper from inside the room but I can't be sure. For all her bluster, I see her hands are shaking so much, it takes three attempts before she can successfully insert the key properly into the roughly hewn lock.

The key turns and she pushes open the door.

The room is dim. The heavy, lined curtains are closed and my nose wrinkles at the smell in here.

She reaches in front of me and snaps on the light, before rushing over to a tangled bundle of clothes and blankets that moves slightly on the floor.

"Grace?" I whisper, almost too scared to hope against hope it's her.

A small hand weaves up out of the pile and as I dash forward, my daughter's fearful, tear-stained face appears.

"Stay where you are!" Angela brandishes the knife close to Grace.

My beautiful girl looks thin and pale. She is dressed exactly as she was when she left home three days ago.

"It's OK, baby, I'm here now. It's over."

Except it looks far from over when someone hisses words into my ear from behind.

"Hello, Lucinda. Long time, no see."

Breath leaves my body as if someone punched it out of my lungs.

The last time I saw this woman, she lay, naked and comatose, on Stefan's bed, having the life apparently smothered out of her. Now, here she is, standing in front of me and very much alive.

Rhonda is heavier now. Her hair is dark and the extra weight around her face makes me shiver because she looks uncannily like Stefan himself.

"Why?" I whisper. "Why did you go along with his sick murder plan... why take my daughter?"

She stares at me with hollow eyes, but stays silent.

"You loved him," I say. "You were always watching us. I felt your jealousy."

"I still do love him," she says coldly. "You don't just stop loving someone because they're dead."

I glance at Grace. Her colour, her vague expression... her blood sugar is low, I can see just by looking.

"My daughter needs medical attention, please let me—"

"The quicker we get this done, the better," Rhonda snaps. "Just tell me what you want. Money? How much?"

"If only it were that simple." Rhonda smiles over at Grace.

Angela's chest is rising and falling too fast. The knife shines in the fluorescent light, reflecting in her mad stare. I have to get Grace out of here.

"Why? Why take my daughter...after all this time?" I say anything, to play for time.

Rhonda shakes her head incredulously. "Angela told me you were dumb, but I thought even you'd have worked it out."

Nothing is making sense. I just want to get Grace and go home. I feel sick and dizzy with the horrible feeling that they don't intend letting us go. I wish I hadn't come here alone, I wish...

"I loved Stefan because he is my *brother*." Her voice shakes. "*Was* my brother, until you took his will to live."

"What?" My mouth is so dry I have to force out the words. "He told me his sister died...she had leukaemia."

"He told you a lot of other things you just blindly believed too, Lucinda," Angela remarks.

She's even closer to Grace now, pressing the knife up close to her throat. My daughter is not crying, not showing any recognition of the fact I'm even here. She's very close to collapsing.

"Ever lost anyone you love so much it feels like a piece of you has been torn away?" Angela taunts me.

"No!" I jerk forward but Rhonda holds me back. I try to shrug her off but her grip is firm.

"Angela *will* do it, she will stab her," Rhonda whispers in my ear. "Stay calm or you'll get your daughter killed."

Stay calm? My legs feel like melting wax, as if they'll not hold me up much longer, and a bubble of panic is rising fast in my chest.

"What do you want?" I shriek.

"A hundred grand. In cash. That's what we want," Rhonda

says slowly. "That's what *Angela* wants, anyway. But me ... I want something different."

"Anything," I whisper. "Anything! I just want my baby back."

"Sweet. But you see, you need to suffer, too. Suffer like I've suffered all these years. You need to experience the empty wasteland of utter loss, Lucinda."

Angela applies pressure to the knife and Grace cries out in pain.

"For God's sake!"

I try to leap forward but Rhonda pulls me back and I feel the ultra-sharp point of a knife pierce through my thin cotton top and into my skin. I cry out, stop struggling.

A wave of hopelessness engulfs me. I feel like I'm drowning, I can't keep my head above water.

I'm going down ... and then I remember. I remember the one thing that nearly destroyed me can save us both.

"You can't hurt Grace," I whisper. "She's Stefan's daughter. She's your flesh and blood, Rhonda."

I feel her freeze at my back and Angela looks like someone hit her with a stun gun.

"She's lying!" Angela yells and Grace screams as the knife blade bites into her again.

"I'm telling the truth." I half turn so I can see Rhonda and she doesn't force my face away. "Stefan came to Nottingham and found me again, ten years ago. He raped me." I'm speaking so fast I'm not sure I'm making any sense. "I found out I was pregnant but I never told him. I thought he was finished, after the car accident ... I ... I ... I just wanted to get on with my life. I thought he'd go to the police about your supposed death, so I just tried to put it behind me."

I want to say how much I hated him. How I would never give him the satisfaction of knowing he had a daughter ... but now is hardly the time.

Rhonda pulls the knife away and steps forward in front of me, staring into Grace's vacant face.

I begin to babble desperately. "See her nose, the fullness of her top lip? Tell me that's not your brother! He's still alive, Rhonda...through Grace."

She believes it. I can see a beam of new hope shining through the dull misery of her face.

"You're her auntie, Rhonda," I sob. "You have to protect her. Let me take her home."

"Don't fall for it!" Angela growls. "She's lying! Stefan would've known if he'd got a kid, he would've—"

"You were different to the others in his eyes," Rhonda says softly. "I don't know why, but that's why I hated you so much."

"She was no different," Angela snaps, shoving at the knife as Grace screams out again. "She was always just another one of his tarts. It's all lies, you silly bitch!"

"Get her away from my daughter!" I scream at Rhonda, suddenly full of fury. "She's Stefan's child!"

"Don't get any closer," Rhonda warns Angela.

"What are you doing?" Angela shrieks. "Don't believe her lies...think of the money."

"The last time I saw you, I thought Stefan had killed you," I whisper. "You don't have to do this, Rhonda. It's not too late to make a fresh start."

Her eyes brim with tears and her expression is wretched.

"I wish I had died that day."

Grace is quiet and terrified. I'm desperate to hold her, to check she's OK.

"Shut up, you stupid bitch," Angela spits and jabs the knife hard into Grace's shoulder. My daughter screams and I dash forward...but Rhonda gets there before me.

I watch in horror as she snatches the knife and plunges it into Angela's neck.

I rush to Grace and she buries her face in my chest as I turn to protect her from the gruesome scene before us.

Suddenly, I lose my balance as something hard thuds into me from behind.

"Jeffery!" I yelp, rigid with shock.

I knew it! I knew our creepy neighbour had something to hide. All this time, Blake has trusted in him, wouldn't hear a word said against him...

"Lucie, move!" I instinctively step aside as he swings a vase at Rhonda's head. She swerves and lets go of the knife.

Jeffery snatches it up and shouts at me.

"The police are on their way...get downstairs with Grace!" He never takes his eyes from Rhonda. "We're taking her home."

He jumps in between us. I see Rhonda snatch up Angela's knife and I rush out of the room with Grace just as Jeffery falls to the floor and as I turn, I see Rhonda pull a bloody knife from his back.

I scream, staggering forward with Grace.

My daughter's eyes are wide but trancelike. If she falls into a diabetic coma, she could die.

We get to the top of the stairs, Grace falling into me. I pick her up to carry her down and jump back at the terrific crash as uniformed officers smash through the door and flood into the stairwell.

An officer takes Grace and we make our way downstairs, into the front room.

Shouting, banging and heavy footfalls echo through the ceiling. I close my eyes against it and hold my daughter close.

The door opens and I see DS Fiona Bean, followed by someone else.

"Daddy?" Grace whimpers as Blake rushes across the room to us.

"I've come to take you both home," he says.

CHAPTER 60

We're both uncomfortable. Dad sits with his fingers laced before him, looking up at me like one of those cute Facebook videos featuring a dog that knows it has done something wrong.

I'm thinking how I can approach the issue from a supportive angle yet show him I'm shocked. Disappointed.

He's put us all at risk.

A distant memory floats to the surface. When I was about eleven years old and in my first year at senior school, I got an invite to hang around after school with one of the "cool" groups of kids. They were going to the bowling alley where someone's auntie worked. I tagged along and ended up buying everyone cans of lager and spending all my lunch money for the week.

I had to come home and admit everything to Dad. He didn't lecture me, he said he could see I felt bad enough and I was suffering because I felt guilty and foolish. And he was spot on. I never did anything like that again.

Standing here now, our roles are now reversed and it feels

wrong. Awkward. I'm trying to think how best to broach the subject when Dad speaks up.

"I'm truly sorry, love," he croaks, his chin on his chest. He looks wretched. Pale and unshaven. I can count on one hand the number of times Dad hasn't had a shower and shave first thing in a morning.

"Why, Dad? Why did you let it get so bad without asking for our help?"

He looks up at me, his eyes red-rimmed and sore. "It happened too fast. It sounds stupid but I didn't know I needed help, love. I thought I had it under control but . . . it seemed to get out of hand so quickly."

Will it help to lecture Dad? Will it make things any better?

Perhaps not, but it might help me.

I feel like I've lived life so long now, biting my own tongue, considering everything I say before I say it. Part of me feels I should tell him how bloody disappointed I am, how he's put us all at risk.

One of the things I've promised myself is to accept the truth of who I am and what I've done. Easily said, but it's a work in progress.

"There are things I need to say to you," I begin, as a heat begins to burn inside my chest.

He looks up quickly, recognising the new, hard edge to my voice.

I realise his blue eyes have paled a little over the years without me really noticing. The lines around his eyes, at the edges of his mouth have deepened. My dad is getting old.

I remember how he put his life on hold to raise me alone when Mum left and then died. How he worked double shifts at the chemical factory for years to give me a decent standard of living.

In my teen years, I'd come home from school and he'd be fast asleep in the chair, still wearing his coat and boots, and he'd wake with a start to make my tea when I got home from netball or art club.

I've seen those tired, beaten eyes before.

And I know I can't do it. I can't tell him how disappointed I am in him because I'm not.

"I'm proud of you, Dad," I say softly. "I've always been proud of you."

"Proud of *me*?" He wipes his wet cheeks with the back of his hand. "I'm a mess. My whole life's a damn mess. After what I've done, the trouble I've caused everyone, I couldn't blame you if you never wanted to set eyes on me again."

"I'm proud of you for getting help, Dad. I'm proud of you for being such a brilliant dad to me for all these years and a wonderful grandad to Grace and Oscar." I sigh. "We all make mistakes. I've made some terrible mistakes I couldn't even bring myself speak about."

"We all make mistakes, lass. Some of us worse than others." He shakes his head and smiles softly. "There's nothing you could ever do that means I'd ever be anything but proud of you, Lucie. I want you to know that."

"Thanks, Dad," I whisper and I take his words and tuck them away in a small, soft place in my heart that I'm nurturing just for me.

CHAPTER 61

Epilogue

Six months later

There's been so much stuff uncovered by what happened to Grace, so much fallout to work through...the last six months feel like a mere six days.

Dad has just been discharged from his rehabilitation programme for his gambling addiction. We begged him to involve the police in the intimidation he'd suffered from the loan sharks but he was adamant he wouldn't do it.

"I borrowed the money. I have to take responsibility for that, love," he told me as I sat holding his hand. "I didn't know it would escalate like it did but you know, I would still have borrowed it if I had."

Blake said he had the right to deal with it as he saw fit but I still feel unhappy they got away with it to do it to others. But Dad is dealing with it in his own way. As part of the work the rehab centre does, he's visiting senior schools and colleges in the area and speaking candidly about what happened to him.

"Hopefully, I can warn young people not to follow the path I did," he told us. "At least some good can come out of it."

The detectives told us that Jeffery would be nominated

for a posthumous bravery award for his actions. When I thought he'd been skulking around making a nuisance of himself, he'd been watching and monitoring and had noticed the woman—Angela—hanging around the house. He'd followed her to the park that day and tracked us to the house. He'd then called the police before coming in to assist me.

The biggest shock has been that he left his house to Blake in his will. He described my husband as his "best and only friend."

Mike and Bev have been our rocks through it all and if anything, I think even more of Bev for helping Dad out like she did. They got over their differences together after Mike looked carefully into the remortgage she'd sorted out for Dad. Although she'd been a little lenient on one or two points, he was satisfied she hadn't broken any regulations.

DI Pearlman called to tell us Rhonda had taken her own life in prison. She'd left a note saying she wanted to be with her brother, even after everything he'd kept from her.

We've all learned painful and valuable lessons about keeping secrets from the people we love the most. We've learned that when the truth comes out of its own accord—as it always does—it can be a hundred times worse to deal with.

That's why I never want to keep another secret from my husband.

That's why the time has come to speak to him about Grace.

Blake sits in his chair and I sit opposite him, on the couch. I pick up a scatter cushion and hug it close to my body. He notices the gesture but doesn't comment.

Despite the calming effect of my medication, I can feel a maelstrom of emotions swirling beneath the surface, kept at bay, for now, with Dr. Mahmoud's help.

Blake's voice is soft when he breaks the silence.

"I know you have something to tell me, Luce, but I want you to take your time. There's no rush now this nightmare is over. Grace is safe, upstairs in her bed. Now it's time to draw a line so we can begin to live again."

I'm so grateful our daughter is OK. She was weak for a few days after coming home and spent some time each day at the hospital—both for treatment and therapy—but she bounced right back and seems her normal self again now, albeit a little more nervous. I now feel fortunate she was in a vague, semi-trance state when I found her because it appears she took in nothing of what was said and done in those awful last minutes in the house.

Blake's words are beautiful when he talks about learning to live again...but they are also naïve. I'm about to rip his world apart, this man who has loved and supported me through so many years, since the day I met him.

But he's right. It really is time to draw a line under the lies, the deceit...time to give up the secrets of the past and free ourselves from its vicelike grip. Whatever the outcome.

It feels strange, just the four of us again in the house. No press gathered at the gate, no Fiona lurking in the hallway.

The living room looks like ours again. Lamps glow warmly, and the fire glow is on. I even lit a candle earlier, and the air is laced with the tranquil scents of lavender and jasmine. It feels like home once more.

"Lucie?"

I look at him now, his handsome face lined with patient concern. I have kept him waiting long enough, but to show him how much I respect and love him, I have to break his heart into a million pieces.

So I tell him what happened that day nearly ten years ago. I take him way back to the night he visited me at Dad's house and I cooked his favourite meal.

"Steak and chips, my favourite." He smiles faintly at the memory. "Some things don't change."

I remind him how we chatted excitedly about our wedding plans, how we couldn't wait for the bright, wonderful future we had planned so enthusiastically together.

"And then you left, you went home," I tell him. "And I had another visitor. Someone I'd hoped never to set eyes on again after university. Stefan O'Hara."

"The abusive relationship you were in?" He frowns. I've only given him the bare bones about my time at Newcastle; I never found the words to admit what I believed at the time were murderous deeds.

I nod.

"Why didn't you tell me, Luce? How did this man know where you lived?"

"He'd turned up at The Carlton a few days earlier and begged me to give him half an hour of my time. He must have followed me, watched me."

I shiver and press the cushion closer to my chest.

Blake shifts in his seat as I continue.

"He explained that he was a recovering alcoholic, and that an essential part of his treatment was to apologise to all the people he'd hurt in his lifetime." I try to disengage myself from the growing pressure inside my head. I've started this, and however bad Blake's reaction is, I must finish. It's the right thing to do and that is my only barometer from now on. "I accepted his apology and he went away again. I thought that was it, the end of the nightmare. I didn't tell you at the time because I didn't want him sullying our happy mood and I genuinely thought it would be the last time I saw him."

"I see." I note his annoyed expression, but I ignore it and press on. There's far worse to come.

"I thought it was you, you see, coming back to the

house for something you'd forgotten. I just opened the door and...he forced his way in."

Blake's face flushes deep red.

"He...he raped me that night, Blake. When he left, he was involved in the road traffic accident at the end of the street."

"Oh no." He covers his face with his hands. "No. No!"

He thumps the chair arm, then stands up and paces around the room, his hands clamped to the top of his head. "I can't believe you didn't tell me this, I can't believe I wasn't there to protect you. I'm so sad you had to deal with this alone and...hang on..." He turns to look at me, realisation dawning. "I *did* come back to the house, because you had a flood!"

He frowns, staring into space. He's trying to remember, trying to join up the dots to make sense of his fractured memory, and he's failing.

"When you left, I set the bath running," I tell him. "Then I heard the door and rushed to open it. Stefan attacked me and left. It was only when the water started dripping through the ceiling that I remembered the bath."

He walks over and sits down next to me on the couch.

"But why didn't you tell me when I came back? You said you were feeling ill, that you'd gone down with some kind of bug. I remember being puzzled that it had come on so quickly." He's lurching between a whole host of negative emotions. "We should've rung the police! Why protect him?" He springs up again, shaking his head like he's trying to expel the terrible thoughts that are flooding in.

"I couldn't get the police involved because I thought he'd use Rhonda's murder." I cry out. "He had photos! I was innocent; I didn't want to go to prison. It sounds far-fetched but you didn't know him. He was so convincing, so plausible."

"We could have fought his allegation together, Lucie. If you'd confided in me, I would've believed you...surely you must know that? Instead, we've had all these...these lies, tainting our relationship for so long. Destroying your mental stability and making me feel like I was never quite enough for you."

It sounds simple now, but it was far from that at the time. Stefan had control over me when I was his girlfriend. I couldn't see it then, but I can see it now. He was skilled at moulding my thoughts into what he wanted from me; so skilled, I thought I was making my own mind up.

I totally bought into his manipulating nature, his ability to get what he wanted.

I believed with every fibre of my body that he'd killed Rhonda that day, and that he would be able to convince the police of my guilt using his plausibility and the photographs he took of me with what I thought was a drugged-up Rhonda.

"You've always been enough for me," I say, pushing the cushion away. "You are more than enough for me. I love you so much."

Blake sighs and reaches for my hand.

"Look. You've told me now and I'm thankful the cloud above us has finally gone. My God, no wonder you've not been in your right mind at times." His face drops. "I wish you could've shared the burden. I wish I could've helped you through it."

I squeeze his hand gratefully.

"We make a fresh start now, deal?" he says, gazing into my eyes.

I can't speak. My throat feels like its closing up and it's all I can do not to stand up and make an excuse to leave the room.

"It's natural for you to worry," Blake reassures me. "You've spent so long living in fear, but Stefan O'Hara is dead. He can never hurt you again, Luce. It's our time now. No more secrets between us, ever...right?"

"But there is another secret," I hear myself say quietly. "There is one more secret."

I wait for him to nod, to say something, but he just stares at me. His entire body seems to freeze, rigid and immoveable as something in him senses the gravity of my next words.

"The night he raped me..." My voice breaks but I push through it. I can't turn back now. "A few weeks after he raped me...I found out I was pregnant."

Blake seems to diminish somehow in front of me. His broad chest, strong shoulders look smaller, his confident demeanour now timid.

He utters one word. "Grace."

I finish his sentence. "Grace is Stefan's child. I'm so, so sorry, Blake."

I can't look at him.

He stands up and walks out of the room. I hear the back door open, and I think he's going to leave, but when I go into the kitchen, he's standing in the garden, staring up at the night sky.

I creep silently out of the house behind him, the invasive cold seeping up from the earth through the thin soles of my slippers.

I move closer to him, but he doesn't look at me.

The sky is black, but the odd star is visible.

"You know, there are millions and millions of stars up there we can't see," he says softly.

"I didn't know that," I say, desperate for him to touch me. Hold me.

"There's so much we don't know about this world. Mostly we focus on the beauty we can see and enjoy and the miracles we take for granted every day."

He looks down at me.

"The joy that Grace gives us, the love we have for her. Those things are real, Lucie; the rest of the stuff that's gone, in the past, it doesn't have to matter unless we let it."

He bends down and kisses me softly on the lips.

"We can work through this together. There's so much more to being a father than mere biology." I hear the pain threading through his words, see the agony-laced hope shining in his eyes. "Grace is mine and I love her with every fibre of my body. Anything else is incidental."

I press my face into his chest and sob softly into his warmth, inhale his familiar scent.

We stand, in each other's arms, for a long time before Blake tilts my chin up to look at him.

"Let's start living the life we're lucky enough to share together," he says.

I nod and slowly, together, we walk back inside.

A LETTER FROM
K.L. SLATER

I do hope you have enjoyed reading *Finding Grace*, my eighth psychological thriller. Reviews are so massively important to authors. If you've enjoyed *Finding Grace* and could spare just a few minutes to write a short review to say so, I would so appreciate that. You can also connect with me via my website, on Facebook, Goodreads, or on Twitter. Please do sign up to my email list below to be sure of getting the very latest news, hot off the press!

www.bookouture.com/kl-slater

Thanks to my publicist, Kim Nash, a seed of an idea from real life sparked off this book, as so often happens. Those of us with children have probably wondered at some point: what age is a good age to allow our son or daughter a little more freedom? Is nine years old too young an age for a sensible child to make the five-minute walk up the street from a friend's house whilst being monitored by adults?

From this initial thought, I began to imagine, from a parental point of view, that most dreaded scenario: a missing child. A parent with a secret past, an impossible choice . . . and soon, I found myself thinking about the story a lot, the characters, how I could tell the story.

The book is set in Nottinghamshire, the place I was born and have lived in all my life. Local readers should be aware I often take the liberty of changing street names or geographical details to suit the story.

As always, I barely finish writing my current book than the character voices for my next story begin vying for attention. It's always an exciting time for me, embarking on a new project. I do hope you'll join me soon for book nine!

Best wishes,
Kim x

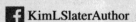 KimLSlaterAuthor

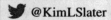 @KimLSlater

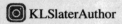 KLSlaterAuthor

www.KLSlaterAuthor.com

ACKNOWLEDGMENTS

I count myself very lucky that I have so many supportive and talented people around me.

First, huge thanks as always must go to Lydia Vassar-Smith, my fabulous editor at Bookouture, for her guidance and suggestions in making the book the best it can be. Thanks to ALL the Bookouture team for everything they do, especially to fabulous publicity manager Kim Nash who inadvertently provided the first seed of the idea that became this book!

Thanks to my agent, Camilla Bolton, who is such a fantastic support in my writing career. Thanks also to the rest of the hardworking team at Darley Anderson Literary, TV and Film Agency.

Thanks to my writing buddy, Angela Marsons, who provides encouragement, support, and laughs on a daily basis!

Massive thanks as always go to my husband, Mac, for his love and support and for taking care of everything so I have the time to write. To my family, especially my daughter, Francesca.

Special thanks must also go to Henry Steadman, who has designed such a striking cover for *Finding Grace*.

Thank you to the bloggers and reviewers who do so much to help authors and to everyone who has taken the time to post a positive review online or has taken part in my blog tour. It is noticed and much appreciated.

Last but not least, thank you SO much to my wonderful readers. I love receiving all the wonderful comments and messages and I am truly grateful for each and every reader's support.

ABOUT THE AUTHOR

K.L. Slater is the million-copy bestselling author of nine psychological crime thrillers.

For many years, Kim sent her work out to literary agents and collected quite a stack of rejection slips. At the age of forty, she went back to Nottingham Trent University and earned an MA in creative writing with distinction.

Now Kim is a full-time writer and lives in Nottingham with her husband.

For more information you can visit:
www.KLSlaterAuthor.com
Twitter: @KimLSlater
Facebook.com/KimLSlaterAuthor